Then Hal saw Sebastian. ⬚ ⬚ ⬚ ⬚ ⬚ ⬚ ⬚
in front of his mother. ⬚ ⬚ ⬚ ⬚ ⬚ ⬚ ⬚ ⬚
stare. Hal was unnerved and ⬚ ⬚ ⬚ ⬚ ⬚
Sebastian. I didn't see you there,' he said weakly.

'Come on, Sebastian,' Jessica said. 'Let's go and find
Tony.'

Hal followed them into the bar, but stood just inside
the doorway and watched. A few feet in front of him, he
saw Jessica bend down to talk to her son. Sebastian
glanced at Hal, still glaring, then returned his gaze to
his mother.

Jessica straightened, and Sebastian walked back across
the room towards him. Jessica was shuffling nervously.

Sebastian reached him. 'Mummy's made me promise
not tell anybody,' he said flatly, 'so I won't.'

Before Hal could respond, Sebastian walked away.
Then he turned back to Hal. 'You're a dead man,' he
said, and hurried back to his mother.

Owen Whittaker is an actor with a strong background in comedy in the theatre and television. He is the father of two young children and he lives in Rutland.

By Owen Whittaker

The House Husband
The Godfather
A Little Trouper

a little trouper

Owen Whittaker

ORION

An Orion paperback

First published in Great Britain in 2001
by Orion
This paperback edition published in 2002
by Orion Books Ltd,
Orion House, 5 Upper St Martin's Lane,
London, WC2H 9EA

A CIP catalogue record for this book
is available from the British Library.

ISBN 0 75284 821 6

Printed and bound in Great Britain by
Clays Ltd, St Ives plc

For my mother,
who still takes the time to worry

I

Hal Morrisey stared around the room, between the oversized pot-plants, at the faces seated around its edge. One of the many depressing things about commercial castings was the feeling that you had been cloned. It was like sitting in a hall of mirrors. Everyone else looked identical to you, with some minor distortions of face, hair colour, or height. In theory, being an actor was supposed to make you feel special. Different. Yet looking around this room, Hal had never felt so ordinary. Looking into the eyes of his rivals he held the proverbial mirror up to his own life: same anxieties, same fading dreams, same air of desperation.

He decided to stop himself wallowing by filling in the compulsory form he had been handed as he came through the door, as at all such castings. He wrote his name, agent, and Equity number at the top of the form, then proceeded to fill in the boxes.

Age: 40.

This did nothing to cheer him up. It seemed only yesterday that he was scribbling '21' in the same box. Those days were gone. The days when he played the sons, not the fathers. Romeo, not Old Capulet. Parts where his character was on heroin, not Viagra.

Hair: Brown.

Such an unexciting hair colour, Hal had always thought.

Black was dangerous. Blond was sexy. Red was wild. Brown was . . . brown. Hal's hair wasn't even a proper shade of brown, but somehow 'mousy' sounded even worse. In truth, it was getting to the stage where he could just as easily write 'grey', were it not for the wonders of Belle Colour – light brown, £5.95 from Boots.

Eyes: Green.

That wasn't altogether true. Hal had unusual eyes – compelling, some might even say sexy. They were a cross between green and blue. On some days, they were predominantly green, with flecks of blue, and on others, vice versa. When he first started out in the business, he used to write green/blue, or blue/green on the forms, until one day, a bitchy casting director, of which there were many, asked him if he had one of each.

Height: 5 feet 11 inches.

Nauseating. Six foot always sounded so much better. Nothing worse than falling just short. Like a horse losing the Grand National 'by a nose'. Or an over-excited teenage boy holding a ruler against his 'hand's best friend' only to read five and three-quarter inches.

Waist: 32 inches.

Hal was proud of that. Pretty cool for a forty-year-old – even if every time he undid his belt and took down his trousers, there were great welts on his hips as deep as the tread on a Michelin tyre.

Inside leg: 31 inches.

Again, Hal didn't flinch. Instead he felt a pang of regret that he was writing it down instead of having it measured by some young wardrobe mistress.

Sex: Male.

How many comedians with great originality had written 'Yes, please' over the years? he wondered. Or 'not unless you kiss me first', or 'only if it's really essential to the plot of this cornflake commercial'.

'Have you finished with that, Hal?'

He looked up to find Jemima Barnes, the casting agent, holding out her hand. Fêted, successful, and as hard as bloody nails, she was middle-aged, hair greying among the highlights, porky of build, fleshy of jowls, but with the eyes of a young, bloodthirsty shark.

'Yes, thanks,' Hal replied, as he gave her his form.

'Nice to see you again,' she said, flatly.

'You lying old prune,' was what Hal wanted to reply, but, of course, he didn't. 'You too, Jemima. Thanks for calling me in.'

'Pleasure,' she responded, and flashed him a professional glimpse of teeth with serrated edge.

Hal held his equally fraudulent smile until her back was turned. 'Yuck,' he muttered, under his breath.

A cheerful thought struck him. Today's casting was for a well-known brand of lager: with a bit of luck he might get a couple of free gulps of beer out of the day. If he messed things up a few times, he might end up drinking a free pint.

'Jim! Hello, sweetie, how are you, me dear?'

'I'm fine. You?'

Oh, God, not that, thought Hal. He hated actors who met other actors they knew at a casting. The never-ever-out-of-work-luvvie cliques, Hal called them. They were always in the West End at night, filming a new drama series by day, and had just turned down a major film due to unavailability.

'Things are good. Listen, you'll never guess who I've just finished filming an episode of *Casualty* with?'

'Who?'

'Guess.'

'Oh, stop. Do tell, *please!*'

'Marty.'

Loud squeal, 'Oh, no! You're joking.'

3

Hal's lip began to curl.

'Can I take a Polaroid?'

Hal looked up to see the latest in the long line of Jemima's assistants. Female, early twenties, cropped hair, jeans, T-shirt, midriff with pierced belly-button.

'Sure,' Hal acquiesced. 'Where do you want me?'

'Just stand where you are. Great. Thanks.'

Still full of energy and the language of enthusiasm, thought Hal. She must be very new indeed.

'Smile for me,' the assistant demanded.

Hal obliged reluctantly. He couldn't understand why these people were still using Polaroids? Wasn't a more effective digital equivalent available? Polaroid cameras always took so long, and everybody always looked so anaemic in the pictures.

'Smashing. Thanks,' said the assistant, as she pulled out the photo, then flapped it about like a Chinese fan to encourage it to dry.

Hal sat down again. He glanced up at the clock on the wall above the receptionist's desk. Eleven a.m. Only forty minutes behind schedule. Not bad, as castings went.

'Hal, you're next. Would you like to come with me?'

Said the spider to the fly, thought Hal, as Jemima led the way along a narrow corridor into the audition.

The room was large and rectangular, the windows blacked out. Left, and towards the rear, was a single video camera with a few lights. Behind this, perched on a bar-stool, sat a scruffy, bearded man. Against the far wall on black-leather sofas was the posse: the art director, copy writers and, worst of all, the clients. These were the people who paid for the whole shooting match. They knew nothing about advertising, acting, actors or direct-ing, but they all became experts upon signing the cheque. It had been a long time since Hal had had the financial blessing of appearing in a commercial, much to his bank manager's dismay.

Only one person remained standing by the sofas. Hal assumed correctly that this must be the director.

'Hal Morrisey,' Jemima announced, handing his form and the Polaroid to one of the clients.

'Hal, nice to meet you,' the director said, in the soft, lazy tones of the self-important. 'Thanks for coming along. Have you seen the script and the story-board?' he asked.

'No, I haven't.' Hal panicked.

The director shot a glance at the clients.

Hal obviously wasn't the first to be thrown unaware to the wolves, and he hoped Jemima would get a rollicking for her slip-up. If not a sound flogging.

'Not to worry,' the director reassured him. 'We're advertising Mandolin lager – do you drink lager?'

'I have been known to,' lied Hal, who was a confirmed bitter drinker.

'Great.' The director smiled half-heartedly, and Hal knew instantly that every other tosser who had been asked that question had responded in exactly the same way. 'There's the bar.'

Hal was staggered he hadn't noticed it. A real set was unusual at an audition. This spelt big budget, lots of dosh. Which made Hal even more nervous.

The director went across the room and stood behind it. Then he leaned on it, and narrowed his eyes, as all directors did before trying to make the story-board sound important. At this stage, they were all Mike Leigh setting up an improvisation that would lead to an award-winning film. 'Okay, you're in a bar, right? Desperate to get a drink.'

So far, so good, thought Hal.

'But the bar's packed, yeah? Chocker. Masses of people between you and the bartender.'

Masses of people, equalled zillions of extras. Hal's heart sank. Loads of people to pay. Maybe not as good an earner as he had thought.

'So you have to get the bartender's attention. With me?'

'Yes,' Hal replied, trying to look intensely serious.

'Now,' began the director, and slammed the palms of his hands on the mock bar, 'do you remember that old pop song that was a hit fifteen or so years ago – the one that went, "Two pints of lager and a packet of crisps, please!"?'

Suddenly Hal felt all of forty: he remembered every tacky line of it. 'Yes, I do,' he confessed.

'Excellent. Well, what I want you to do, Hal, is pretend there's loads of people between you and the bar and jump up and down to attract the bartender's attention. As you do this I want you to shout, "Two pints of lager and a packet of crisps, please." Okay?'

'Fine,' Hal lied. He was already dying of embarrassment. Three years of classical training, twenty years of theatrical experience, had brought him to this.

'Right, there's your mark.' The director pointed to a cross of black gaffer-tape on the floor. 'Could you give your name and agent to camera, please?'

'We're rolling,' the camera operator muttered.

'Hal Morrisey, and I'm with Pippa Grey.'

'Okay,' said the director. 'Whenever you're ready.'

Hal swallowed his pride and began to jump. 'Two pints of lager and a packet of crisps, please!' he yelled.

'Good,' encouraged the director. 'Keep going.'

'Two pints of lager and a packet of crisps, please!' Hal yelled, and jumped five more times.

'Right, stop!' the director barked. 'Fine. We need you to get a bit more height, Hal. You see that trampet on the floor there?'

'Pardon?' Hal gasped.

'Trampet. On the floor to your right.'

He did now. On the floor some two feet to his right was a small square trampoline. 'Yes.'

'Good. Use it to get as high as you can while you say the line.'

Hal walked over to the trampet, teeth gritted. He summoned up a mental picture of red, glowingly unpaid bills and threatening solicitors' letters.

He stepped on to the trampet and bounced. 'Two pints of lager and a packet of crisps, please!'

'Good. Louder, Hal. You're dying of thirst.'

'TWO PINTS OF LAGER AND A PACKET OF CRISPS, PLEASE!'

'Even louder, Hal. That bar's very crowded.'

'TWO PINTS OF LAGER AND . . . A . . . A PACKET OF CRISPS . . . PLEASE!' Hal screamed.

'Wonderful. Now I want you to say the whole line while you're still in the air!' the director roared.

'*What?*'

'Say the whole line while you're in the air.'

Hal was still bouncing, incredulous.

'You understand, Hal? The whole line—'

'– while I'm in the air?'

'That's right.'

'You sure?' Hal questioned.

'Absolutely. You can do it. Now, come on!'

'Two pints of—'

Bounce.

'Two pints of lag—'

Bounce.

'Two pints of lager an . . .'

Bounce.

'Two pints—'

Bounce.

7

'Two pints . . .'

Bounce.

'Two pi . . .'

Bounce.

'Two pi – (bounce) Two pi . . . (bounce) Two pi . . . (bounce) . . . oh bollocks!'

No more bouncing.

Hal stepped off the trampet and ran his hands through his hair in frustration. 'Sorry, folks. I just hit the wall of my limitations,' he declared, then turned and made his way out of the room.

His heart was pounding as he reached the foyer. He had never before walked out half-way through an audition. Not once in twenty years.

'Oh, hello, Hal,' said Jemima. 'You all finished?'

'Probably,' he replied, as he exited through the swing doors on to the street, gulping for air.

Hal never felt good after a commercial casting, but today he felt worse than ever. He had just offended one of the biggest ad agencies in the industry. More importantly, he doubted that Jemima Barnes would call him for another casting. And that was serious. Jemima cast a lot of major television programmes and a fair number of the films still made in the UK.

He needed to talk to someone. If he spent money he didn't have on a taxi, he had time to sponge a cup of coffee off Belinda before dashing across to the Queen's Arms for the half.

Hal stood on Belinda's doorstep in Crouch End waiting for her to answer the door. He hoped she was in. If not he'd just wasted ten pounds he was unlikely to recoup. Especially after this morning's escapade.

Belinda was an old friend from more years back than

either of them cared to remember. They had met at college where Hal was busy having a good time, drinking, smoking, partying, and failing English and History A Level, and Belinda was drinking a bit, partying a little, tutting every time someone lit up a fag, and gaining top grades in relentless pursuit of her chosen career. They were part of a larger circle of friends, and although most were taking different subjects, they were drawn together socially by a shared sense of humour. Then Hal went to drama school and gradually lost touch with everyone except Belinda.

Belinda had been inadvertently responsible for introducing Hal to his ex-wife. He had just about forgiven her for that now, a year after the divorce. When the decree absolute had slid through the letterbox, and blown what was left of Hal's world apart, Belinda had nursed him through the ensuing difficult period.

Belinda opened the door. She wore a tweed business suit, and opaque blue tights. Her soft features were crowned with tousled, blonde hair. Her spectacles were perched precariously on the end of her nose, and she was holding a lipstick. She was wearing a full professional smile, which collapsed rapidly into an expression of mild confusion. 'Oh, hi,' she said.

'I missed you too,' Hal said.

'I'm in a bit of a rush.'

'You're looking very smart,' Hal said. 'What's happened to my baggy-sweater-and-leggings girl?'

'I'm on my way to work, Hal.'

'Shouldn't you be there already?'

'I've spent the morning working here,' she told him.

'You've been skiving, you mean.'

'No. I've been catching up on paperwork.'

'Paperwork, of course. *The Times*, the *Sun*, *Red*, *Marie Claire*—'

'I'm half-way through making up,' Belinda inter-rupted. 'I have patients to attend to. Is it something important?'

'I've popped round for a whinge.'

Belinda grimaced. 'Do you have to whinge to me?'

'Well, who else can I whinge to? Look, I haven't got long myself. I'm due at the theatre any minute. Come on, Belinda, you know the drill. I have a good moan, and you tell me to stop grumbling and bloody well grow up and do something about it. You've had plenty of practice.'

'Ten minutes.' Belinda walked back down the hall.

'I've had a terrible morning.'

'Poor you,' Belinda said, with as much sympathy as she could muster. She sat down at the kitchen table. A small mirror was propped up against a milk jug, next to which lay an open makeup bag. 'You don't mind if I carry on patching myself up, do you?' she asked.

'Not at all.'

Belinda removed her glasses and took an eye-liner pencil from her bag.

'Don't I get a cup of coffee?' Hal asked, as she started to draw a line under one eye.

'I haven't got time to make it. You can have a glass of wine, if you like. There's a bottle of red open.'

'I can't. I'm on stage in a few minutes.'

'It's never stopped you before.' Belinda grinned.

'Go on, then, just the one.'

Belinda stood up, and crossed to the drinks cabinet. 'Now,' she said returning with the bottle and a wine glass, 'are you going to whinge away? I hate to tell you this but you have five minutes for a self-pitying gripe before I have to leave.'

'Fair enough,' Hal conceded. 'I walked out half-way through an audition.'

'Why?' she asked, pulling out the cork.

'They were making me look a prat.'

Belinda smiled. 'So what's new? What did they do?' She poured wine into Hal's glass. 'Make you recite your speech backwards? Deliver your Hamlet in the manner of an Asian shopkeeper?'

'Worse than that.'

'Oh, Hal! I don't know why you stay in acting. It's always made you so damned unhappy. I hate to see you so wretched.'

'That's rich coming from you. Being a shrink doesn't always make you permanently cheerful. Sometimes your face can be so long after a day at the loony-bin, it looks as if it's been stretched on the rack.'

'Never mind that now. What did they do to your party piece?'

'Nothing. I didn't do an audition speech – it wasn't for the theatre. It was a commercial casting.'

'What?' Belinda exclaimed. 'You can't afford to do that.'

'They made me jump on a trampoline, and I had to say the whole line while I was suspended in mid-air, and I'm not a performing monkey!'

'No, you're not. But at least a monkey gets paid peanuts, which is more than you do from acting.'

'Belinda!'

She sighed. 'I'm sorry. That was unfair. But, Hal, I wouldn't mind acting not making you rich if it made you happy. I just think it would be so much healthier for you if—'

'Let it go, Belinda. You're beginning to sound like Amy.'

'Well, as you know, I agreed with her about that, if not about much else. Maybe if you'd swallowed your pride now and again, and tried another profession, you and she might still be together.'

'Do you really think that was why she left me?' Hal asked, taking a gulp of his wine.

'If you think about it logically.'

'Funny. I thought it had something to do with her shagging another man.'

'She had an affair, yes,' Belinda conceded.

'She ran off with him, Belinda,' Hal reminded her. 'That's why I divorced her.'

'I'm aware of that.'

'She bloody hurt me, Belinda.'

'I know. But maybe you should ask yourself why she did it?' Belinda suggested.

'Because the man was solvent?' Hal spat.

'Maybe.'

'Sensible?'

'Perhaps.'

'Decisive?'

'Yes.'

'Everything I'm not. In theory.'

'Well?'

'Then why aren't they still together in their little love nest?' Hal challenged. 'Because he was a self-obsessed, gutless, fucked-up arsehole. That's why.'

Belinda giggled. 'You may be right about that, but he did offer stability – he wasn't depressed all the time. That's the point I'm trying to make. You're bright and funny, but the profession you've chosen is so difficult and it just brings you down.'

'Yes, but—'

'Don't interrupt me. Remember I'm a shrink.'

Hal held up his hands. 'I'm sorry. You're right, Belinda. I've had enough. I think I'm going to jack it in.'

'You're not serious?'

'I am.'

Belinda had heard Hal mention quitting the business before.

'You've had a bad day. You'll be fine tomorrow,' she said.

Hal shook his head. 'No, it's not just this morning. I've been fed up with it for ages. Unemployment, rejection, poverty. I'm not getting any younger and I just can't see it happening for me, Belinda.'

'What will you do instead?' Belinda asked. 'Not that it's anything to do with me.'

'Haven't got that far,' Hal admitted. 'Any ideas? Perhaps we could pop out for a drink one night? Bang our heads together. See what we can come up with – if you can spare the time.'

'Maybe. When are you thinking of calling it a day?'

'Soon.'

'The new Mr Decisive, eh?' Belinda smiled.

'Yeah, right. I'll jack it in at the end of this play.'

'Really?'

'Yeah. Probably.' Hal weakened. 'I'll call my agent and do it. Look, we'll talk. Bugger! Is that the time? I'll be lucky to make the curtain, let alone the half.'

'The half?' Belinda queried.

'The half. I'm supposed to be there thirty-five minutes before curtain up. Listen, I'll call you. Talk some more about it,' Hal said, as he stood up.

'Of course you will, Hal.'

'No, I mean it,' he yelled, as he sprinted for the door.

'I won't wait in,' she shouted as it banged behind him.

Belinda groaned. It was true: acting *had* been bad for Hal. It had become like a drug to him: he had had just enough success in the early stages of his career to keep him going. But, like most addictions, it had been full of false promise. Now it kept him low and depressed. And Belinda hated to see him like that.

What if he really did give it up? He wouldn't: Hal would go on dreaming, no matter what it cost him. He'd hang in there waiting for the big break, the one that was always just around the corner.

2

The Queen's Arms Theatre was at the back of the Queen's Arms pub in Islington. According to some, it was 'compact and bijou', but others described it, accurately, as 'small and tatty'. Atmospheric, said some. Claustrophobic, said Hal. He rushed through the bar, where they still rang up your bill in pounds, shillings and pence, into the theatre, and went backstage to what was laughingly known as the dressing room. This consisted of a long, communal tunnel that ran parallel to the back of the stage and bore a strong resemblance to a subsection of a London sewer. Everybody, men and women, changed together. It was a paradise for voyeurs, of which there were a fair few in the acting profession. Hal blinked as his eyes adjusted to the glare of the bulbs around the makeup tables.

'You're late for the half, Mr Morrisey,' the crop-haired company manager barked at him. 'We were getting worried.'

'Sorry. Commercial casting. Ran late. I need the job to subsidise what I'm not earning out of this little venture,' he said, sitting down in his allotted chair.

'Oh, Hal, nice of you to join us,' quipped Michael Skinner from the next chair, as he applied a white stick under his brows. 'Skin of your teeth, my friend. We were just dividing up your lines between us.'

'Sod off.' Hal laughed. Michael was playing his older brother and he was a good egg.

'How'd the audition go?' Michael asked quietly.

Hal gave Michael the thumbs-down.

'Balls! Get your makeup on quick. You're on in a minute.'

'What's the point of wearing makeup? The audience is only six inches away. The front row of tables is so close they could reach up and pick your nose for you if they so wished. I think they can see clearly without you going out there looking like a drag-queen.'

'Tut, tut, tut. These rebellious young actors. Turn up late, won't wear makeup. So unprofessional, darling.'

'Hal, hi! Where did you get to, you naughty boy?'

His leading lady's exaggerated American accent grated on Hal's already frayed nerves. 'I was at a—'

'Never mind, sweetie-pie. No time. Listen, have you seen this wonderful review in the *Guardian* today?'

'No,' Hal confessed.

'Lorna!' Michael barked at her.

'It's an absolute rave. Well, for most of us, anyhow. I'll leave it with you,' she said, dropping the page on Hal's lap.

Lorna May was tall, blonde and blue-eyed. This play required a quick change backstage, when Hal was also 'off', which left her naked for at least thirty seconds. Every day Hal bore witness to the fact that she had a fantastic body. Even so he couldn't forgive her for being such a complete cow.

'Don't read it,' Michael warned – pointlessly as Hal was already half-way through it. '*Hal Morrisey plays the unhappy leading role with the same hang-dog expression on his face throughout the play. To such an extent, that I had to check my programme notes to make sure the part was not being played by the cartoon character, Droopy.*'

16

'The bastard!' Hal swore. '*Even if this is a comedy, Mr Morrisey, might we suggest adding a second dimension to the part to complement the one you appear to be stuck in?* Who does this tosser think he is?' he asked.

'Act One, beginners on stage, please,' came the call.

'Shit! Costume.' Hal tore off his street clothes.

Michael ran to the rail and retrieved his friend's costume. 'By the way,' he announced, 'you've had a message. Jake's out front today.'

'Great timing,' moaned Hal. 'Confidence-sapping review, followed by the news that I have friends in to watch the show.'

'Lorna's such a monster,' Michael said, as he helped Hal on with his shirt. 'I don't know how you manage to kiss her on stage every day.'

'I'm a professional.'

'*Touché.*'

'I tell you something weird, though,' Hal began, as Michael helped him into his trousers and braces. 'She hates me but in every performance she insists on ramming her tongue into my gob.'

'How disgusting!'

'You're telling me. But if she's stupid enough to do it today I'm going to bite it.'

'Fiver says you don't.'

'You're on.' Hal sprinted for the stage.

Jake was waiting at a small table in the bar as Hal left the auditorium. He was easy to spot: his nose was large, full, and shiny, and it glowed like the dying embers of an open fire, due to countless bottles of red wine. Jake's huge physique had been nurtured by days filled with nothing to do but eat.

He had covered his ageing bulk with an artist's smock, a Paisley cravat tied jauntily around his thick neck, loose cotton trousers and, on his feet, Jesus creepers, with faded grey socks. A uniform which told everyone no woman loved him enough to try to turn him into the kind of man she usually found attractive.

'Hal, dear boy! Take a seat, I have a foaming pint of our host's finest ale, resting in anticipation of nothing more than the caress of your lips.' Jake said, in the honeyed, resonant tones Hal would have killed to possess.

' 'Ello, Professor, 'ow yer doing?'

This greeting was a running gag between them. Hal had met Jake on his first professional job out of drama school – a French farce in rep, somewhere in Devon. Despite three years of training, Hal had been struggling with his received pronunciation. Jake had taken him under his wing, Professor Higgins style, and honed his standard English during the course of the run.

'How am I, dear boy? Still railing against the injustices of a profession that uses family, shared religion, anal sex and the old school tie to exclude the shining aura of true talent,' he moaned. He took a sip of the house wine and winced. 'Speaking of talent, young Hal, you were truly wonderful today. A shining example to your fellow players. You lead by example and with courage. Never was there a captain who less deserved to go down with his sinking ship.'

'You hated the play, then,' Hal said, smiling as he picked up his pint.

Jake leaned across the table. 'I think Shakespeare, Wilde, Pinter and Stoppard can rest peacefully. I doubt this young playwright is likely to wrestle the crown of greatness from their reputable heads. As for the production, I think the standard was so akin to a Gang Show that I spent the entire ninety minutes waiting for someone to sing out that they were riding along on the crest of a wave.'

Hal sighed. 'I know. As swan-songs go, it's pitiful, isn't it?'

'Swan-songs?' Jake raised a greying eyebrow. 'Whose? Please tell me it's that appalling leading lady of yours. She gave a very bad impersonation of Vivien Leigh in *Gone With the Flatulence*.'

'You were impervious to the charms of the delightful Lorna May, then?'

'Not at all. I'd love to compromise her on a casting couch any day of the year. She just couldn't act. Why did she scream like a snared mink when you kissed her?'

'I've no idea.' Hal blushed. Jake would not approve of his schoolboy-type revenge and lack of professionalism. 'Anything happening in your neck of the woods?'

'One or two things in the pipeline.' Jake winked. 'Can't say much more. Don't want to tempt fate. Bit superstitious like that, don't you know?'

It was a euphemism for sod-all, and meant that there was no sign of work.

Jake was approaching sixty-five. He had lost the wife he loved due to his lack of success and, worse still, the respect of his two children, who had emigrated. More recently, his house had been repossessed. Now he was old, lonely and penniless, spending his evenings drinking and cooking for himself on an ancient Baby Belling in a damp bed-sit in Tooting Bec. For a brief moment, Hal felt he was looking at his future self.

'You all right, Hal?'

'Sorry, I was in a world of my own.'

'Are you sure?'

'All right,' Hal said. 'You wanted to know whose swansong it was? It was mine. I've had enough, Jake. I want out.'

'You speak blasphemy, dear boy!'

'No, really, it's true.'

'Nonsense! Bad play, a bitchy leading lady and a ghastly review have conspired to bring you to a low point. Happens to the best of us. But we dust ourselves down, pick ourselves up gracefully from the furnace of failure and move on.'

'It's different this time. I'm not enjoying it any more, Jake. I have to get real. I'm forty, and the chances are that I'm just not going to make it.'

Jake took a slurp of his wine and stared at him. 'No. You have real talent. You don't have to end up like me, old boy.'

'Jake, I really didn't mean . . .' Hal felt his cheeks burn as words failed him.

'Liar!'

'Jake . . .'

'You can bloody well get off that ridiculously gifted backside of yours, and buy me another glass of wine to make up for your tactlessness.'

Hal stood up. 'What is it?'

'Actually, I think I'll try a glass of the Chilean red this time, if you don't mind. The French acid has numbed my palate.'

'Chilean it is.'

'Hal,' Jake said, stopping him in his tracks.

'Yes?'

'Come to dinner next Friday. Quaff a glass or two of fine Burgundy warmed in a rusting saucepan of tepid water, on a hob still burning off the aroma of the previous night's cooking. Eat vegetables stewed into a flavourless mulch, potatoes roasted until they are each wearing their own suit of armour-plating, and a lamb joint cooked so rare, you won't even be sure if the sheep is dead. And discuss your plight with old Jake, for friendship's sake. Do not make a decision until you have done so. Promise me?'

'Sure,' Hal said, even though he knew there was nothing his friend could do to change his mind.

Hal sat glumly on the District Line. After his separation from Amy, he had taken the first decent affordable flat he'd seen, which happened to be in East Ham. Not unnaturally, he viewed it as a bit of a come-down from Hampstead. Having been born and raised on the glamorous piece of Essex coastline that is Southend-on-Sea, he had gradually fought his way up to the prestigious north London suburb. Now it was as if he was gradually working his way back to where he'd started.

He walked the seven minutes home from the station. The road he lived in was reasonably quiet, filled with Victorian terraced houses. A small Asian child riding a bike along the pavement nearly knocked him over. Hal turned into the entrance of number forty-seven and let himself in.

Hal lived upstairs and Mrs Worrel, his eccentric landlady, downstairs. There was one communal entrance, with Hal's front door at the top of the hall stairs. His landlady's door opened just as he reached the first step. Hal muttered an expletive under his breath and braced himself to face her.

Mrs Edith Worrel, widowed, was in her late seventies. She was short and stout. It was hard to differentiate between the various parts of her body: from just below her chin to the top of her ankles she appeared to have been squashed into one square lump, not unlike a car that had been written off and crushed into a cube of indistinguishable metal.

'Could I 'ave a word, Mr Morrisey?' she asked, in the husky voice of a heavy smoker.

He sighed resignedly. He'd already been dragged into her kitchen that morning. 'Mrs Worrel, what can I say? I know I'm a little late paying the rent this month . . .'

'Mr Morrisey, you're a little late wiv your rent every month,' she reminded him, pulling together the ends of the tatty pink crocheted shawl she always wore. 'But be fair, I always wait at least another week before threatening you with eviction.' She grinned, displaying a row of nicotine-stained teeth.

'You're very patient with me,' he admitted, returning her smile.

'I 'ave something I want to show yer, Mr Morrisey. There are things you need to know.'

Hal's heart sank. This could only mean one thing. She'd been slurping the Earl Grey all day without using a tea-strainer. He might have to suffer her Madam Za-Za routine yet again. She was a fortune-teller from a family of fortune-tellers, with the gift of foresight handed down through generations – or so she said.

'I'm a bit snowed-under at the moment, Mrs Worrel. A bit later, perhaps?'

'Mr Morrisey, it won't take long. And you wouldn't want me washing-up your future in Fairy Liquid, now would you?' she asked. Her eyes twinkled above her round puffy cheeks, reminding Hal of a benevolent toad in a children's book.

'Go on then, but I've not got long,' he lied – he had neither the funds nor the invitations to go anywhere that evening.

He followed Mrs Worrel along the hall, through the sitting-room that smelt like all grannies' houses the world over, and into the kitchen.

'Take a pew,' she said, sitting down and gesturing to one of the grey vinyl-covered chairs that stood around the circular table. The brown china teapot sat next to two matching cups and saucers, directly in front of the chair in which Mrs Worrel now sat. Alongside these lay a half-empty packet of Embassy, a lighter, and a butt-filled dessert bowl, overflowing with ash like a miniature Krakatoa.

She stared intently into Hal's eyes. 'I know you think I'm cracked but you're wrong. An' I may be seventy-eight and proud of it, but that doesn't mean I'm senile either. I still have all me marbles,' she said, tapping the side of her head with her index finger. 'Me body may be collapsing, but me mind's as sharp as a tack.'

'I've noticed that when you count out the rent money,' Hal acknowledged.

Mrs Worrel pulled out a cigarette. She lit it then took an exaggerated drag, tilted back her head and blew the smoke at the ceiling.

She picked up one of the teacups. From the chip in the side, Hal knew it was the one he had drunk from that morning.

'I've bin studyin' this all day,' she informed him.

'That's very sweet of you, Mrs Worrel, but really there's no need—'

She silenced Hal with a wave of her hand. 'Wanted to get it right, yer see. It's not like the usual tea-leaves. Bit more complicated. Take a look.' She thrust it under his nose.

As far as Hal was concerned it was a stained teacup filled with tea-leaves that should have been flushed down the sink hours ago.

'Can yer see the pattern?' she said.

'Hmmm, it does look a bit odd, doesn't it?' he humoured her.

'Yeah. But what does it mean?' she asked him.

'I thought you were going to tell me.'

'I can't.'

'Oh. Well, then, why—'

'Not exactly,' she clarified. 'The leaves are too spread around. Too . . . separated.'

'Oh, Lord, you're not going to give me more bad news about my ex, are you?' Hal enquired.

'No, it's nothing to do with her. Although it *is* something to do with a woman.'

'Really? Can I marry someone rich next time?'

Mrs Worrel tutted angrily. 'No, no, no. It's nothing to do wiv that. It's definitely career I'm seeing. You're going to be offered a job,' she stated firmly.

Hal's ears pricked up. 'What kind of job?'

'Not sure. But it'll be different in some way. Not what you're used to.'

So, maybe it wasn't an impossible dream: he could give up the theatre and some dozy employer would give him a proper job.

'What's the money like?' he asked.

'Good. Oh, yeah, it's good dosh.' She stared at him. 'This is the point, see. It's not the gift it appears to be. There's something wrong. Problem is, I'm just . . . not sure what.'

'Christ, if the money's good, and it doesn't involve trampolines, that's enough for me. Nothing's ever perfect, is it?' Hal said.

Mrs Worrel stiffened, then gave a little shudder. 'Don't take it.'

'What?'

'The job. Just don't take it.'

'But you said the money was great.'

'I know, dearie.'

'So I'd be mad to turn it down, wouldn't I?'

Mrs Worrel stared at Hal. 'I can't explain why, see. It's . . . I don't know, a feeling. At least let me do another reading before you take it.'

Hal scratched his head. It seemed that every friend or

acquaintance of pensionable age had decided to appoint themselves his career adviser. Then a thought struck him. An eccentric old woman was predicting his future based on the contents of a packet of Twining's. And he had taken it seriously. This showed just how sad his life was. 'Yeah, sure, no worries. Now listen, Mrs Worrel, I've really got to dash. I have a stack of phone calls to make.'

'All right, darling,' she said, as he stood to go. 'But you make sure you remember this: appearances can be deceptive.'

'I'll remember,' Hal said, and left as speedily as etiquette would allow.

Hal sat in front of the television, picking half-heartedly at some overcooked lasagne.

His sitting room was relatively spacious, filled with a few bits and pieces he'd salvaged from the divorce: a table and three pine kitchen chairs, a rug, which covered the swirly patterned carpet, a few prints on the bland magnolia walls, and an old hi-fi system.

He watched the television screen as the credits rolled for the end of *Coronation Street*. A lager commercial followed. 'That's it, go on, rub it in,' he shouted.

Then a still photograph of a middle-aged man filled the screen, and Hal listened to the accompanying announcement. **'The following repeat episode of the comedy *Bringing Up Ralph* will be shown as a tribute to actor Ian Wilson, who died tragically at the end of last month.'**

Hal had read all about Ian Wilson's death. Frankly, you'd have to be illiterate or living on the moon not to have done so. *Bringing Up Ralph* was the most popular situation comedy on TV and had been for the past three or four years. It was about a couple who were divorced

25

and the subsequent raising of their six-year-old son, Ralph. Hal thought it was trash, but because of the divorce theme, he watched it fairly regularly.

The child playing Ralph was a young actor called Sebastian Taylor. His face was all over the screen now as the title credits rolled: big blue eyes, blond hair, angelic. The star of the show. He played six years old, he looked six years old, but by Hal's reckoning he must be at least nine. Everybody loved Sebastian Taylor. He was known as 'The Nation's Poppet'. Everyone loved him. Everyone thought him a wonderful natural acting talent.

Sebastian Taylor: barely out of nappies, untrained, plucked from nowhere and given his own television series while Hal slogged his guts out at the Queen's Arms for nothing. The kid was probably loaded. God knows what they were paying him. Nine years old and he probably had a garage full of sports cars he wasn't even old enough to drive. And next week he was probably playing Hamlet at the RSC because he could put coach loads of bums on seats.

Something inside Hal Morrisey snapped. Enough was enough. Tomorrow he would go and see his agent and tell her he was quitting acting. Mrs Worrel had said he was going to be offered a proper job, and he'd damn well take it and hang the consequences.

He had communication skills. He could become a salesman, perhaps. After all, he'd been selling himself for years, and there couldn't be a more difficult product than that. Or public relations: he quite fancied buttering up wealthy clients in a hospitality tent at Wimbledon. Perhaps he could become a theatre critic and savage some other poor sod's performance.

His dream had ended.

And, to his surprise, he didn't feel sadness. He felt relief.

3

Belinda arrived at the Fairview Psychiatric Hospital in Highgate, where she worked. She checked her watch and realised that there was still over three-quarters of an hour to go before her working day was due to begin. She was feeling a little hung-over and somewhat low, a dangerous combination to carry into her working environment.

In need of a chat, she left her office and made her way to the staff kitchen on Churchgate Ward, in search of her friend Mary.

Mary was a psychiatric nurse in her late twenties. She was tall, muscular, and strong as a gorilla, which was useful when one of the patients decided to work off his frustration by throwing a bed or two around the ward.

The pair had met at the staff Christmas karaoke party. They had both been volunteered by their colleagues to sing Madonna's 'Like A Virgin', Belinda because nobody had ever seen her with a boyfriend, and Mary because she had been seen in the company of more men than the commanding officer of a large garrison. They had met up at the bar, chatted, compared notes, and looked out for each other ever since.

They were an odd combination: Mary was outrageous, outspoken, continually seizing the day, while Belinda was reserved, polite, and idealistic.

When Belinda shuffled through the door Mary was making her pre-battle cup of coffee.

'It's being so cheerful that keeps you going,' Mary commented, studying her friend's expression.

'Sorry.' Belinda grabbed a coffee mug.

'You all right?' Mary asked.

'I feel a bit down actually,' Belinda confessed.

'Well,' Mary began, clapping her hands. 'If you want some hot news to cheer you up, the new duck has let it slip that he fancies the knickers off you.'

'Duck' was a standing joke between them: they were convinced that most of the other doctors working in the hospital were quacks.

'Which one?' Belinda asked.

'The one who looks like a mature Brad Pitt.' Mary poured water over the coffee granules in her mug. 'I had a drink with him last night and all he wanted to talk about was you. You're lucky we're still speaking.'

'Brad Pitt? Don't mention actors to me,' Belinda said. 'Hal came round yesterday.'

'That's the one who used to be married to your friend, right?'

Belinda made her coffee. 'He rang me last night, too, pissed, from a pub to tell me he's giving up acting, even though he'd already told me that morning.'

'He's said that before, hasn't he?'

'I think he means it this time. He's going in to see his agent to break the news today.'

'So why has that made you miserable?'

Belinda sat down in the one armchair and put her mug on the table. 'I've pushed him into it a bit – and I think it's the right thing for him to do. Being an actor hasn't made him happy. But what if giving up makes him even more miserable?'

'Look, he's a grown man. He has to learn to make

decisions for himself. Why should you be trying to wipe his arse for him? Unless . . .'

'Unless what?'

'You fancy him – don't you?'

'He's just an old friend. I've known him years—'

'You do, you know. You're always going on about him. You want him to tear off your blouse buttons with his teeth, don't you?'

'*Mary!*'

'Go on, girl. Why don't you give him one? Get it out of your system.'

'Do you have to be so crude?'

Mary finished her coffee. 'Belinda, you're too moral for your own good. You never allow yourself to have any fun.'

Belinda huffed.

'Time to go.' Mary walked towards the door, then stopped. 'You really like Hal, don't you?'

'Of course I do. He's a good friend. I feel sorry for him.'

'*Sure*. See you at lunch-time.'

Belinda stared out of the window at the pretty parkland surrounding the hospital. An apple tree stood just outside and she could see the buds appearing, heralding the onset of spring. A tear eased its way out of her left eye. She had spent her life looking for the ideal man, the perfect love. Now, at thirty-five, she had begun to think she was destined to spend her life alone.

'Monica – *Monica*! My love, my dear, you must listen to me. Things have become desperate.'

Mr Warburton stood before her, resplendent in beige pyjamas.

Belinda looked up. 'Mr Clinton,' she said, 'you know we're not supposed to see each other.'

'But you don't understand, Monica. Hillary is furious.

There are women coming out of the closet every day with some new accusation. Congress want to impeach me! And all for a few precious moments between those cherry lips of yours.'

'Don't worry, Mr Clinton. I'm sure a scandal will be avoided.'

'But it won't, you floozy. I've read it in the stars.'

'I didn't know you were into astrology?'

'The *Daily Star*, you nincompoop!' He corrected her.

'Come along, Mr Warburton. Let's have you back on the ward now.' Mary's reassuringly large frame appeared and she grabbed the patient firmly by the arm.

'But you can't take me away!' he screamed. 'You don't know what she's doing to me. Don't give them the tapes,' he hollered, as Mary dragged him from the room. 'Or the dress! For God's sake, where did you keep the dress for all those months?'

Mr Warburton was a long-term inmate. He always cast Belinda in the role of a high-profile mistress. She had been Josephine to Warburton's Bonaparte, Cleopatra to his Mark Anthony, Lillie Langtry to Edward VII and Marilyn Monroe to his Jack Kennedy.

Belinda stood up and shook herself. Mary was right. Why was she spending so much time worrying about Hal? He was just a friend, after all.

The office of Hal's agent, Pippa Grey, was in a high-rent block in Piccadilly. He hadn't telephoned to say he was coming: he didn't want to be put off. He slipped past the token security guard slouching behind the desk and took the lift to the third floor. He still had to get past the officious Janice, Pippa's secretary.

'Janice, how lovely to see you again,' he said.

She scowled at him. 'Do you have an appointment, Hal?'

'No.'

'Well, Adrian Mullender does.' She gestured to the fresh-faced youth standing next to her.

'Damn. What about if I begged? I really need to see Pippa.'

'No, Hal.'

'Sorry, Janice, but it's urgent. Look, you don't mind if I barge in, do you? I won't be ten minutes,' Hal said to Adrian.

'Not at all,' replied the young man.

Must be a rookie, straight out of drama school, if he doesn't mind me pushing in, thought Hal.

'Well, I do, Hal,' Janice snapped.

'Don't worry, Janice, you won't have to put up with me for much longer,' he said, blew her a kiss and walked into his agent's office.

'Hal? What are you doing here?'

When Hal had first met Pippa Grey she had been doing Janice's job as assistant to Peter Matthews, Hal's original agent. An ambitious gold-digger, she had stomped around his office, bra-less and with short skirts, until the poor man had dropped dead of a heart-attack. Then she had taken over. Peter had been of the old school, a big drinker and socialiser, a man who cared about his clients' welfare. Pippa's level of concern depended on how much commission she was raking in. Consequently, she couldn't give a toss about Hal.

Peter's office had been above a knocking shop in Soho, small and tatty. Pippa's office was huge, the walls plastered with photos of her with her star clients, a montage from which Hal was notably absent.

'Sit down, Hal. Good to see you,' she said.

Hal was taken aback. He'd barged in without booking an appointment, and had been anticipating her usual level of contempt, yet she actually looked pleased to see him. In fact, she was smiling.

'I've been trying to phone you all morning,' she informed him.

'I'm not in.'

Hal had never seen her in professionally charming mode before, and even now he found her intimidating. Of Amazonian stature, with cropped red hair and matching lipstick, she was okay as an agent, but Hal remained convinced that she was just the centre-half England had been crying out for since Jackie Charlton retired.

'I've come to tell you something,' he announced.

'Oh?'

He took a deep breath. 'I'm giving up. I've had enough, Pippa. I thought I'd better tell you in person.'

Pippa's eyes widened. 'I don't believe you. I take it you've given this some thought?'

He was gratified by her attempt to show she cared. 'I've agonised for days and I'm convinced I've reached the right decision.'

She stood up and strode over to the window. 'So, there's nothing I can say to persuade you to change your mind?'

Now Hal was nonplussed. He'd expected her to show him the door straight away.

'No,' was the best he could manage.

'You don't want me to put you forward for anything else? Ever again?'

'That's right.'

'Or tell you about any auditions that come in?'

'Absolutely not.'

'It's set in stone, then?'

'Yes.'

'Let me get this right. You don't want me to tell you about the audition I've lined up for you this afternoon?'

'Oh, come on, Pippa, stop playing games with me.'

'Even if I were to tell you it's a telly?' She turned away from the window and faced him.

'Another commercial casting?' Hal flushed. 'Huh! I couldn't think of anything worse.'

She came to her desk and sat on the edge, crossing her legs slowly. It was almost as if she was flirting with him.

Hal had had enough of being dangled at the end of her line. He stood up.

'Sit down, Hal. It's not an advert. It's a television.'

'Look, I've said it's no-go. What more do you want me to say, except . . .' Hal withered under the weight of her stare. 'Oh, go on, then. Who's casting it?'

'Jemima Barnes.'

'Well, there's no way she'd cast me in anything after I walked out of the—'

'Ironically enough,' Pippa interrupted, 'that's why she's called you in. Your feisty behaviour rather impressed her.'

'You're joking.'

'Actually,' she said, brushing imaginary fluff from her skirt, 'it rather impressed me. I didn't know you had it in you, Hal.'

'Look, I want security, I want regular work, I want money . . . Speaking of money . . . how much?'

She gave an exaggerated sigh. 'A little disappointing, really. They're only offering fifteen hundred a week. Though I suspect I can push them up to two grand. That's two weeks location, plus six weeks' rehearsal and studio recordings. That's a minimum of sixteen thousand. Plus any overtime and other bits and pieces. It's not great, but it's okay.'

Inwardly Hal whimpered. That was more than he'd earned in a year since he had left drama school.

'Still not interested?' she asked.

'I'm probably unsuitable, anyway.' Hal's resistance was faltering.

'Not according to Jemima. You're the right age, right type. It would appear she spread word of your James Dean-style defiance. It impressed someone with influence, she says.'

'The director? The show's star?' Hal asked.

'Maybe, maybe not.'

Hal sighed. 'Pippa . . .'

'It's a situation comedy. A regular character.'

'They'll kill it after the first series.'

'It's been running for years, Hal. It's massively successful. Your money would go up next series as well. Still,' she shrugged, distractedly, 'you're not interested.'

'Come on, Pippa. Situation comedy? I mean it's not me. Which situation comedy?'

'*Bringing Up Ralph.*'

'I thought they'd decided not to carry on with that after Ian Wilson died.'

'How long have you been in this business, Hal? That's just publicity nonsense. Didn't you see the tribute episode last night?'

'Yes.'

'Well, you'd be replacing Ian Wilson.'

Hal's mouth dropped open. 'I'd be playing the father?'

Pippa smiled. 'If successful.'

'Why do they want to see me?' he asked.

'They've been auditioning for weeks. Not found anyone suitable. They start filming the week after next.'

'How come?' Hal said, scratching his chin.

'Sebastian Taylor's being fussy. He was rather fond of Ian.'

Hal sat silent.

'It's up to two thousand a week and a chance to work with the Nation's Poppet. What more do you want?'

34

'The audition's today?'

Pippa went for the kill. 'This is the final day. All the other actors are on recalls. One reading, and you'll know by tomorrow morning at the latest whether they want you or not. You've a good chance here, Hal. This might be big-break territory. If you don't get the job, I'll leave you to enjoy your retirement. What do you say?'

Hal sighed. 'All right. One more for old times' sake even though I won't get it.'

'Four o'clock at the Jester TV production offices.'

She slipped off the edge of the desk, grabbed a pen and pad, jotted down the details, then handed a piece of paper to Hal. 'That's the address,' she informed him. 'Now, haven't you an entirely worthless profit share to perform in?'

Hal glanced at his watch. 'Bloody hell, yes. I must go.' He made his way to the door in a daze.

'Hal.' Pippa stopped him in his tracks.

'Yes?'

'It's looking good. Don't fuck it up.'

4

Hal was running. He had to tell someone! Somehow it wouldn't be real until he did. He raced through Highgate Village, hurdling small children, dogs and shopping bags as he headed for Belinda's place of work.

Yesterday afternoon he'd sat outside the audition room, mouth dry, palms sweating. He had looked at the scene he was to read, practised it in his head. Inflections, character, timing.

The actor before him left, smiling, and Hal's heart had sunk.

Then Jemima collected him and took him into the audition room. In the corner behind the door sat a woman, her face half hidden behind the script. He presumed he would read with her. She never looked up. Jemima introduced him to the producer, the writer, and the Nation's Poppet, Sebastian Taylor. Hal was to read with Sebastian. Which he did, three times. Sebastian knew the scene and did not take his eyes off Hal. By the third reading Hal was word-perfect too.

It was odd, the way the child looked at him. He didn't act with Hal, he just said the lines and stared at him, which made Hal uncomfortable.

The producer, a man called Tony, had said, 'Good, very good' after each reading. He asked Hal to remember that he was not in a theatre, and to bring his performance down to a more subtle level.

After the third reading the producer whispered into the writer's ear, who whispered into Sebastian's ear. The boy glanced briefly over Hal's shoulder, then nodded. It was the only time Sebastian's eyes had left Hal during the entire audition. Hal glanced behind him, but the woman was hidden once more behind her script. He had almost forgotten she was there. Then it was the usual handshakes, and a promise to telephone his agent by tomorrow lunch-time.

Sebastian Taylor had stared until Hal closed the door behind him.

Still Hal ran, out of Highgate Village and up the backroads to the hospital.

When he'd left the audition Hal had gone into the nearest pub, shaking. It had been the easiest he had ever had. He felt good. It had gone well. He knew he had done himself justice. The producer had congratulated him. The writer had complimented him on his reading. Never had a pint tasted so sweet, transformed into the nectar of the gods with the fantasy of fame and fortune that raced through his mind. Until just after six o'clock that evening. He knew Pippa would have closed the office by then, that no call would be forthcoming until the morning, and his optimism had faded.

The road to the hospital seemed never-ending. His heart was racing, his lungs felt as if they were about to explode, and his legs became heavier with every step. 'Almost there,' he told himself.

From ten o'clock the next morning, when Pippa's office opened, Hal had paced backwards and forwards around his flat. He stared at the telephone, willing it to ring, *begging* it to ring. When it did it was Jake, reminding him about dinner on Friday night. When it had rung the second time, Hal knew. Every fibre in his racked body, every cell in his shattered mind, had told him that this was the call.

Still Hal ran. He had now entered the grounds of the hospital, full of greenery and peace, so at odds with the busy streets he'd left behind. He held aloft the champagne he had brought to share with Belinda, like an athlete carrying the Olympic flame.

When Hal eventually forced himself to lift the receiver, he closed his eyes and braced himself for bad news. 'Hello.'

'Hal?'

'Hello, Pippa.'

'Oh, damn, I'm sorry. What am I doing ringing you?'

'What?' Hal had exclaimed.

'You've retired, haven't you?'

'Pippa.'

'You're going to be a meat-packer, or was it a traffic warden?'

'*Please!*'

'So you really wouldn't be interested to hear you have just been cast as the father in the next series of *Bringing Up Ralph*, would you?'

'What?' Hal had whimpered.

'Yes. They want you. For some obscure reason they thought you were fabulous. They've also optioned you for a further two series.'

'Oh, God.'

'And thanks to my brilliant negotiating skills they've gone for the two grand a week.'

'Er . . .'

'They're biking the scripts for the six episodes round to you later in the day. You start the job Monday week. I'll let you know the times and places later. Oh, and you'll have to go for a wardrobe fitting, but some woman called Jennie will be ringing you about that.'

'Er . . .'

'Hal? Say something.'

'I think I'm going to be sick,' he had replied.

'Tell the press that in your first interview. They love all that crap.'

'Press interviews, wardrobe fittings, biked-over scripts, two grand . . . TWO GRAND! Pippa, is this real?'

'Of course!' She laughed.

'It can't go wrong, can it?'

'No! Look, Hal, the pubs are open. Go and get nicely plastered. You have my permission. Not too sloshed to open the door to the courier with your scripts, just pleasantly oiled. I'll call you back again this afternoon. It'll probably make more sense when you've had a few.'

'Thanks, Pippa, thanks for everything.'

'My pleasure, my fifteen per cent. Congratulations, Mr Morrisey. I'll buy you lunch at the Ivy later in the week to celebrate. 'Bye for now, star.'

The phone went dead.

And that was when he had begun running to tell Belinda. She had recognised how unhappy the business was making him. She knew how close he had come to giving up his dream. She had witnessed the years of struggle. He knew that when he had shared his news with her, it would start to feel real.

Hal fell through the doors into the hospital's reception area and sprinted to the desk. 'Dr Belinda Marsh, please, and hurry,' he said, puffing, to the security guard on the desk.

The man checked down his list, picked up the phone, and dialled the extension number. 'What's your name?' he asked.

Hal knew how tight security was in this type of

hospital. Amy had worked in similar establishments. He thought quickly. 'I'm her husband,' he blurted. 'Hal M M Marsh.'

The guard's eyebrows furrowed. 'I never knew she had a husband.'

'Well, you do now,' Hal bluffed.

'You sure? Only we have to be careful here, mate.'

'Of course I'm sure,' Hal barked.

'How come I've never seen you before, then?' the guard enquired.

'What? Well, I've hardly been in a mad rush to visit this place, have I?' Hal was thinking on his feet.

'So what are you doing here now, then?'

'I have to see my wife. Tell her it's urgent.'

The guard put the telephone down. 'Can't get through, I'm afraid. All hell's broke loose up there this morning.'

'But it's an emergency!' Hal persisted. 'Er . . . her mother has passed away.'

The guard looked at the champagne bottle. 'Organising a quick wake, are you?'

'It's to soften the blow. Her mother's been ill for some time. She made us promise to toast her parting with her favourite champ— Why am I telling you all this?' Hal said, through gritted teeth.

The guard weighed Hal up. 'This is on the level, is it?'

Hal crossed his fingers. 'Why would I lie?'

'Righto.' He dialled a number. 'Sam, can you come down and cover me for a few minutes? I've got to escort a gentleman up to Churchgate.' He hung up. 'Okay, mate, as soon as he gets here, I'll take you up.'

Hal had been ushered into the Churchgate ward staff room by the formidable Mary and told to wait. He opened the champagne, found a couple of mugs and filled them. It had been a lively morning on the ward, and everybody was frantic. He had to spend a full fifteen minutes sitting on his excitement before she walked through the door. 'Belinda!' he shouted and ran to her. 'I've done it, girl. I've only gone and done it!'

She stared at him, saw the joy in his face and she knew: she understood exactly what he was saying to her. 'I never believed it would make you so happy,' she said.

'Didn't you? All those years of miserable struggle and now it's all over. Have some champagne,' he said, handing her a cup.

Belinda's smile widened. 'Hal, I'm so happy for you.'

'I knew you would be. That's why I ran all the way here. I wanted you to be the first to know. I knew you'd understand what it meant.'

'Oh, Hal, I'm so proud of you. It's amazing to think that after all these years you've finally managed it.'

'I know!' Hal laughed.

'You've actually given up acting!'

Hal was temporarily dumbstruck. When the power of speech returned he said, 'Er . . . no, it's not quite as simple as that. You see, I've got a job—'

'A job!' Belinda interrupted. 'Already! That's fantastic! You certainly haven't let the grass grown under your feet.'

'I mean an acting job.'

'Hal?' Belinda's face showed her disappointment.

'No, wait a minute. It's a big job.'

'*Jack and the Beanstalk* in Bloxwich?'

'No, I'm talking money here.'

'Going to pay you Equity minimum for this one?'

'Belinda! Listen, I'm going to be famous!'

'No, Hal, *you* listen. I've had a lousy morning. One of my patients tried to strangle me, and you come in here, pretending to be my husband, and letting me believe you've given up something that has always made you miserable—'

'Look,' said Hal, picking up the champagne, 'would I have brought this if it wasn't big news?'

'I don't care! And my mother is alive and well and living in Weymouth.' She raised her cup and hurled its contents into Hal's face.

'Belinda?' Hal said, spluttering.

'How much longer before you realise? How many more false dawns? Once this job is over you'll be miserable again. How much longer do I have to listen to you saying you're giving up acting when it's not going to happen?'

'Belinda, you don't understand,' Hal cried. He caught her wrists and held them tight.

'Unhand her, Arthur!'

Hal looked round to see a tall man, who appeared to have no arms, standing in the staff-room doorway.

'Oh, no, that's all we need,' gasped Belinda.

'Unhand her, or face the consequences!'

'Don't be ridiculous,' Hal said.

'She may be your wife, but she's my mistress!'

'I beg your pardon?' Hal exclaimed. 'Who the hell is this?' he asked Belinda.

'I've told you about him. This is Mr War—'

'You may be King Arthur, but I am a knight of the Round Table, and Guenevere and I are lovers.'

'What's he talking about?' Hal asked Belinda.

'I am Sir Lancelot. And you are a blackguard!'

It was at this point that Hal noticed the man had arms after all. But they were encased in a strait-jacket.

Then Mr Warburton lunged forward and head-butted him. He collapsed on to the floor. 'Hal! I don't believe this,' he heard Belinda scream.

As he lay there, blood pouring down his chin, he

wondered if the scriptwriters of *Bringing Up Ralph* might be prepared to work a broken nose into the story-line.

5

Hal's nose still throbbed like a recently banged cymbal, but, as he stared at his reflection in the shaving mirror, he saw signs of improvement. One of the psychiatrists at the hospital had declared that he didn't think Hal's nose was broken, which was confirmed by the fellow he saw at the nearest A&E department. It still glowed alarmingly red, but he had to concede that it would probably be fine in a day or so. He breathed a sigh of relief as he switched off the light above the mirror and went into his sitting room where his tea was steaming on the coffee table. He flopped on to the sofa and took a comforting slurp then heard a key turning in his front-door lock. Just in time, he pulled his towelling-robe around himself.

'It's only me, love. Don't mind me lettin' meself in, do yer?' Mrs Worrel asked rhetorically.

'Would it make a difference if I did?'

'Not when yer as much behind in the rent as you usually are,' she confirmed. 'That smells nice. Any more in the pot?'

'I'm strictly a tea-bag-in-the-mug man.'

'Philistine,' Edith muttered. 'You may scoff at my Gift,' she remarked as she crossed the room, 'but I'm not as daft as yer think.' She eased her way into the narrow chair that stood opposite Hal's sofa. 'Oh, Gawd, what the bleedin' 'ell 'appened to yer nose?'

'I got nutted by one of Belinda's fruitcakes.'

'Getting into fights at your age? Your trouble is you've been on yer own too long. You've no woman in yer life. Or yer bed, come to that. Except me, of course, and I'm afraid the days when I used to leap from inside me wardrobe wearing nothing but a smile are long gone, dearie.'

Hal couldn't help grimacing at this graphic picture.

'You need to get yerself a girlfriend.'

'Mrs Worrel,' Hal said, with dignity, 'have you just come up to give me advice on my love-life? Or was there some other—' He was interrupted by the telephone. 'Excuse me, I must answer that.'

'Don't mind me.'

Hal picked up the receiver.

'Hal?'

'Yes?'

'It's Pippa. Listen. You have a costume fitting tomorrow. Have you a pen handy? Take down this address.'

'Got it,' Hal confirmed, as he finished writing.

'You've got to be kitted out quickly because they've brought your filming dates forward. You travel on Monday and start shooting on Tuesday. Your schedule will arrive with the scripts. It'll tell you what scenes you're filming on what day. Just learn the relevant scenes over the weekend. This isn't theatre – you're not expected to know the whole episode back to front on day one. Okay?'

Hal grinned like a man who had just slapped custard pie into the face of an uncooperative bank manager. 'It's better than okay, Pippa. It's fantastic. Where is the filming taking place? Mauritius? Tahiti? The Maldives?'

'Bournemouth, and it'll probably be freezing so take a sweater. Best of luck. I'll call you if there's anything else.'

'Thanks, Pippa. When will I have a contract to sign?'

'About three weeks after you've finished the job, if

45

things run true to form. Don't worry – they'll give you expenses while you're on the shoot.' And she was gone.

Hal glanced at his answering-machine as he hung up. There was a message, and he made a mental note to listen to it when he had got rid of his landlady. 'Mrs Worrel, I don't want to be rude, but that was an important phone call, and I've lots to do—'

She put up a hand to stop him. 'It's all right. I knows when I'm not wanted. Just help me out of this chair, will yer?'

'What was it you came to see me about?' Hal asked, as he manoeuvred her to the door.

'Doesn't matter. It'll keep.' She turned to face him. 'You took it, didn't yer?'

Hal was startled. 'Took what?'

'The job. The one I told yer not to take. Yer did, didn't yer?'

Suddenly he remembered her prophecy of doom. 'Oh, no, actually. It didn't turn out to be a proper job, it's an acting—'

'I never said it'd be a proper job.' Mrs Worrel's face was a picture of concern.

'Didn't you? Well, listen, it's amazing news. I'm going to be a regular in *Bringing Up Ralph*,' he told her excitedly.

'What's that, then?'

'Everyone's heard of *Bringing Up Ralph*, Mrs Worrel. It's the biggest sit-com on television.'

'I only watch soaps and documentaries,' she informed him.

'Well, it's massive and I'm taking over as Ralph's father.'

'What happened to the last one who played it?'

Hal's face took on a more serious expression. 'Ah, that was all rather sad. He died unexpectedly.'

Mrs Worrel's face was grave. 'Not many laughs in that.'

'No,' Hal agreed, deflated.

'I knew you'd taken the job,' Mrs Worrel informed him.

'I suppose the phone call rather gave it away.'

She shook her head. 'It was your bloody nose. It's not too late to change yer mind, you know.'

Hal gasped. 'I can't just walk out on the biggest break of my career!'

Mrs Worrel sighed. 'Think about it,' she said, and disappeared down the stairs.

'Batty,' Hal whispered, as he closed the door. Then he went to the answering-machine and pressed play.

'Hal, dear boy, it's Jake. Forgive my impudence, but although you have a brain capable of memorising vast quantities of blank verse, on a day-to-day level you have the memory of a rabbit with Alzheimer's. I hope you haven't forgotten you are to do me the honour of joining me for supper in the bijou hovel I call home. Shall we say eight o'clock for the half, dear boy? Farewell until then.'

Indeed, Hal *had* forgotten. Worse still, he had been looking forward to a night in with his scripts. He thought about ringing to cancel. Then he remembered that Jake thought he was about to spend an evening talking him out of quitting the business. His old friend would be genuinely pleased for him. On the other hand . . .

Hal headed for the shower, and began to rehearse in his mind exactly how best to broach things with Jake.

'I just got angry with him, Mary. He'd convinced me he was going to give up acting and then he'd done the opposite.'

'I can't imagine any actor giving up the minute they land their big break,' Mary said reasonably.

'I know, and I feel terrible. It's only one job, though, isn't it? It's not exactly the starring role. He wasn't even first choice. I mean, he only got the job because the original actor slashed his wrists. If that isn't a bad omen I don't know what is. Five minutes of fame, and he could be back doing end-of-the-pier stuff, couldn't he?' Belinda sat on one of her two large, dark blue sofas, her feet tucked under her.

'You're just wound up because he got battered in his hour of glory – and you've got the hots for the bloke,' Mary declared.

'I'm the psychiatrist so I'll do the analysing, and that's nonsense,' Belinda snapped.

'Oh, cobblers, Belinda,' Mary retorted, waving her glass. A splosh of red wine fell on to the cream carpet. 'Why don't you give him a ring and see if his swelling's gone down?' Mary suggested. 'Where are you going?' she asked as Belinda stood up and headed for the door.

'I'm going to get a cloth before *that* becomes a permanent feature of my carpet.' Belinda pointed at the wine stain.

Mary apologised sheepishly. 'Perhaps we should drink white from now on.'

Belinda went into the kitchen for the salt-cellar and a J-cloth.

She had known Hal for so many years. After his marriage had ended and Amy had moved to Manchester, he had regularly called round to talk to her about the divorce. She had heard all Amy's criticisms of Hal. His lack of practicality, which Belinda had found endearing. His obsession with succeeding as an actor, which she found astonishing yet somehow admirable, his bizarre sense of humour, which she found sexy. In fact, she had been smitten with Hal for as long as she could remember. Once, she had intended to tell him so. That was why

48

she had invited him to visit her at university. She had planned to tell him at the party where Hal had met Amy. She had kept quiet. Since the divorce she had known Hal still felt raw. In any case, he had never indicated that he was attracted to *her*.

'Give him a ring,' Mary suggested, appearing from nowhere and handing her the telephone.

'Who?'

'Hal.'

'Don't be silly.'

'You'll only worry if you don't.'

'I'll be fine.'

Mary sighed. 'Give me those.' She snatched the salt-cellar and the cloth. 'I spilt the wine so I should clean it up. I think we need to talk.' She headed off to do battle with the carpet.

Hal pressed Jake's intercom and waited to be buzzed in. The door to the bedsit was ajar, and when he went in he felt instantly depressed, as usual, by the drab old floral wallpaper, stained with the nicotine of hundreds of chain-smoking tenants, the green floral carpet, with large threadbare patches, the ageing sofa and chair covered in green Dralon. Then he remembered the scripts tucked into his rucksack and felt better. He had just begun to think excitedly about showing them to his friend when Jake emerged from the bathroom.

'Hal, dear boy, how nice to see you. On time too. Welcome, once again, to my little palace. As you can see, I've had the hit squad in from the BBC's *Changing Rooms* since you were last here. Clearly those overpaid interior designers have made a complete fuck-up of the place. Now, plant your rear on the sofa, and I'll pour you a glass of the embalming fluid that that con-man of a wine merchant assured me was a fine claret.'

Jake filled two glasses and made his way carefully across the room. Hal saw that he was swaying slightly. He wondered how many other empty bottles were already in the bin next to the fridge. He knew Jake well enough to tell that he was having a bad day.

'Here you are,' Jake said, as he handed over the glass. 'Best to hurl it quickly at the back of the throat. Don't want it lingering too long on the old tastebuds.'

Hal took a sip and flinched. 'I see what you mean.'

Jake sank heavily into the chair opposite. 'I don't suppose the happy wanderer has a bottle of vintage Mouton Rothschild in his little knapsack, has he?'

'Not exactly. More sort of Beaujolais *nouveau*.'

'Never mind. Perhaps we'll save that for later. Well, are you hungry, dear boy?'

'I am actually,' Hal replied. He had learnt from bitter experience that the best way to get through a meal at Jake's was to fast all day and arrive hungry enough to eat anything.

'Sit up at the table, then, and I will deliver a lovingly prepared starter for your delectation, while my Hungarian goulash congeals to perfection in the oven.'

'I thought you were going to do a roast?'

'I was. Unfortunately I had to go into town earlier and was a little late arriving back. I'm afraid it's foreign stew with rice, supplied by good old Mr Ben.'

'Uncle Ben,' Hal corrected as he sat down. 'Mr Benn was a little man in a bowler hat who used to have wild adventures in a fancy-dress shop.'

'And we've all had a few of those, dear, haven't we?' Jake said with a wink. He put the open wine bottle on the table with his own glass, then returned to the kitchen area of the room.

'I'll just check the main course,' he said. He bent down opened the oven door, put on an oven glove, then lifted the lid of the casserole dish. 'Oh, yes, very *Quatermass.*'

He stood up, wheezing, picked up two bowls and brought them to the table. He put one in front of Hal. Hal stared down into an orange and green concoction. 'Jake, I don't wish to appear rude, but what is it?'

'What is it?' Jake echoed. 'Prawn cocktail, of course,' he informed him.

Hal picked up his spoon and took a mouthful. 'But there aren't any prawns in it. It's just lettuce and Thousand Island dressing.'

'Oh, damn, I knew I'd forgotten something. Sorry, dear boy. Not to worry, the main course is just waiting for the bell to come out fighting, and I can assure you it's a heavyweight.'

Hal chuckled.

'Now, then,' Jake began, as he topped up Hal's glass, which was virtually untouched, and refilled his own, which was empty, 'if I remember rightly, the purpose of this evening, apart from the usual attempts at botulism, salmonella and liver damage, was to discuss your intended retirement from the cruel and merciless profession we share.'

'Yes, it was,' Hal agreed. 'Which brings me—'

'Please, Hal,' Jake raised his right hand, 'there will be ample opportunity for you to have your say on the matter, but I beg of you, allow me to teeter precariously on a mythical soapbox and deliver my speech. Lord knows, I have precious few chances to do so professionally, these days, and it's good to keep one's hand in.'

'But, Jake, you don't understand—'

'Oh, but I *do* understand, Hal,' Jake insisted. 'Believe me, dear boy, after the day I've had, perhaps more than ever.'

'Why? What happened?' Hal asked, suddenly concerned.

'I'll come to that later. Now please don't spoil my soliloquy. I came into this business with the same hopes, dreams and ambitions as you. I trained at RADA, and was seen as a leading light. A major career was predicted by staff and fellow pupils alike. At the beginning it seemed the prophecy was to come true but, like a runner who has sprung forth too quickly from the block, I became stale, and have watched everyone else catch me up and pass me by. For a sad, randy old man like me to confess it is not pleasant to be lapped, something must be terribly wrong. And it is.'

Jake took a sip of wine.

'This profession is vicious, Hal. We spend our lives being rejected and humiliated. We suffer any indignity to stay in work, allowing worthless individuals to treat us like dogs because of the power they have over us. We metamorphose into grovelling hypocrites. We pretend to have such camaraderie within a company, while all the time we are looking after our own interests. We stab each other in the back to avoid returning to the dole queue. Actors change into people their own mothers wouldn't recognise. Worse still, they change into people they themselves would cross the street to avoid. And every time the likes of you and I become rational human beings again, Hal, wise to all the falseness and misery, our profession teases us by tossing us some pathetic little job. Just enough to keep the dream alive. Which is why I am still waiting for the big break.'

Hal could see tears forming in his old friend's eyes.

'I was called into town today to see Marcus.'

'Your agent?' Hal queried. Jake had several acquaintances called Marcus.

'I thought he was my agent. And, indeed, he was until four thirty this afternoon.'

'I don't understand.'

'I have been tossed off his books. He's pruning his list, and his secateurs have closed themselves around my professional testicles. Thirty years I've permitted that incompetent to manage my career. I should have known something was up when he took me to lunch for only the second occasion. I should have guessed things were not all they should be when he failed to flinch as I ordered wine costing twenty-five pounds. The ignorant little man probably thought that I was about to do the decent thing and fall on my sword.'

Hal patted his shoulder. 'And you had no idea this was about to happen?'

'None. We talked over lunch about the things we usually talk about in his office over a cup of instant coffee. We joked, laughed and gossiped until I was half-way down my liqueur when he said he'd decided to let me go. He confessed that he had singularly failed to find me work in recent years, and felt sure my luck would change if I were to find alternative representation. He even provided me with a list of possibles. All losers, all further down the ladder of personal management than he is, and heaven knows Marcus is pretty bottom-rung, these days.'

'Well, then, it's no bad thing, is it? Marcus is an old has-been. You need someone younger, more enthusiastic, taking care of you.'

'Hal, just how many young agents are going to want to represent me at my time of life and with my work record? They'll be trawling their nets around the drama-school final-year shows, fishing for the stars of tomorrow. They're not going to want a tired old trout like me on their books. I'm a reminder to their young hopefuls of how most people in this business end up.'

Hal ran his hands through his hair. 'I don't know what to say, Jake.'

'Say nothing, old boy. It's too late for this old fool. But it isn't too late for you. I brought you here tonight to talk you out of quitting acting. I was one step away from committing a heinous crime. Hal, get out while you can.'

'*What?*' Hal exclaimed.

'I mean it. This has nothing to do with what I feel about your talent, but that isn't a guarantee of success any more. If it ever was. You're still young, Hal. If I encouraged you to continue I might be condemning you to end up a sad old bastard like me, and I simply can't do it.'

'But, Jake—'

'Hal, listen to me. You're forty. You can use your talents in a way to make you money, not misery. Have a normal life filled with all the simple things people enjoy. That's my advice to you. I owe it to you to speak the truth for the first time in the eighteen years I have known you.'

Jake picked up a napkin and wiped his eyes. 'There. I've said my piece. I will now go and retrieve Frankenstein's monster from the oven, and you can spend the rest of the evening telling me why you are going to ignore me.'

But Hal didn't argue against what Jake had said, or tell him about the scripts in his bag. He couldn't. He suddenly felt foolish: he had forgotten how the profession worked. Jake wouldn't be pleased for him, not really. Actors are selfish: they always think they are the one who deserved the lucky break. Jake had told Hal he thought of him as his theatrical son, convinced him to believe in his talent, assured him that this day would arrive, but he would feel bitter, angry and jealous at Hal's good fortune. Especially today when the business had treated him so cruelly.

Instead Hal spent the rest of the evening feeling guilty about his success. For the first time in eighteen years, he had to find other subjects to talk about with his friend. Jake drank heavily, while Hal hardly touched a drop. It felt like the longest two hours of his life. Eventually he made his excuses and left. He had got half-way downstairs when he realised he had left behind his bag with the scripts. Cursing, he made his way back to Jake's door and rapped on it.

When Jake opened the door he was holding Hal's open rucksack. 'Sorry, dear boy, I've run out of wine and I remembered you said you'd brought a bottle with you. Why didn't you tell me your good news?'

'I wanted to, but you'd had such a bad day and—'

'So you let me waffle on about giving up when your star was in the ascendant. Congratulations. I'm thrilled for you. Never has a bit of luck been more deserved.' Jake handed the bag to Hal then threw his arms around him in a bear-hug.

'We shall arrange a night on which to toast your success.'

6

Even though *Bringing Up Ralph* was broadcast on BBC1, it was made by an independent company called Jester, whose production offices were in London's West End. This was where Hal's audition had taken place and where he returned for his costume fitting.

He breezed through the door of the large, plush offices into the reception area. Two well-dressed young women sat behind an enormous desk. Both had in front of them large switchboards, and they wore headsets with small microphones attached.

'Hi, I'm Hal—'

'Oh, lookie here! It's the new kid on the block, all sweaty palms and virginal. Just how we like them,' said someone behind him. Hal turned.

A tall man of about six feet six stood before him. He was in his fifties, had broad shoulders and a receding hairline. What hair remained on the back of his head was as curly as a poodle's. He was wearing white jeans, and a V-neck T-shirt, which showed off bulging biceps, and enough chest hair to stuff a small cushion.

'I'm sorry,' Hal said, taken aback, 'you're . . . ?'

'Peter, sweetie. I'm your dresser. For the next seven or eight weeks I shall be zipping and unzipping your flies like a porno film on fast-forward. So I think we should be on first-name terms, don't you?'

'Fine,' Hal muttered.

'Good. You're not all starry, then? Lord knows, we have enough divas on this show as it is. One more and I'd have considered retiring and opening a safe-house for battered rent-boys. Wenches,' he said, to the two receptionists, who scowled at him, 'I'm going to take Mr Morrisey through to the torture chamber to see which frocks we can squeeze his manly frame into. If Mini the Mona rings again, tell her Jennie has found her a fabulous nightdress for that scene she was worrying about, but on no account are you to put her through to either Jennie or me, *comprende*?'

They smiled tolerantly.

'Right, then.' Peter crooked a finger at Hal. 'Follow me to the sweat-box.' He led the way down a corridor.

'Who's Mini the Mona?' Hal asked.

'Penny Davenport, the old ham who plays your screen wife – or ex-wife, I should say. Don't tell her I call her that – you wouldn't want to get me into trouble, now, would you?'

'No, of course not. Is she that bad, then?'

'Haven't you met any of your fellow cast members?'

'Well, I read with Sebastian at the audition, but I didn't speak to him.'

'At least you've bowed at the feet of the star. No, Penny's okay, I suppose. Wardrobe hate her because it's like dressing lettuce. Whatever you put her in just hangs limp. No tits, poor love. Trouble is, she thinks she's Joan Collins. Keeps trying to get us to buy her all this sexy stuff, and she ends up looking like a teenage boy in drag. Now, if she had Jessica's figure—'

'Who's Jessica?'

'Crikey, they really have kept you wrapped in cotton wool, haven't they? Scared of frightening you off, probably.'

'And who's Jennie?'

'This,' said Peter, as he turned off the corridor into another room, 'is Jennie. She's the costume designer for the whole shebang, head honcho, so be nice to her, Hal. Otherwise millions of viewers will see you on their screens dressed like an advert for the Oxfam chain.'

'Take no notice of him, Hal.'

Jennie sat cross-legged on the floor. Spaced lengthways across her thighs was a dress on top of which was a sewing set. She offered her hand to Hal. 'Forgive me for not standing up, but I'm half-way through something here,' she said.

Jennie was young, short, had mousy hair and was dressed appallingly. Typical, Hal thought. Most of the costume designers and wardrobe mistresses with whom he had worked had abysmal taste when it came to their own clothing.

'Peter will give you some things to try on,' Jennie told him.

He glanced around the room. Along one wall was a trestle table covered in clothing, scissors, and a number of drawings. Along the other three walls were mobile clothing rails from which hung garments of all shapes and sizes. Peter plucked a pair of denim jeans and a black roll-neck sweater off one, and a pair of light-coloured leather boots from under another.

'Start with smart but casual. We'll save the sequins for later,' he said, as he handed over the collection.

Hal looked around the room a second time. 'Er, where do I change?'

'Oh, lights-out-under-the-duvet type, are we?' Peter teased. 'That'll have to change. I can't dress you in the dark, you know, not with my eyesight. It's only vanity stops me wearing glasses.' He glanced at Hal's expression and relented. 'Just joking. He crossed to the wall where the table stood and opened a door just to the left of it. 'Dressing-room off. Now, get a move on. We've several more outfits to make you look ridiculous in.'

Hal went in and pulled the door to behind him. He emerged a few minutes later dressed in the clothes he had been given.

'Oh dear. Why are all actors such liars?' Peter asked. 'I thought you said you were a thirty-two-inch waist?'

'I am.'

Peter lifted up Hal's jumper. 'So what's this hanging over the top of your trousers, then? A rubber ring?'

'These jeans must be a size smaller,' Hal argued.

'Let's hope so, or they'll all have to go back and we're short of time. When's your first day of shooting?'

'This Monday. I travel down on Sunday afternoon,' Hal informed him.

'No time to diet, then. Even Rosemary Conley couldn't help you now. Get those off and I'll try to find a pair of extra large to save the day.'

Hal trudged despondently back into the dressing room.

An hour later, there had been little success. Hal stood before Peter and Jennie, his early enthusiasm dissipated, his ego bruised.

'Are you thinking what I'm thinking?' Peter asked Jennie, his eyes wandering to a certain rail of clothes.

'Hmmm,' she responded.

Peter took some items from the rail. 'See if you can get into these,' he suggested, handing Hal a pair of grey chinos and matching sweatshirt.

Hal did as he was asked, and the pair exchanged a knowing look.

'Not bad. Now, what about this little number?' Peter said, picking out a shirt, tie, and dark blue suit. 'Slip into them, then come out and give us a twirl.'

Hal did so, and Peter wolf-whistled. 'Bingo! I think we've finally won the lottery. What about you, Jennie?'

'Hmmm. It'll see us through till the studio dates, anyway.'

'Oh, Hal, like the song says, you may be little more than a second-hand Rose, but you carry it off to such perfection,' Peter said. 'Which means we can all go home to a hot bath and, for the lucky few, a good rub-down with a lavender-perfumed aromatherapy oil from a close friend dressed in leather.'

Hal laughed. 'What do you mean, second-hand Rose?' he asked.

'The last two outfits were Ian Wilson's. It appears your frame is identical to his. Isn't that a Twilight Zone type of coincidence? He had a spare tyre the size of a tractor's as well.'

'*You mean I'm wearing the clothes of someone who died?*'

'Well, he didn't die in them!' Peter shrieked. 'Not literally, anyway. Professionally Ian used to die in them on a weekly basis – the studio audience hated him. He had so much canned laughter taped on to his laugh lines, the sound crew called him Heinz.'

'Peter!' Jennie chastised him.

'You're missing the point,' Hal argued. 'It's bad enough stepping into his shoes without—'

'But you're not stepping into his *shoes*, are you?' Peter retorted. 'The shoes we bought for you fit perfectly. We're only asking you to wear his shirt and tie, and it's not as if he hanged himself with that, is it?'

'But—'

Hal was interrupted by a cough. 'Hal,' Jennie began softly, 'I understand what you're saying. Of course, if it makes you uncomfortable we won't make you wear Ian's costume. But it will only be for the duration of the location shooting. We're just short of time. We promise we'll get you lots of nice things to wear by the time we get into the studio. Honestly, you'd be doing us a big favour.' She smiled hopefully.

Hal didn't want to ruffle anyone's feathers before he'd even officially started the job. 'Well . . .'

'Oh, thank you, Hal,' Peter exclaimed. 'You've just leapt straight to the top of the wardrobe department's Christmas-card list.'

Hal went into the dressing room to change back into his own clothes. For the first time, he felt uneasy about replacing someone who had committed suicide. What misery had brought the poor bugger to that? He knew it was a cut-throat business but there were limits. It had taken someone ending their own life to save Hal from Jake's fate and he felt guilty. This wasn't like taking over from an actor in a long-running West End show. It was tinged with tragedy.

'Fuck,' Hal muttered, under his breath. Then, as he squeezed into his own jeans, waist size thirty-two inches, he said, to his reflection in the free-standing mirror, 'I need a drink, mate.'

Belinda put on her reading glasses and stared at the two front-door bells to the right of the red door. She could never remember which one was Hal's – she hadn't visited him here very often. She peered at the small labels on the door frame, then pressed the bell that bore his name. She tucked her glasses back into her handbag. No answer. Her courage failed her and she turned to leave, but then the door opened and before her stood the tank-like figure of Edith Worrel. 'Hello, love. It's wass-yer-name? Belinda, isn't it?'

Belinda felt flattered that she was so memorable. She had only met Hal's landlady twice, fleetingly.

'Come to see His Majesty, 'ave yer? I suspect he's off

rubbing shoulders with the stars, now he's become so grand. Still, I expect he'll be back soon. Do you want to come in and wait?'

'No, it's not urgent, and he's not expecting me, so—'

'Oh, come in for a minute. Tell you what, I'll put the kettle on an' make a brew for us. If he's not back by the time you've finished yer cuppa, you take yourself off home and it's his loss. What do yer say?'

Part of Belinda wanted to refuse politely, but on the other hand, it was a long, awkward trek from Crouch End to East Ham, and she had come to apologise. She hadn't telephoned to let Hal know she was coming so it was hardly his fault that he wasn't home.

'Thank you. You're very kind.'

'Bloody lonely, more like, but don't tell Mr Morrisey that. He thinks I've got a string of admirers as long as me arm.'

Belinda smiled. 'It will be our secret,' she said.

'Come in and make yourself at home, then.' Mrs Worrel let the door swing open, and went down the hall. 'We'll sit in the kitchen, if you don't mind. I don't use the lounge much, these days. Gotta telly in me bedroom, see. Much nicer watching the box snuggled up under the blankets with a hot-water bottle glued to your toes, don't yer think?'

'I couldn't agree more,' Belinda responded.

Mrs Worrel cackled, then rounded it off with a hacking cough. 'Girl after me own heart,' she said. 'Sit yourself down while I sort us out.'

Belinda sat down on one of the grey chairs, her nostrils flaring in distaste at the overflowing ashtray.

'So, have you seen Gawd's gift to acting since one of your nutters – sorry, dear – patients punched him?' Mrs Worrel asked, as she filled the kettle.

'You heard about that, did you?'

'Yer couldn't 'elp but notice 'is 'ooter.'

Belinda winced. 'How is it now?'

'Looked fine when I saw him on his way out this afternoon.' Mrs Worrel scooped tea-leaves into the brown china teapot.

'He didn't say anything about being a bit cross with me, did he?' Belinda asked.

'No. Would yer be bothered if he was?'

'Well, yes, I suppose. I mean, Hal's an old friend.'

'Course he is, duck.' Mrs Worrel grinned to herself. 'So, that's why you're 'ere, then. Come to say sorry for his war wound?'

'Partly.'

'Don't tell me you've something else to be sorry for?'

'Yes and no.'

Mrs Worrel set the teapot on the table. 'Tell me more,' she said.

Belinda felt she had already said too much.

The old woman noticed her concern. 'I know, I know, I'm a nosy old cow, but what else 'ave I got to look forward to in me old age if I can't interfere in me tenant's life, now and again?'

Belinda laughed. 'It's not that interesting, really. I've known Hal a long time. I'm always nagging him to give up acting. Based on his track record, who wouldn't? Then he got his big break. He ran miles to tell me his good news – and I'd had a bad day and I thought he'd come to tell me he'd taken my advice and . . . I suppose I felt cross or something and I didn't . . . Instead of—'

Mrs Worrel placed a hand on Belinda's. 'You're rambling, dearie. Let me pour us a cup each.'

Belinda blushed.

'So, you're feeling bad because you've sensibly told him to pack it in, and then he goes and gets this cracking job.' Mrs Worrel stared into her teacup. 'Well, supposing you were right to tell him to give it up, in spite of this thing on the telly? I mean, supposing this job isn't what it was cracked up to be?'

Belinda took a sip of tea, and was surprised to find it was Earl Grey. 'I've thought about that, but I mean, *Bringing Up Ralph*? There aren't many more high-profile jobs on television, are there?'

'Dunno. Don't watch comedies. But what if this isn't the big break it was cracked up to be? What if it proved to be about as lucky as a rabbit's foot with myxomatosis?'

'It can't be, can it?' Belinda said.

'I'm not so sure, girl. I've got a bad feeling. I saw . . . something. About this telly thing. Something about bein' a father, too. He never had a child with his first missus, did 'e?'

'No.'

A memory flashed in Belinda's mind, of Hal sitting on one of her sofas, complaining that his landlady fancied herself as a fortune-teller. Suddenly things made sense. 'Look, you mustn't worry, I'm sure Hal will be fine,' she said reassuringly, hoping she didn't sound patronising.

Mrs Worrel grinned. 'He's told you, hasn't he?'

'Told me what?' Belinda feigned ignorance.

'About the tea-leaves.'

'Well . . .'

'It isn't really the leaves, love. They just give me something to stare at. Helps me concentrate. It's more about voices, and messages, and . . . me instincts, I suppose. I've had these feelings for years. When it started it was a bit like early wireless, all crackle and interference, everyone talking at once. Gradually it changed, like someone twiddled the old fine-tuner between me ears. I hated it at first, wanted it all to go away. Then I gradually got used to it. Anyway, by the time I was in me twenties I was using it to 'and out advice. Little things

64

mostly. I tell yer, I'm never wrong. With the exception of Gillian, my niece, of course, but I was unlucky there.'

'What happened?'

'I told her not to go within a hundred miles of the Taj Mahal. You see, her husband had a good job with a tea company. Those were the days. So, he gets the chance to go and work in India for a couple of years. This was only a day or two after I've said this to her. Gillian thinks I'm a genius and thanks me for warning her, like, and he turns down the offer.'

'So?'

'I got the wrong Taj Mahal, didn't I? Turned out to be a curry house in the East End. She got knocked over by a taxi on a zebra crossing right in front of it.'

'Oh dear.'

'She was fine – well, apart from a broken ankle. Never forgave me for ruining her husband's career, though. Hasn't spoken to me since. That's the only mistake, mind, in more years than I care to remember. You may mock, but I still say this job of Mr Morrisey's isn't all it seems, and he should be careful.'

'I'm sorry, Mrs . . .'

'Worrel, dearie.'

'I'm sorry, Mrs Worrel, I'm a trained psychiatrist and I'm afraid that makes it difficult for me to believe in the kind of things you're talking about. I know how our imaginations—'

'Oh, I keep forgetting you're one of them as well,' Mrs Worrel interrupted.

'As well?'

'Like that other one he was married to. Wassname? Amy. Nasty piece of work, if you ask me, carrying on with another man.'

'It wasn't quite that simple, really,' Belinda said.

'You speakin' as a woman now or as a trick-cyclist?' Mrs Worrel asked.

Belinda blushed. As a woman, she could never condone Amy's behaviour, though this was an opinion she felt best kept to herself.

'You wouldn't treat a man like that, would you? Any more than you'd stand for a man cheating on you.'

Belinda gazed at the floor, hot with embarrassment.

'Look at yer, girlie. Blimey, you're as old-fashioned as me, you are.' Mrs Worrel cackled.

Belinda looked up and smiled at her. 'Maybe you should consider doing my job if you read people that well, Mrs Worrel.'

'Look an old girl in the eyes and tell me you don't fancy the Y-fronts off young Hal.'

'*Mrs Worrel!*'

'I didn't mean to embarrass yer, dearie. I suppose it's one of the perks of gettin' older. When you're a kid you can be rude, cheeky, nosy, truthful, and then you have to wait until you've virtually got one foot in the grave before you can behave that way again.'

Belinda drank the remains of her tea. 'Mrs Worrel, Hal and I are just old friends. We've known each other for years. We've teased each other, helped each other, argued with each other. We've been there for each other, but always as friends.'

'Yes, dearie, and there's your problem.'

'I'm not sure we should be having this conversation.' Belinda wriggled in her seat.

'What yer worried about? No one ever listens to a word I say anyway. Not Mr Morrisey. Not even you. So why not talk?'

'Because this is a conversation based on imagination, not fact,' Belinda argued.

'Is it?'

'Has Hal ever mentioned me in any context other than as a friend?'

Mrs Worrel considered this. 'He mentions you, all right.'

'Maybe. I bet he doesn't tell you he wants to rip my clothes off and ravish me on the kitchen table, though, does he?'

'Young men don't talk dirty to old duffers like me! It'd be unseemly. Anyway, it's my job to embarrass people of Mr Morrisey's age by talkin' about sex. It's tradition. The same way it's a mother's job to dig out that picture of her son willy-waving at the age of four and show it to all his girlfriends,' Mrs Worrel stated.

'You're not answering the question.'

'Trouble is, you're not confident enough. I've seen nuns dressed sexier than you. Get the stockings out. Buy a pair of 'igh 'eels.'

'Oh, don't you start,' Belinda begged.

'Didn't think I'd be the first to give you that advice. Look at that jumper yer wearin' – you could fit me in there with you and it would still look three sizes too big.'

'Just answer me, please. Has Hal ever given you the impression that he is in any way attracted to me?' Secretly Belinda was hoping that he had.

'Trouble is,' Mrs Worrel began, 'she 'urt him, didn't she? He's still licking his wounds. Every time he thinks about another relationship, he sees the ghost of his ex-missus. All covered in chains with her 'ead tucked under 'er arm, and holdin' 'is balls in 'er other hand, isn't she?'

Belinda burst out laughing. 'Mrs Worrel, you're incorrigible,' she told her.

The old woman joined in with Belinda's mirth.

When the laughter had subsided, Belinda looked at her watch. 'I don't think Hal's going to show. It's time I was leaving.'

'Don't go yet. Not just when it's gettin' interestin'. Give it another ten minutes,' Mrs Worrel urged.

'I can't. To tell the truth, I feel too embarrassed to see him now, after all the nonsense we've been saying.'

Mrs Worrel conceded defeat. 'Fair enough,' she said, picking up Belinda's teacup and staring into it. 'Before you go, are you sure you wouldn't like me to—'

'No! Thank you, but no,' Belinda said firmly, getting up. 'I've had enough for now.'

'You want me to tell His Nibs you came round?' Mrs Worrel asked, as she opened the door and Belinda stepped outside.

'Is there any chance of you keeping it a secret?'

'Shouldn't think so. You know what an old gossip I am.'

Belinda smiled. 'Tell him I'll give him a ring.'

'Right-oh.'

'Goodnight, Mrs Worrel.'

'Goodnight, dear. Sweet dreams,' she said, cackling as she closed the door. She waddled back along the corridor into her kitchen. She'd guessed that Belinda was attracted to Hal. Well, you don't travel all that way to say sorry to someone who's just a mate. You ring them up, or send a card. Mrs Worrel didn't want Hal to give up acting altogether . . . but she did want to get him out of this job. Maybe Belinda could help.

She couldn't resist it. She walked over to Belinda's teacup, and stared into it, trying to tune the wireless in her head to the right station.

7

Hal had had a few, not that many, but a few certainly. Which wasn't helping the situation. Back in his flat, he was all packed and ready to go, but he couldn't remember his lines. And it wasn't as if there were that many of them! He'd played Richard III, for heaven's sake, and anyone who has ever tackled Dick the Shit would tell you the bloke's never bloody off-stage. Reams of dialogue. Now Hal had a few phrases to remember, and he was blank. He needed help, someone to read the scenes with him. Normally he would have asked Jake, but after the other night's dinner he didn't think it was a good idea. Anyway, Jake had shut himself away. Hal had telephoned, left messages, but he hadn't replied. Hal knew he should go round to check that he was okay, but there'd been no time and he was going away on location tomorrow.

Mrs Worrel? No. In *Bringing Up Ralph* Hal's character, Michael Pilton, was recently divorced. Art mirroring life rather ironically, Hal thought. Several scenes that he needed to learn were played opposite his ex-wife in the show. The script said there was still a high level of sexual tension between the characters. Somehow sexual tension and Mrs Worrel didn't go together. So . . .

Belinda. She'd left a message on his answering-machine apologising for being horrible about his success.

Hal picked up the phone and dialled her number. 'Come on, come on. Please be in,' he muttered.

'Hello?'

'Belinda?'

'Hal! Thanks for ringing back.'

'Sorry I missed you the other night. I'd had a stressful day. Popped into the pub after the costume fitting and bumped into an old friend. I think he was the first person I told who was actually thrilled I'd got this job so I stayed on to celebrate.'

'That's okay. I popped round to say sorry for not being overjoyed at you getting *Bringing Up Ralph*. You were obviously right not to give up your dream and it was naughty of me to behave so badly about it.'

'You're feeling terrible about it, are you?' Hal said, meanly.

'Yes, all right, I am.'

'Want to make it up to me?'

'I suppose . . .' Belinda sounded suspicious.

'Busy tonight?'

'No. I'm just drowning my stress in a little red wine and half-heartedly tinkering with a bit of paperwork. Why?'

'I'm after a favour. Truth is, I'm struggling. I'm going away on location tomorrow.'

'Oh, are you?' Belinda hoped she didn't sound disappointed.

'Yes. Thing is, I've a few short scenes to learn, and I'm having a memory block. I was wondering if you could help me with my lines.'

'Are you sure I'm the right person to do it?'

'No, but no one else is available, and I'm desperate.'

'Oh, thanks very much. What do you want me to do exactly?'

'Well, I've got a short speech for a start. I'd just want

you to look at the script while I try to remember it, and give me a prompt when I dry – sorry, I mean forget,' Hal said.

'Oh, I'm not sure about that, Hal. I mean, I'm not an actress.'

'I'm not asking you to audition, just read a few lines so I know where to come in!'

'Don't shout at me!'

'Sorry, sorry. Look, you don't mind helping me, do you?'

'As long as you promise not to get cross.'

'I won't. Thanks, Belinda, you're a brick. Okay if I come over in about an hour?'

'Fine. Bring another bottle of wine, will you?'

'You got it. 'Bye.'

Belinda put down the telephone. How odd that Hal should ring, just when she'd been thinking about him. Though, if the truth be told, she'd thought of little else since her chat with Mrs Worrel. That silly old woman had rattled her. But Hal must have loads of actor friends who could help him . . . What if he wanted to come round tonight because he wanted to see her? After all, the reason she was glad he was coming over wasn't because she was a good friend who wanted to help him learn his lines, it was because she wanted to see him.

Maybe she should just be brave, take the bull by the horns, and tell him how she felt about him. No, that might frighten him off.

Belinda poured herself another glass of wine. She knew she shouldn't. She'd had far too much already, and she hadn't eaten.

There was something else the old woman had said. That Belinda wasn't confident in herself as a woman. She giggled as she thought this: everyone gave her flak for the way she dressed down. All her friends said she sent out the wrong signals to men by the way she behaved: disinterested, untouchable, shy, virginal, gay, asexual, spinster. *Spinster?* Who had called her that? Amy. Maybe they had been right. It couldn't hurt to tart herself up a bit, could it? She took a healthy slug of wine. By the time she had put her glass down, she had decided to plumb the depths of her wardrobe to see if she could concoct an outfit that, if not sexy, did not bring 'frumpy' to mind.

Forty minutes later, Belinda sat on one of the blue sofas in her sitting room. She felt odd. She was wearing a skirt and she never wore skirts in the evening, only for work. She hoped she wouldn't get confused when Hal arrived and ask him to lie down and tell her about his childhood. She giggled. Red wine had that effect on her. Which was why usually she only drank it at home. Elsewhere she stuck to bottled beer.

She had changed clothes at least ten times in forty minutes – which must be some kind of record. Her bedroom looked as if it had been rifled by enemy spies. She had settled for a plain black skirt, the hemline just above the knee. She had even found a pair of sheer black tights buried beneath a pile of knickers and put them on. Even Belinda had to admit that they flattered her legs more than the hard-wearing, opaque ones she usually favoured. To top this off she'd settled for a pretty white silk blouse, which she had bought to wear at a wedding. Daringly, she had left the top two buttons undone. Rather racy, she thought.

The doorbell rang. Belinda finished her umpteenth glass of wine, then poured some more. 'Coming,' she yelled. She stood up and looked at her reflection in the mirror that hung above the fireplace. Her hair looked a mess, she thought and frantically ruffled it with her fingers.

The doorbell rang a second time.

'Just a minute,' she called.

She did up one of the buttons on her blouse, then undid it again. 'Damn, damn, damn, should have stuck with the sweaters.'

The doorbell rang a third time. 'To hell with it!' she muttered. Then, 'I'm on my way,' she shouted, and ran to the door.

Three-quarters of an hour later Hal and Belinda were in the sitting room, chatting away. Belinda had shown enthusiasm about *Bringing Up Ralph*, and Hal had told her the whole story.

At one stage, he had paused and said, 'You look different tonight. Have you had your hair done or something?' She was a little disappointed that after all her effort with her clothes he had noticed only her hair, especially as she thought it looked like a recently abandoned bird's nest. But at least he had noticed something. Eventually he said, 'Well, if it's okay with you, I wouldn't mind trying to do a bit of work.'

'No, that's fine. That's why you're here. Where do you want me?' she asked, then giggled.

'You telling the jokes now?' he asked, as he opened his rucksack. '*This* is supposed to be the funny stuff,' he tossed her a script.

'Sorry,' Belinda said. 'I'll be good, I promise.'

'Page twenty-two, the telephone-box scene.'

'Telephone-box scene. Page twenty-two, page twenty-two,' she echoed, flicking through the pages of the script.

'Come on,' Hal chivvied her.

'I know, I know.'

'Belinda! What's taking you so long, for heaven's sake?'

Belinda shifted uncomfortably. 'Nothing . . . It's just . . . I'm not wearing my reading glasses.'

'Why not?'

Belinda thought her glasses made her look like a constipated owl, but she wasn't going to tell Hal that. 'I don't know,' she said.

'Well, how did you think you were going to read without them?'

'Erm . . . squint?'

'Well, would you mind putting them on? Speed things up a little?'

'No, of course not. I don't know why I didn't think of it earlier.'

Neither do I, thought Hal.

Belinda picked up her handbag, retrieved her glasses and put them on. 'Okay. Got it. Page twenty-two. Whenever you're ready.'

Hal tried to recite from memory: *'Hello, son. No, listen, don't fetch Mummy. It's you I want to talk to—'*

'Hal?'

'What is it?'

'Why do you look as if you're about to punch yourself?'

'What?'

'Why are you holding your fist up by your face like that?'

'I'm supposed to be in a telephone-box. I'm just pretending I'm on the phone, okay?'

'Oh, you're *acting*!'

'Of course I'm bloody well acting! What did you think I was doing?'

'Sorry, I thought you were just going to say the lines, you know, try to remember them.'

'Well, it goes together. It's when I try to act them that I forget them. Anyway, what are you watching me for?

You're supposed to be looking at the script in case I go wrong.'

'You won't hear another peep out of me, I promise.'

'Unless I forget my lines,' Hal reminded her.

'Exactly. Yes. Carry on,' she said, looking down at the script.

'Er . . . where was I? Oh, yeah. *"Listen, don't fetch Mummy, it's you I want to talk to—"'*

'Why is he in a telephone-box? Why can't he just use his mobile?'

Hal tried to remain calm. 'Because he's lost it. He's left it at his ex-wife's house and he doesn't want her to listen to his answer message, okay?'

'Why doesn't he?'

'Why doesn't he *what*?'

'Want his ex-wife listening to the answer message on his mobile.'

'Because he's put a message on it saying that he's no longer married to that sour-faced, fat old cow.'

'But wouldn't she hear the message when she rang him?'

'She doesn't have his new number. That's why he felt safe to leave the message.'

'But she still wouldn't—'

'Belinda! Please! I haven't got time to explain the plot of every episode, nor to discuss the merits of the writing. I go on location tomorrow. I'm desperate. Can we please just get on with it?'

'Sorry,' Belinda said sheepishly.

Hal began again. *'Listen, don't get Mummy, It's you I want to talk to—'*

'Daddy wants you to do something for him,' Belinda put in.

'What are you doing?' Hal asked, startled.

'I prompted you. You'd dried.'

'No, I hadn't,' Hal assured her. 'I paused.'

'Oh, it was a dramatic pause,' Belinda said, hoping theatrical jargon might save her.

'Actually, I just took a breath and you jumped in. Look, I tell you what, if I need a prompt, I'll ask for one.' Hal put his fist back up by his ear and tried again. *'Daddy wants you to do something for him. Only it's a secret. So don't tell your mother. You remember Daddy's . . . Daddy's . . . Daddy's . . . YES!'*

No reply

'YES!' Hal barked again.

No reply.

'YES!' Hal repeated tensely.

'Yes, you were very good as far as it went.'

'No, I mean yes I want a prompt. I can't remember the colour of the bloody mobile phone.'

'So when you scream yes you want a prompt?'

'Yes. You say yes to the assistant stage manager, or whoever is prompting.'

'No. You *shout* "yes" at them. I bet the assistant stage manager is usually a woman.'

'Belinda, will you get off your feminist soapbox and—' Hal stopped himself. 'All right,' he said, fishing a second script out of his rucksack. 'Let's try something different. This is a scene between my character and his ex-wife's parents. My lines are the ones marked in yellow highlighter. You read the other character's lines for me.'

'Sure,' Belinda promised.

'Top of the page. I speak first. You ready?'

Belinda gave Hal a thumbs-up.

Hal cleared his throat. 'Where's that daughter of yours, Eric? Out sucking the blood from some poor beggar's neck again, is she?'

'Now, now. Don't be too hard on Priscilla, James.'

'Why are you speaking in that voice?' Hal asked. 'You sound like Darth Vader with a bad dose of bronchitis?'

'Well,' Belinda began, a smile breaking across her face, 'he's a man. I was just trying to sound *basso profundo*, a bit butch, you know,' she said, starting to giggle.

For some reason, Hal found himself smiling. 'Why do you want to sound butch?'

'To help you,' she said, still laughing.

Hal chuckled. 'You make him sound like some young buck. He's in his sixties, this bloke.'

'Well, he'd have to be, if he was supposed to be old enough to have fathered the "fat old cow", wouldn't he?' she quipped.

'He speaks very well of you.' Hal was laughing now. 'Can we cut the hysteria and try again, please?'

'Yes, of course.' Belinda stopped giggling abruptly and straightened her face in the way of one who is trying to hold back laughter.

'From your line, then.'

'Now . . . now . . .' Belinda gurgled.

Hal and Belinda were hysterical with laughter. Belinda was holding her stomach and kicking her legs in the air.

Good legs, Hal thought. Then he leaped on to the sofa and began to tickle her mercilessly, speaking amid his own guffaws. 'You aggravating woman! I come over here for help, and you're argumentative, dim, nit-picky—'

'NO! STOP!' Belinda screamed.

'Taking the piss in my hour of need . . . no, no, *no*!' Hal shouted as Belinda began to tickle him back.

Soon the tickling turned into grappling, and the grappling to caressing, and before Hal had time to realise what was happening, Belinda was kissing him as she had in a thousand guilty dreams.

Hal pulled away suddenly. 'Whoa! Stop! What's going on?'

Belinda stared helplessly at him. 'I don't know. It just sort of happened,' she said.

'Well, it shouldn't, it mustn't,' Hal insisted. 'I mean we're friends, right? It just mustn't.'

'Why not?' Belinda was brave enough to ask.

'What?' Hal spluttered. 'I just said, we're old friends. It could ruin things. Crikey, Belinda, it'd be all complicated and . . . Oh, what a bloody mess.'

'Hal?' Belinda said, 'it's okay. Calm down.'

'Is it?'

'Yes. We only had a kiss. We've had a few drinks and we got silly. There's no need to panic.'

'Isn't there?'

'No,' she reassured him. 'These things happen. There's nothing to worry about. We were just a bit daft.'

'We're still friends, right?'

'Of course.'

'I haven't upset you or anything? Only I'd hate to do that. I didn't mean it to happen, Belinda. I wasn't trying to take advantage of you—'

'Hal, stop it. I was as much to blame as you.' She met his eyes. 'More so, if anything.'

'What do we do now, then?'

'Forget it. Come on, you've got some lines to learn.'

'Yes. You're right.'

Hal felt distinctly uncomfortable, mixture of guilt, shock and confusion. 'Belinda, I don't seem to be concentrating very well here. Perhaps I should go through my lines at home.'

'Oh, okay.'

Hal collected his scripts and put them back in his rucksack. 'Right. I'll be off then. Thanks for trying to help.'

'I'll see you to the door.'

When they got there, Hal opened it, slipped out and turned to face her. 'Goodnight, then,' he said.

'Safe journey tomorrow, and I hope it all goes well.'

'Thanks.'

'Ring me when you get back, maybe?'

'Of course I will.' With that he scurried off down the street, and Belinda closed the door.

There was no goodnight kiss.

8

Hal sat on his bed in a hotel room in Bournemouth. Scripts were strewn over the duvet, and a gin and tonic with ice clinked in his hand. He had a juvenile habit of raiding the mini-bar the minute he checked into any hotel room. He had played with most of the toys: set his alarm call via the telephone, flicked through the satellite channels on the television, and watched his free two minutes of soft porn, then switched the television off in case *Naked Babes in the Wood* appeared on his bill. He had ironed his tie in the trouser press.

Now he picked up the telephone-box scene: they were to shoot it the following morning. This made him think of Belinda. He liked her. A lot. They had hit it off from the moment they met but last night's kiss had shocked him. Had he ever felt attracted to her before? Suddenly he remembered the time he had stayed with Belinda when she was at university – he had crashed on her sofa. When she had come down for breakfast the next morning in her bathrobe, she had leaned across him for the newspaper or something, and it had gaped open. Hal had been transfixed by the sight of her breasts. When she sat down, oblivious to this, and spoke to him again, he had blushed and stumbled over his words.

That evening they had gone to a party and Hal had met Amy. She had run rings around him, taken him to bed, then taken over his life for the next thirteen years. She had gone into psychiatry and everything about her had become increasingly clinical: her attitude to life, career, their home, sex, and the affair that had destroyed their marriage. It wasn't until it was all over that Hal realised how little affection Amy had shown him.

It had been just over a year since the decree absolute and he had yet to sleep with anyone else. He'd had a couple of dates, but he just couldn't get into it. Maybe that was why he hadn't thought of Belinda romantically. Or maybe the idea of getting involved with another psychiatrist was too much to contemplate.

He was shaken from his thoughts by a knock at the door.

'Hal Morrisey?' said a man of about forty, with prematurely greying hair.

'Yes.'

'Glad I found you. I'm Brian Matthews, and it's money time!' He waved a small brown envelope under Hal's nose. 'Can I come in?'

'Yes, of course.'

'I don't usually hand out gratuities on a Sunday, but as you've just arrived I thought I'd make an exception. I know what you actors are like – half of you arrive strapped for cash. Sign this for me, will you?' He handed Hal a piece of paper and a biro. 'And do me a favour? Don't count it until I've left the room. I always find that rather offensive.'

'I'm sure it's all there,' Hal said, and signed the form.

'Oh, and one other thing. Don't tell the other actors I've given you your expenses early. The rest of them won't receive theirs until tomorrow.'

'Your secret's safe with me.'

'Good. Speaking of actors, there aren't many for you to meet tonight. Sebastian's here, but he's gone out for an early meal with Tony, the producer, which leaves Penny Davenport. As you're going to play screen ex-husband and wife, Tony thought it would be a good idea if you ate together tonight.'

'Sounds great.'

'We've reserved a table for you at eight. I suggested to Penny that you met in the bar for drinks at seven thirty.'

'Fine.'

'All evening meals and drinks are paid for by us. Just sign for them on your room number. Anything else has to come out of the little brown envelope. 'Bye for now.'

Hal closed the door behind him, crossed to the dressing-table and picked up the brown envelope. This was an unexpected treat.

Hal was in the bar, pint in hand, at seven twenty-five. At a quarter to eight, Penny Davenport arrived, in a knee-length black dress, with a red silk scarf and Victorian-style ankle boots. As she walked towards him Hal understood the problem Wardrobe had with her costumes: she was straight up and down, no waist to speak of and her chest not so much flat as concave.

'You must be Hal,' she said, in husky, breathy tones. 'So sorry I'm late, darling. There's no hair-dryer in my room. It's an outrage. I had to ring Reception and beg for one. It took the silly little man ages to bring it and then he had the bare-faced cheek to expect a tip.' She lit a More menthol cigarette.

'Not to worry. I haven't been here long. Drink?'

'Please! I'd just die for a vodka and tonic. With ice and lemon.'

Hal went to the bar, ordered Penny's drink and another for himself. Hell, he thought. It's free. Why not? It was already shaping up to be a long night.

By the time Hal returned to their table, Penny was stubbing out her cigarette.

'Oh, God, darling, I need this,' she said, and took a generous slug of the vodka. Then she said, 'How are you settling in?' she leaned forward and put a hand on his knee.

'Fine. I've only been here since this afternoon.'

'No, darling, I mean how are you settling in general?'

'I film my first scene tomorrow. Other than that, the most exciting thing that's happened so far is the costume fitting.'

'You haven't met any of the others?' she said.

'Nope.'

'So you have that treat in store.'

Why did everyone keep saying that, Hal wondered. It was as if they all hated each other. 'You're the first member of the cast I've met.'

'Well, aren't I the lucky girl?' She smiled insincerely. 'I can honestly say,' she fished out another cigarette, 'that I'm delighted to have you on board. I couldn't stand Ian. Oh, Lord! Am I awful? I know one shouldn't speak ill of the dead, and he was tolerable when we made the first series, but then success went to his head. Big-time. And he couldn't act if his life depended on it. Well, you must have seen him.'

'I don't think I should comment,' Hal told her.

'No! Of course not, sweetie. What am I thinking of? I shouldn't be talking like this at all, really. Not to you. He went all secretive and shifty on the last series as well,' she informed Hal, ignoring her own advice.

'What made him . . . you know?' Hal enquired diffidently.

'Top himself? Gambling. Horses, casinos, everything. Huge debts, sweetie.'

'I didn't know.'

'Press let him off lightly. Shall we eat?' she suggested. 'I'm ravenous. The food here is ghastly, by the way, so be careful what you order.'

During dinner, Penny savaged the rest of the regular cast, while pawing Hal's knee. Edwin Sullivan, who played her father in the show, was 'all right. He carries his scripts around with him in a cloth bag. Spends most of the time sitting in the corner doing *The Times* crossword. He's rather like his acting. Bit of a bloody bore, darling.' Elizabeth Sage, who played her mother, was, 'Senile, sweetie. Mind's gone. Can't remember her lines. The retake queen, we call her. Writes her lines on her hands, as if she were on the stage. Trouble is, she's too blind to read them.' Carla Morris, who played Penny's best friend, was 'just so wet! She's an actress, darling, you'd expect a bit of life but I think she'd be happier serving coffee after mass on a Sunday. She's sick before every show, can you believe it?' Various members of the crew, production staff and, of course, Wardrobe were subject to similar character assassination.

As Penny was playing Hal's ex-wife in the show, his character was supposed to have a love-hate relationship with hers. After tonight, Hal doubted he would have to dig deep into his acting reserves to portray this successfully.

Unfortunately, Penny's room was on the same floor of the hotel as his. Now, as they walked along the corridor, she was still at it. 'As for Tony, our beloved producer, well! Couldn't direct his way out of the proverbial paper bag. You do know that in situation comedy the producer usually does the directing, don't you, darling?'

'Of course,' Hal lied.

'And as for that precocious little – Oh, hello, Jessica.'

A woman of about thirty-five was walking down the corridor towards them. Her hips were swaying in a slightly exaggerated manner but her stride seemed purposeful. She was tall, with flowing red hair and large brown eyes that radiated intelligence and vulnerability. She had full lips, and her breasts pressed against a tight-fitting, short, dark blue dress, which exposed long legs that seemed to Hal to go on for eternity. She was voluptuous, curvaceous, beautiful. Drop-dead gorgeous, leaped into his mind and groin.

'Hello, Penny,' Jessica said. As she passed she smiled at Hal, whose knees wobbled.

'Fuck, that was close,' Penny exclaimed.

'Who was that?' Hal asked breathlessly.

'Sssh!' Penny put a finger to her lips. 'That, my dear, is Sebastian's mother. Strange woman. Never says much. Just sits around whenever Sebastian's on set. But you can feel her presence.'

'Oh, I think she was at my audition.'

'Just watch what you say about the child when she's around. There have been a few mysterious sackings. I wasn't the first person cast in my role, you know. My predecessor never made it past the pilot episode. Several guest artists haven't got beyond rehearsals.'

'I see.'

'Don't worry, Hal. Stick with me and you'll be all right.' She kissed both of his cheeks. 'Goodnight, darling. I'm off to bed before I get into trouble.' She went into her room and closed the door.

Hal sighed with relief. As he walked into his own room, he pictured the way Sebastian's mother had smiled at him. She had something about her. Charisma, perhaps?

Then the thought of the telephone-box scene interrupted his dream, and he knew he would have to have one last look at the damn thing before lights out tonight.

*

It was late afternoon, and Belinda was huddled on the blue sofa. The numerous sections of the *Sunday Times* were draped around her, and she held a mug of hot chocolate. At least the hangover had gone.

The doorbell rang.

'Oh, who's that at this time on a Sunday?' she said aloud. It had become a bit of a habit: one of the problems of living alone for so long. She hauled herself up and shuffled to the front door.

'Afternoon. I've just split up with Danny so I thought I'd come round here and cry on your shoulder, preferably over a glass or six of wine,' Mary said, and stomped up the hall.

When Belinda joined her, Mary was in the kitchen, pulling an open bottle of white wine out of the fridge. 'Is this all you've got?' she asked.

'Yes.'

'Oh, well, it'll have to do, I suppose. I can always get some more.'

Belinda handed her a wine glass. 'Help yourself.'

'You not having any?'

'I had more than enough last night.'

'Must have been some session.'

The two women made their way to the sitting room, where Mary plonked herself on a sofa, and slammed the bottle on to the coffee table. Belinda tucked her knees up under her jumper and tried to look concerned. 'What went wrong?' she asked.

'He just dumped me.'

'His reasons?'

'Apparently, I'm too domineering, especially in the bedroom department.'

'And are you?'

'Honestly, he was such a wimp. There's nothing wrong with a girl knowing what she likes, is there?'

'I suppose not.'

'Women have the right to be assertive. Why should only men get pleasure out of shagging?'

'Why do you always have to make it sound so sordid?' Belinda wailed.

'Oh, don't be so prudish. Just because you're the eternal virgin,' Mary snapped.

'I'm not a virgin,' Belinda assured her. 'I believe in long-lasting relationships rather than quick flings, but that doesn't make me a prude, a virgin – or a lesbian.'

'But you just spend all your time waiting for Mr Right to come along and whisk you up the aisle. Well, you're thirty-five, Belinda, and I hate to be blunt, but I think he's stood you up. You seen Hal lately?'

Belinda was startled. 'What makes you ask that?'

'Because you always go all funny after you've seen him.'

'I do not!'

'Yes, you do. Why don't you just admit you fancy him, give him a good session and get it out of your system?' Mary suggested.

'It's not as simple as that.'

'Only because you make it complicated for yourself.'

Belinda sighed. 'He was here last night. I kissed him.'

'I knew you fancied him! Tell me more.'

'It was a disaster. I frightened the life out of him. He leaped into the air as if he had just sat on a butcher's hook and now I don't know what to do.'

'Did you tell him how you feel?'

'Of course not!'

'That's the trouble with you psychiatrists. You ask all the questions and never give any answers. You lose the art of opening your gob, letting your emotions go and regretting it the next morning.'

'You've got a point there,' Belinda admitted.

'Ring him up, invite him round, and tell him how you feel. If he's interested, great. It's knickers-flung-over-the-shoulders territory. If he isn't, sod him. You can move on.'

'I can't ring him. He's on location.'

'So, ring him when he gets back. Stop making excuses for yourself.'

Belinda looked at her friend, drew a deep breath and said, 'All right. I will.'

'Good. That's you sorted. This wine is disgusting. I'm going to pop out in search of decent booze. Then I'm going to come back and finish my story about the fuck-wit who's just blown me out. And you're going to be sympathetic. Okay?'

'Yes, miss.'

'Good. Don't go away.' Mary headed for the front door.

Belinda knew her friend was right. Common sense told her that this Hal thing would fester away if she didn't confront it. When he came back, she *would* tell him how she felt.

9

Hal's alarm went off at four thirty on Monday morning. He got up, took a shower and went through his lines, panicking. At six thirty on the dot, he walked into the hotel dining room.

There he was met by a tall moustached man, wearing a skiing jacket and carrying a clipboard. 'Hal Morrisey?'

'Yes.'

'I'm Steven Young, first assistant director for the location.'

'Oh, hi.'

'Listen, change of plan, I'm afraid. The weather is cocking up the itinerary. Your scene's been put back. Can't say exactly when we'll get to you, but I'd be surprised if it's before eleven. Sorry I didn't let you know sooner but I've only just found out myself. Just hang out in your room, and we'll send someone for you when we're ready.'

'Okay,' Hal said, turning to leave.

'No need to rush,' Steven assured him. 'Why don't you have some breakfast now you're up and about?' He dashed off.

Hal looked around the dining room. Early though it was, one or two people were there: a couple of old ladies in one corner, a few sales reps, a family. He decided to order from room service and turned away.

'Hello again.' Sebastian's mother was sitting at the table behind the door. She wore a black jacket, unbuttoned, with matching short skirt, black tights, with expensive-looking black knee boots, and a cream camisole fringed at the top with lace. She looked as if she had just walked off the set of a remake of *The Avengers*, Emma Peel and Purdy rolled into one. 'We met briefly last night.'

'You're Sebastian's mother?'

'I see Penny has filled you in. Care to join me?' she asked, smiling.

Would I! thought Hal. 'Okay. If you don't mind.'

She smiled again. A smile that said, 'Come to bed,' although Hal was prepared to admit that that was probably wishful thinking on his part.

'Where's Sebastian?' he asked.

'He's with Tony. He wants to direct when he's older so he sometimes watches other people's scenes. Gives everyone his expert opinion.'

Jessica took a bite of toast. Butter dripped off it and landed on her blouse. 'Oh dear,' she said, picking up the table napkin and rubbing it over her left breast.

It was almost more than Hal could bear.

She looked up suddenly, caught him gaping, and shot him a rueful smile. Hal blushed. 'It's only a blouse,' she said. Her voice was soft, tinged with seductive warmth.

'So tell me about yourself, Hal,' she said.

'There's not much to tell,' Hal replied, modestly.

'Well, start with your family. Do you have brothers and sisters?'

'No. Only child, me. Explains a lot, doesn't it? Probably why I've never grown up. I suppose it's why I'm in this game. Still dressing up and pretending to be someone else.'

Jessica smiled again.

'Are your parents still alive?'

'Sadly not. They were both knocking on a bit when they had me. Pity really, they'd have been dead chuffed to see me land this job. Especially Mum.'

'That's sad. And are you married? Partnered?'

'Divorced.' Hal felt uncomfortable.

'Your fault?'

'She had an affair.'

'No children?' Jessica asked.

'You're very direct, aren't you?'

'Do you mind?'

Hal looked into her eyes. There was something about her gaze, he thought, the intensity in her eyes, that meant you couldn't look away. 'No. And no current girlfriend, no children.'

'It's sad when you lose your partner, isn't it? I'm used to it, but I'm not sure I like being alone,' Jessica mused wistfully.

You don't have to be! Hal wanted to scream. He was glad she had answered the question of her availability without him having to ask it.

'Though, of course, I have Sebastian,' she added. Her eye drawn to something over his left shoulder. Hal turned to look.

When he turned back, Jessica had stood up. 'Sorry, I don't mean to be rude, but I must go. Edwin's arrived and I'd rather not talk to anyone else in the cast. I'm sure I'll see you again.' She made her way out of the dining-room.

Hal watched her until she was out of sight. She was the type of woman who made most men dribble, so why was she on her own?

'Mind if I join you?' Edwin was smiling benignly down on him. 'You must be Hal. I bumped into Penny on the way down and she described you to me.'

Hal dreaded to think how Penny's summary of him might have run.

Edwin sat down. 'She was in a foul mood. They've changed the schedule and she'd thought she had time for a lie-in but they've just dragged her out of bed.'

'It's the other way round for me,' Hal informed him. 'I was up at sparrow-fart, and now I'm not needed until after eleven.'

'You'll get used to it. Have you breakfasted?'

'No one's come to take my order.'

'It's self-service, through that door over there,' Edwin said, pointing.

'Oh, right. I'll go and have a look.'

'I'll come with you,' Edwin declared, and they stood up. 'You don't do crosswords, do you? Only I'm having a devil of a time with three-across. "In the eye of the beholder with conjunctivitis." '

'I don't do them, I'm afraid,' Hal confessed as they walked together. 'Though as a shot in the dark, could "in the eye of the beholder" have something to do with beauty?'

'Of course. Conjunctivitis. Sleep as in eye, sleeping beauty. Thanks, Hal! Speaking of which, was that Jessica I saw leaving the restaurant?'

'Er, yes.' Hal was irrationally embarrassed.

'Attractive, isn't she?' Edwin commented.

'Do you think so?'

'Oh, come on. We all think so. Word of warning. I shouldn't get over-ambitious, there.' Edwin lowered his voice. 'She dotes on Sebastian. They're thick as thieves. You couldn't slip a piece of Spam between them. Just be careful what you say about the boy in front of her. We've had a bit of trouble in the past. Still, I expect Penny's already told you.'

'Yes. So,' Hal tried to sound casual, 'she's never . . . I mean, there's never been any rumours about her and—'

'Lord, no. She's very aloof – you'll be lucky if she deigns to talk to you,' Edwin replied.

But she *has* spoken to me, Hal thought, as they arrived at the self-service buffet. She didn't want to talk to members of the cast, but she wanted to speak to me.

He picked up a plate and bounced towards the bacon, his flagging ego boosted.

When Hal reached the location the weather had brightened. The April rain had subsided, though the sun was still dancing in and out of the clouds. A car had brought him to a suburb of Bournemouth, full of leafy avenues, thirties and forties houses with people-carriers parked in the drives, and a variety of corner shops.

The telephone-box was situated in a narrow gravelled path, sandwiched between two fences. The camera and television monitor were positioned tight against one fence, and there seemed little room for the crew and the director to squeeze in around them. The kiosk was surrounded by two large lights, shining directly onto it.

Hal had been sent to another room in the hotel to be made up. Then Peter had dressed him – inappropriately in Hal's opinion: blue jeans, a loud sweater and a leather flying jacket. 'Now you're not going to start complaining, are you? There's an unfunny running gag about your character's lack of dress sense. Sad thing is, Ian loved his outfits. He thought he looked so trendy.'

When Hal arrived he had been given some coffee and Steven, the first assistant, had said, 'We won't keep you long.' Then everyone had ignored him.

It was a further twenty minutes before Steven reappeared. 'Can you stand in now, please?' he asked.

Hal followed him to the telephone-box.

'There's the marker for your position.' Steven pointed to two pieces of gaffer-tape in the shape of an X stuck to the floor of the phone-box. 'We'd like you to stand on there facing left. Lean against the coin-box casually, pick up the phone and put it to your ear.'

'Sure,' Hal said, and his stomach turned a somersault. 'Do you want me to do all that now?'

Steven looked at him in a way that told Hal he couldn't quite believe how green he was. 'Yes, please. Then Tony can check he's happy with the shot.'

'Right.' Hal took up his position.

He waited. And waited.

He could see the cameraman and the producer whispering conspiratorially, and he wondered if he'd somehow managed to cock-up already.

The lighting cameraman climbed down from behind the camera. 'Bloody sun,' Hal heard him say. He looked up at the sky, then down at a small light meter. He walked across to the phone-box, and leaned inside. 'Sorry about this, the sun's playing silly buggers.'

He pushed the light meter directly under Hal's nose. It was square, about the size of a small transistor radio, and at its top-end sat what looked like half a ping-pong ball. 'Just ignore me,' the cameraman said. 'You don't have to look at it.' Hal had gone cross-eyed. 'I'm just taking a reading . . . Bill,' he called, 'can you get me another flag for this arc-light?'

Bill arrived with a large piece of polystyrene, which he attached to a pole. The cameraman adjusted it, took another reading, then said, 'That'll have to do, haven't got time to fart about any more,' and went back to his camera.

A quick exchange of words, then Hal heard Tony say, 'Okay, let's rehearse one.'

'Okay, we're going for a rehearsal. Nice and quiet, everyone,' Steven shouted.

'Okay,' Tony said, 'and – action!'

It was the first time Tony had spoken to Hal since he arrived at the location. He was taken by surprise, and froze.

'What's wrong with him? Is he deaf?' Tony asked. 'Action!' he yelled again.

'Oh, right,' Hal said, unprofessionally. Then he began his speech. 'Hello, son. No, listen, don't fetch Mummy. It's you I want to speak to. Daddy wants you to do something for him. Only it's a secret. Remember, Daddy knows best. So, don't tell Mummy. You remember Daddy's blue phone? You know—'

'Hold it!' Tony screamed.

More conferences, this time with a woman holding the script.

Hal was distracted by the arrival of Jessica. She looked as immaculately stunning as she had at six-thirty that morning. It took Hal a little while to register that she was holding Sebastian's hand. The star had arrived.

If anything, the boy looked even smaller than he did on screen. Wispy blond hair flopped about a round, cherubic face. The atmosphere tensed.

Sebastian's innocent eyes stared coldly at Hal.

Hal gulped.

'Okay, Hal. Listen, it's a red phone,' Tony barked.

Hal cursed.

'We're running really behind here,' Tony said to Steven. 'Let's shoot one.'

'Right, everyone, we're going for a take. Complete silence, now, please,' Steven shouted.

A woman ran into the telephone-box and attacked Hal with a hairbrush. 'You look great,' she said, then disappeared. Hal hoped she was right: he felt sure that in her haste she'd removed several layers of skin from his ears.

'Okay, mark it,' Tony shouted.

A man with a clapperboard stood in front of the camera. '*Bringing Up Ralph*, series three, episode four, scene sixteen, take one,' he said, opened the clapperboard and banged it shut.

'Okay, we're rolling.'

There seemed to Hal to be an enormous pause before he heard Tony shout, 'Action!' '. . . so don't tell Mummy. You remember Daddy's bled phone—'

'*Cut!* What the hell's a bled phone?'

'A cross between a red phone and a blue one. Sorry,' said Hal.

'Okay, let's go again,' Tony shouted.

Hal looked at Jessica and Sebastian. The child was grinning at him. No – that would have meant he was sharing the joke. He was smirking at him.

Hal tightened his jaw in resolve. He was determined to get this right.

'Action.'

'. . . remember Doddy's red phone—'

'*Cut!* Action.'

'. . . remember Daddy's bread phone—'

'*Cut!* Action.'

'. . . remember Diddy's red pheene. Balls!'

'*Cut!* Action.'

'. . . remember Daddy's red fart. What am I saying?'

'*Cut!* Action.'

'. . . remember Daddy's red phone, don't you . . . *Yes! I did it!* Oh, sorry, I should have just carried on with the speech, shouldn't I?'

'Oh, for God's sake, *cut!* Action.'

Take seven was word-perfect, right to the end of the speech, much to Hal's relief. 'We haven't got time to bugger about getting this thing just so,' he heard Tony tell Steven, who shrugged in response.

'Okay, check the gate!' Tony hollered.

A member of the crew seemed to open the camera lens. 'Gate's clear,' he shouted.

'Right, it's a wrap. Let's strike and move on. I want to get the ballroom scene started before lunch,' he declared.

There was a sudden flurry of activity. Hal was unsure what to do. Then Steven appeared. 'That's you done for the day, Hal. Give me a couple of minutes, and I'll organise a car to take you back to the hotel.'

Hal slunk out of the phone-box. It was at moments like this that he wished he hadn't given up smoking.

'You weren't very good, were you?' a high-pitched voice said, from somewhere just above his waist.

Hal looked down, to see the Nation's Poppet staring directly into his eyes. 'No, I don't suppose I was,' he admitted. 'I was a bit nervous. First day and all that.'

The child tilted his head to one side. Suddenly he looked like a quizzical puppy. 'You *are* a professional, aren't you?' he asked.

'Yes. It's just that I've not done much telly before,' Hal explained.

'I'm never nervous,' Sebastian said.

'Well, then, you're lucky, aren't you?' Hal tried to fake a smile. 'Perhaps it's one of the advantages of being so young,' he added.

'Yes,' Sebastian said, looking Hal up and down. 'I suppose you're pretty old. But Edwin's ancient. Even he could remember the colour of a telephone.'

'Perhaps I should get Edwin to give me lessons,' Hal suggested sarcastically.

'You've got to relax. I could see you acting. Nobody can see me acting, because I'm a natural,' Sebastian boasted.

Hal felt his temper fraying. 'Is that right?' he said, through gritted teeth.

'Sebastian.' Jessica had appeared at her son's side.

97

'We have to go on to the next location. Say goodbye to Hal.'

Sebastian produced the most sickly smile Hal had ever seen. 'Goodbye,' he said, taking his mother's hand.

Jessica smiled – far more appealingly. 'See you later,' she said, over her shoulder, as she led her son away.

Hal sighed dispiritedly.

It was eleven o'clock at night. Hal had had several consolatory beers and a few glasses of wine, which had finally hit the spot. He was a bit sloshed. He knew he shouldn't drink when he was depressed and now, as he teetered up the corridor towards his room, he was regretting his foolhardiness. He had a heavy day tomorrow, three important scenes, and the last thing he needed was a thumping headache.

He had skipped lunch, and spent the afternoon cursing himself for cracking under the pressure that morning. He had worked and worked on his scenes for the next day until he was convinced he was word-perfect. Yet this hadn't lifted his spirits. The producer hadn't spoken to him, the star of the show had criticised him, and his fellow actors, Penny and Edwin, had patronised him all through dinner.

As he turned the corner, he came upon a delightful sight.

Jessica Taylor was standing outside a door in a full-length white silk nightdress, her bare feet visible at the bottom. A thin pretty layer of white lace decorated her ample cleavage. Admittedly she was smoking a fag, but the way she tilted back her head to blow the smoke at the ceiling made even that filthy habit look erotic.

'Hello again,' Hal said, as he reached her.

Jessica jumped, looked over her shoulder, then put a finger to her lips. 'You've caught me,' she whispered, stubbing out her cigarette in the glass ashtray in her right hand, then placed it on the floor by her feet.

Hal tried not to look down the front of her nightdress, but failed.

'Sebastian's asleep,' she told him. 'He doesn't like me smoking. Thinks I'll get cancer. Do you smoke?'

'Used to,' Hal whispered back.

'Don't tell him you discovered my guilty secret, will you?' She winked.

'I wouldn't dream of it,' Hal promised.

'I thought you did well, today,' she said, much to Hal's surprise.

'Really? I don't,' he said.

'It was your first day. Everyone else has been working on this programme for ages. It's not easy coming in cold.'

'Mummy!'

Jessica's eyes widened in panic. 'Yes, poppet, I'm coming.'

Hal thought fast. Swooping down, he picked up the ashtray and hid it behind his back.

A second later, Sebastian appeared in the doorway.

'Mummy, what are you doing?' he said, rubbing his eyes. 'And what's he doing here?'

'Nothing, little one. I heard a noise and came to see what it was. Hal was just passing, that's all,' Jessica told him.

'He probably made the noise,' Sebastian said, stabbing a finger in Hal's direction.

If only the nation could see him now, Hal thought.

'Don't be silly, Sebastian. Now, come on, let's go back to bed. Goodnight, Hal,' Jessica said, as she steered Sebastian through the door.

Hal walked a little way along the corridor and waited. Within a minute, Jessica reappeared, her eyes on the floor.

99

Hal coughed.

She looked up at him and he held up the ashtray.

She smiled broadly, blew him a kiss and closed the door.

Hal closed his eyes momentarily, trying to feel that kiss. The world started to spin so he opened them again, took a deep breath and swayed towards his room.

He had just undone his trousers and slid them down to his ankles when there was a knock on the door.

His imagination ran riot. Had Jessica been overcome by lust? Was she outside his room, bosom heaving, in anticipation?

Hal fought back into his trousers and went to open the door.

It was Steven. 'Sorry to bother you so late, but Penny and Edwin said you'd only just left the bar. My room's next door, so I thought I'd give you this, now,' he said, thrusting some pages into Hal's hands.

'What is it?' Hal asked.

'New scene. We've ditched one that you weren't in and replaced it with this. Hey, your part's building already,' Steven said enthusiastically. 'Bit late in the day, but the writer was insistent. It's going to be shot first thing on Wednesday morning, so I thought the earlier you had it the better. Take it to bed with you, eh?' Steven suggested.

A poor substitute for Jessica Taylor, Hal thought. 'Yeah, sure.'

'Happy studying,' Steven said, and let himself into his own room.

Hal closed his door, bimbled across to the bed, and flopped on to it.

Steven had a point. After the start he had made, it was nice to be given an extra scene, rather than having lines cut. But when was he going to learn it?

He lifted the pages above his head, and stared at them.

Oh, no. The new scene was with the Nation's bloody Poppet.

IO

Jake sat at the table in his bedsit, a copy of the *Stage* spread in front of him, a glass of red wine in his hand. It had been a long time since he had scanned the job pages of the trade paper, yet he had been staring at this edition since the previous Thursday. That was something beginners did. Or losers. Now he felt he was both.

He had circled an advertisement in red pen. An open audition. Oh, the indignity. It wasn't even an open audition for the West End but for Theatre in Education, a schools tour of salubrious Lambeth and Elephant and Castle. On the plus side, at least that unpalatable phrase 'profit-share' was nowhere to be seen. The play was also to his taste, *Romeo and Juliet*, and there were two parts for which he was suitable: his advancing years gave him a shot at old Capulet while his balding head and ever-increasing paunch made him physically perfect for Friar Lawrence.

The money would be poor, but every little helped. And even if a schools tour was the lowest of the low, it would be good to do some real acting. It might even boost his confidence.

Jake gulped down the contents of his glass.

The audition was today. What was the alternative? Something about beggars and choosers leaped into his addled brain. 'How appropriate,' Jake said, to the four walls that surrounded him.

Hal was freezing. When he had dreamed of being on location filming a starring role, it had not featured an indoor swimming-pool in Bournemouth at seven o'clock in the morning.

He stood in the shallow end, awaiting the appearance of the Nation's Poppet. Next to him, and visible beneath the ripples, was a small set of steps. Sebastian wasn't the tallest individual in the world, and everyone was less than keen for him to drown.

Some extras were also in the pool, which had been hired for the morning to the exclusion of the public: a couple of kids, who were screaming and dive-bombing into the water, an old woman, who Hal was convinced would die of hypothermia at any minute, a fat man, a few thirty-somethings, and a couple, also in the shallow end. The shot was to open with the couple fondling each other, then the camera would move down the track, panning, until it alighted on a two-shot of Hal and Sebastian. Then the scene would begin. That was how Steven, the first assistant, had explained it to Hal.

When Sebastian arrived, he was flanked by his dresser and his mother. He looked like a champion boxer making his entrance into the ring.

Hal watched Jessica cross to a chair against the wall and sit down. He waved to her and she smiled at him.

It was as if she had dressed especially for the occasion: she wore a pink T-shirt, a short white skirt, ankle socks, and trainers. As she crossed her legs, he caught a flash of black undergarment atop perfect thighs and his body responded. Hal panicked, and thought of cold showers, cold sores and runny noses. Sebastian was about to get into the pool. He could just see the headlines: *'Television*

Company Sack Paedophile From Award-winning Comedy'. That did the trick.

'You're a bit weedy, aren't you?' Sebastian said, in a piercingly loud voice.

'Morning,' Hal replied.

'Okay, Sebastian, we're ready for you in the pool, now.' Steven appeared at his side. He picked Sebastian up and lowered him gently into the water on to the steps. 'How's that looking?' he called to the cameraman.

'Too high, try the lower step.'

'Sebastian, would you mind?'

Sebastian sighed, and lowered himself on to the lower of the two steps. 'Is that okay?' he asked sulkily.

Steven looked over his shoulder, and gained a thumbs-up from the cameraman. 'That's just great,' he told the boy.

'Are you going to get your lines right this time, Hal?' Sebastian asked.

Before Hal could reply, Tony appeared and crouched down before them. 'Okay, chaps, lots to get through this morning. I want to move as quickly as possible as we only have the pool until lunch-time, so no time for rehearsal. Steven's explained the shot. Remember, don't start the dialogue until the camera reaches its mark at the end of the tracking. Okay?'

'Okay,' Hal replied.

Sebastian nodded.

'Fine, we're almost ready to go,' Tony said, and walked back towards the camera.

'You've not got many hairs on your chest, have you?' Sebastian commented.

Hal looked down. 'Five a side around each nipple,' he confessed.

'I thought men were supposed to have hairy chests,' Sebastian snarled.

'Not all men.'

'He has,' Sebastian said, pointing to the male half of the courting couple.

'You're right. Mind you, so has she,' Hal quipped, with a false laugh.

Sebastian was stony-faced.

'Sorry,' Hal apologised. 'I'm not very good with kids.'

'I'm not a kid,' Sebastian spat. 'I'm a young man.'

'Of course. I should have realised. Look—'

'Okay, quiet, everybody, please, we're going for a take,' Steven bellowed.

'Good luck,' Hal said to Sebastian.

'I don't need luck,' Sebastian assured him.

'You need a frontal lobotomy,' Hal muttered, under his breath.

'What?' Sebastian asked.

'I said, you've obviously done a lot more than me,' Hal lied, with a grin.

'*Action!*'

The camera rolled along the tracks, panning from the courting couple, who had begun kissing, until it reached its destination in front of Hal and Sebastian.

'Dad?' said Sebastian. 'What are—'

'Cut!'

'Hal?'

'Yes, Steven.'

'General rule. Never look directly into camera unless specifically asked to do so. Okay?'

'Damn! Yes, sorry.'

'Don't worry. Just look at Sebastian. Act with him as you would in the theatre. We'll go again.'

Sebastian sniggered.

Another take was marked and action called. This time Hal kept his eyes fixed on his young co-star, and the scene began.

Sebastian pointed to the courting couple and said, 'What are those two doing Dad?'

'The breast stroke, by the look of it, son,' replied Hal. 'Cut!'

'What went wrong this time?' Hal asked Sebastian.

'They messed up. Someone would come and tell you if it was your fault again,' Sebastian informed him.

'What's going on, sweetheart?' one of the extras, the old woman, asked Sebastian.

Hal saw Sebastian's eyes shine, and a sickeningly perfect smile spread across his innocent little face. 'A problem with the camera, I think.' He oozed charm.

'Only it's freezing in here,' the old woman complained, and Hal nodded in agreement.

'I'm sure it won't be long. Would you like me to ask them if you can have a rest?' Sebastian enquired.

'Oh, that's ever so kind of you but I'll be all right. I'm a big fan of yours,' she told Sebastian. 'You're a real little trouper, aren't you? I can't wait to tell my friends I've met you,' the old woman gushed.

'Thank you. You're very kind,' Sebastian replied.

Hal had to admit it: the boy could act.

'Cheerio,' the old woman said, and went back to her starting position, ready to swim across the background of the shot.

'I've got lots of fans,' Sebastian boasted.

'I'm not surprised,' Hal replied, with a shiver.

'Okay, we're going again,' Steven said.

Three full takes later, of which two had been aborted due to technical errors, Hal was sure he was turning as blue as a stag comedian's jokes.

'One more straight away, please,' Steven yelled, and they began again.

They hadn't got far before Tony yelled, 'Cut! What's

that clicking noise every time you speak Hal? You got a set of castanets down your trunks, or something?'

'It's my teeth chattering,' Hal confessed.

'Should do what I do, love,' the old woman shouted. 'Take the buggers out!' she showed the world her gums.

Everyone laughed, the crew and the extras. And they all seemed to be laughing at Hal.

'Hal, I'd get you out but we're running out of time,' Tony said. 'Let's just try another quickly.'

'Okay, settle down, now. We're going again,' Steven roared.

Once the laughter subsided another take began, and everything seemed to be going okay. Then Hal heard an unexpected burbling noise, like a diver rising to the surface followed by the sound of laughter behind the camera.

'Cut!' Tony called. 'What happened there?' he asked.

'He blew off!' Sebastian screamed with laughter and pointed at Hal, who blushed. Everyone was pointing at him and laughing. He felt humiliated. Admittedly he was numb in the nether regions by now but not so much that he was unaware of his bodily functions. He looked at the giggling culprit.

What was the use? No one would believe it was Sebastian and not him. Nobody would want to. Nobody would dare to.

Three takes later, they were approaching the end of the scene.

Hal: 'Yes, of course, Daddy knows best. So why don't we invite the pool attendant for coffee. Maybe he can find a way of distracting your mother while I search her handbag for the mobile.'

Sebastian: 'You are silly, daddy.'

'Cut! Check the gate.'

'Why do I always say, "Daddy knows best"?' Hal asked Sebastian.

'It's your catchphrase, silly. You say it every week. It makes people laugh.'

'Does it?'

'It did when Ian said it.'

'Oh, well, that's all right, then,' Hal said.

Silence followed, and Hal sent up a silent prayer asking to be released from his torture.

'Okay, that's a wrap, let's set up by the diving-board for Penny and Sebastian's scene.'

Hal breathed a huge sigh of relief.

Suddenly he felt a small hand on his back. 'Well done, you did really well there.'

Such high praise from Sebastian, of all people, took Hal by surprise. 'Thanks,' he mumbled.

'You look really cold. You'd better get out of the water quickly,' Sebastian suggested.

'You're right. I'm frozen.'

Hal placed his hands, flat on the poolside and attempted to heave himself out. He failed. He looked at Jessica, and noticed her watching him closely. He summoned up his strength, pushed down hard on the side of the pool, bent his legs and leaped upwards.

He hadn't noticed that Sebastian's hand slid down to the back of his shorts. He didn't feel the boy's fingers take a decisive grip. In fact, he was unaware that anything was wrong until he heard coarse, raucous laughter. Then he knew. His trunks were bunched on his thighs, and what remained of his masculinity after hours in cold water was on full view. The crew were clapping and cheering.

He dropped back into the pool and heaved up his trunks.

He considered drowning the child, then realised Sebastian was already out of the water. Tony waved a reproachful finger at him, laughed again, and ruffled the boy's hair.

Hal looked across at Jessica, who was in hysterics. Game over, Hal thought. All his fantasies faded. Not only did the woman of his dreams think he suffered from irritable bowel syndrome, she had now had a full-frontal view of him in all his shrunken glory.

Slowly he ploughed his way to the steps at the side of the pool, and braced himself for an endless barrage of cheap laughs at his expense.

Hal had to wait until after lunch before a car could take him back to the hotel.

A location catering truck had been set up, and everyone had lunch there.

'Having the sausages, are we, Hal? I would have thought a chipolata was more your size.'

'What you drinking with your meal, then, Hal? Miniatures, is it?'

Hal pretended to take it all in good heart, but died inwardly.

The minute he got back to the hotel he ran to his room: he needed to speak to someone who would not only sympathise but talk him out of his artistically suicidal state. He thought of phoning Belinda, but it was too soon after the other night's unexpected drama. Instead he rang Jake.

'Hal, dear boy, how kind of you to call.'

Hal felt instantly comforted by his familiar tones. 'What are you up to?' he asked.

'At the moment I'm playing a little guessing game. I have just returned home with John from Oddbins' recommended buy-of-the-week. He finds me a wine, within a certain price range, then removes the label. I have to guess its country of origin, the grape it's made from, et cetera, and if I get it spot on three times in a month, he gives me another bottle free.'

'Sounds fun. So what's your guess this week?'

Jake sighed. 'My palate is struggling to determine exactly which nation has inflicted this poison onto the mass market. Bulgaria is a possibility. There has, in recent years, clearly been a communist plot to rot the livers of decadent westerners. Argentina is another potential culprit, still remorselessly unforgiving over the Falkland Islands, they've been shipping bottles of mustard gas into the British Isles, cunningly labelled as Cabernet Sauvignon. Or perhaps it's the Chileans? Frankly, if they make their own people drink the antiseptic mouthwash they called wine, then the United Nations should need no further proof of their appalling reputation on human rights.'

'Should you be drinking by yourself at this time in the afternoon?'

'I'm celebrating. You can congratulate me, if you like. I've just been offered employment.'

'Fantastic!'

'Don't get excited. I shall be touring Shakespeare around schools. I shall be speaking blank verse to pupils who think *Hamlet* is a cigar, *Lear* is a jet, and *As You Like It* is a pornographic magazine.'

'Still it's work, Jake. Listen, after the day I've had—'

'Hal, today I had to suffer the indignity of an open audition. Forty years in the profession, and I have spent the day playing silly buggers with a bunch of fresh-faced youths still trying to get their hands on their Equity cards, a fistful of middle-aged nobodies who had recklessly given up jobs in Asda to pursue an ambition it was far too late to achieve—'

'Yes, but, Jake—'

'—plus a bunch of senile old duffers who had never risen any higher than spear-carrying or singing out of tune in the chorus of a tacky musical.'

'Never mind. Listen, I've had the most awful—'

'The director flicked peanuts in his mouth while I performed my audition speech. Can you imagine?'

'Oh dear,' Hal replied, deflated.

'Sorry to go on, dear boy, but it really was one of the most humiliating days of my professional life. But I'm ranting. What was it you were trying to tell me?'

'Oh . . . nothing, really. I was just wondering how you were.'

'Ah! Unfortunate timing then.'

'I tell you what, Jake, I'll give you a call when I get back to London.'

'That would be most appreciated.'

' 'Bye till then.'

Hal left his room and went to the bar, using his expenses to drown his sorrows.

Mentally he recapped. Professionally, so far, this job had been a disaster: forgotten lines, staring into camera, chattering teeth. And Sebastian Taylor, the Nation's Poppet, all-powerful star of the show, had turned out to be a right little shit. Worse, the child had taken an instant dislike to him. And there seemed little Hal could do about it.

Personally, things looked even worse. He fancied Jessica – no, lusted after her, longed for her, dreamed of her. She had stirred feelings in him he had sworn never to entertain again after his divorce from Amy. But Jessica had made his head spin and his heart pound. And she was out of his league. He had been made to look a fool in front of her. And to top it all, she happened to be the mother of his number-one fan.

Hal wanted another drink, but he didn't want other members of the cast and crew to arrive back and start teasing him again.

'Room service,' he muttered to himself.

Just as he was about to leave, he noticed a fine pair of thighs slip effortlessly on to the stool next to his. 'Buy a girl a drink?'

He manoeuvred his eyes up until they were met by Jessica's.

'Sure. What would you like?' he asked nervously.

'Pimms, please. I know it's not summer, but I fancy something fruity.'

He ordered Jessica's drink, with another for himself, and tried to remain composed. 'Where's Sebastian?' he asked.

'With his tutor. English and geography. It's the law, you see. So, I've popped down for a quick drink.'

'You deserve a break. It can't be easy raising a child by yourself.'

'No, it isn't.' She raised an eyebrow. 'Whereabouts in London do you live?' she asked.

Another opportunity to be singularly unimpressive, Hal thought. 'You don't want to know,' he replied.

'Oh, yes, I do.' Jessica shifted around on her stool.

'East Ham. Another reason to be embarrassed today.'

'What do you mean?'

'Oh, come off it. Today's been a nightmare for me.'

Jessica laughed – a surprisingly deep, sexy laugh. 'I thought people were very cruel to you today,' she said.

Not least your son, Hal thought. 'Really?'

'I thought you behaved with great dignity under difficult circumstances.'

'Thank you.'

'Most of the other actors would have joined in and made jokes at their own expense, but you didn't, Hal. You smiled, but I could tell you were dying inside.'

Hal blushed. 'I was, actually.'

'You're so sweet.' Jessica slid her hand along the bar and squeezed Hal's. 'I've always found theatricals heartless, vicious people. I'm so scared my Sebastian might grow up like that.'

Hal was convinced he already had. 'I'm sure that won't happen,' he said.

'They're so cruel and self-obsessed. You don't think that, in some way, he might be poisoned by them, do you?'

Hal shook his head reassuringly. 'No chance.'

'I don't speak to the other actors. They're afraid of me. They think I got somebody sacked for upsetting Sebastian. It's not true, of course, but I haven't discouraged the rumour. That way they leave us alone and I can protect Sebastian. Don't tell them I told you, will you?'

'Scout's honour,' Hal said, putting his hand on his heart.

'Meeting someone like you gives me hope. You're really sensitive.'

'Am I?'

'I must go,' she said suddenly, and stood up.

'Listen, before you leave,' Hal said, 'I just want to apologise for my performance this afternoon.'

'Why apologise to me?'

'I don't really know.' Hal floundered. 'It's just . . . well, it wasn't very impressive, was it?'

Jessica smiled wickedly. 'Considering the conditions,' she said, shooting a glance at Hal's crotch, 'I thought it *extremely* impressive. Must dash.'

With that, she headed for the exit. Hal watched her go and saw cast members and crew entering the bar, Tony at the helm, with Elizabeth Sage's arm tucked under his, all in high spirits.

Elizabeth looked at Hal, and then at Jessica.

'Everything all right, dear?' the old woman asked.

Jessica smiled in return.

'Jessica,' Tony roared, as she passed him, 'you off?'

'I must check Sebastian's okay,' she said, and departed.

'Ah, Hal!' Tony called. 'I almost didn't see you there. But, then, you're quite difficult to see without a magnifying glass, aren't you?'

More laughter. More humiliation. When would it ever end?

11

It was Sunday and, once again, Mary was opposite Belinda on one of the blue sofas, quaffing white wine as though it was water. This time, though, free of a hangover, Belinda was keeping pace with her.

'So have you heard from lover-boy, then?' Mary asked.

'No. I've been using the time Hal's been away to think things through. Analyse how I really feel.'

'Yuck! So what was the upshot?' Mary asked, cutting to the chase. 'Are you going to go for him or not?'

'Well, I think so.'

'Yippee! Thank Gawd for that.' Mary topped up Belinda's glass. 'A toast. To the shrink and the thespian, though I'm not sure which is which, and a well-planned night of romantic seduction! When's he back?'

'I'm not sure. Soon, I think. I've left a couple of messages asking him to call me and . . .' Belinda trailed off.

'You've rung him already! And?'

'And I've dialled 141, then rung a couple more times. Well, I didn't want Hal to think I was hassling him.'

Mary cackled. 'Poor cow! You've got it bad, haven't you?'

Belinda nodded. 'I'm scared, Mary.'

'Don't be. Leave it to Auntie Mary. First thing we're going to do is take you late-night shopping after work tomorrow.'

'Why?'

'*Why?*' Mary repeated and looked Belinda up and down. 'Because you couldn't seduce a man who'd just walked out of jail after serving twenty years dressed like that. You've got to speculate to accumulate. Dust the cobwebs off your purse and we'll choose you a nice frock, underwear, the works.'

'I'm not sure that's really me.'

'Of course it isn't. None of this is you, is it? We've got to stop you thinking like you, haven't we?'

'I suppose so.'

'Trust me, the right clothing will make you feel different. It'll give you confidence. It might even convince you that you can be sexy!'

Belinda giggled. By general standards, Mary was not a beauty. She was a big girl, and her face was plain, but she radiated personality and sex appeal, and men loved her. If just a little of Mary's magic rubbed off on her, maybe she stood a chance with Hal.

'Okay, anything else?' Belinda asked.

'I suggest you cook him a nice meal. Show a lot of leg as you flounce around the kitchen. Be flirtatious. Pick imaginary bits of fluff off his jacket. Pounce on him over the After-Eights.'

'I tried it once and I made a complete mess of it.'

'That's because you didn't do it properly. Tell you what, let's pop out, get a couple more bottles of wine and then you can practise on me?' Mary suggested.

'I beg your pardon?'

'You need lessons, or you're going to screw it up again,' Mary replied firmly.

'But—'

'Oh, come on. It'll be a laugh,' Mary interrupted. 'Get your purse. We need to buy you some Dutch courage.'

'I might have known I'd be paying.'

'For my expertise,' Mary informed her.

'So how come you've been missing from work these last few days?' Belinda asked, as they grabbed their coats from the stand in the hall.

'I was due some leave.'

'I tried ringing you at home but there was no reply. You must get an answering-machine.'

'I haven't been at home . . . I've been at Paulo's,' Mary confessed.

'Who's Paulo?'

'He's my new man. And I tell you, Belinda, when he took off his pants it was like "Jake the Peg".' Mary said cackling, again. 'Do you remember the old Rolf Harris song? I'm Jake the Peg, diddle-diddle-diddle-dum, with an extra leg, diddle-diddle-diddle-dum. Oh my word!'

Belinda burst into hysterics. 'Mary, you're incorrigible!'

'I know, that's why you love me.'

The two friends left the flat still giggling. Belinda was beginning to doubt that Mary was the right person from whom to take lessons in love.

As Belinda and Mary stepped on to the streets of Crouch End, Hal sat on a train bound for London. He had been due to finish shooting two days earlier, but there had been problems with the weather. This meant he had only one day off before rehearsals began before shooting in the studio.

Most of the cast travelled back together, and Hal found himself in a carriage with Penny, who fell asleep within two minutes of the train pulling out of Bournemouth, and Edwin, who was wrestling with the crossword.

Hal tuned in to the conversations taking place around him. Behind, Elizabeth Sage was holding court with some bit-part actors, telling them about the good old days. Across the aisle were Tony, Steven and the Nation's Poppet with Jessica.

Occasionally, she glanced at him out of the corner of her eye and smiled. And he smiled back.

At first Hal had tried not to look at her but she had caught his eye. She had driven him mad. She had slipped off her shoes seductively, rubbed her thighs, run her fingers through her hair, yet never made Hal feel that it was for his benefit. He felt as confused, as he was excited.

'Anyway,' Tony announced, raising his fifth whisky and ginger, 'to absent friends.'

'I miss Uncle Ian.' Sebastian sighed, lips quivering. 'He was such a good actor.' He looked directly at Hal, whose eyes, for once, were not trained on Jessica's thighs.

This was too much for him. He did not want to sit and listen to the first assistant, the producer and the two-faced brat of a star sing the praises of his predecessor. He glanced at Jessica, who also seemed uncomfortable. He leaned across to Edwin and said, 'I'm going to the buffet car. Can I get you anything?'

'The answer to three across if you could. "Hairy men with good voices are brought to their knees by same *femme fatale*"?'

'Delilah,' Hal suggested, standing.

'Pardon?'

'Delilah. As in Samson, and Tom the Song.'

'Who?'

'Tom Jones.'

'I see. Of course. I see Samson. Yes, obvious. It was the second half of the question that confused me. I'm not very good on popular music, I'm afraid.'

'It's not unusual. Now, are you sure I can't get you anything?'

'Yes, please, that's kind. A coffee.'

Hal looked at Penny, whose eyes were still closed, her mouth open. 'What about Sleeping Beauty?' he asked.

'About twenty years of her life if she wants to go on partying at the same level. Other than that, I shouldn't bother.'

On his return journey, Hal bumped into Jessica. 'Hi,' she said softly.

'Hello there,' Hal replied, almost coyly.

'I'm just on my way to the buffet car,' she said.

'You should have said,' Hal told her. 'I could have saved you the walk.'

'I needed a break,' she confessed.

An almost enjoyable silence passed between them, as if neither really wanted to pass the other.

'Well, I'd better get Edwin's coffee back to him, I suppose.'

'Yes, of course,' she said, and began to move past him. As she did so she caught his arm. 'I just wanted to say,' she whispered, 'that I've been thinking about you. A lot.'

Hal was speechless. Before he could gather his senses he heard one of the electric doors slide open and Elizabeth Sage stepped through. For a moment she seemed to glare at them. Then she smiled, said, 'Excuse me, dears,' and went past.

Jessica watched her go. 'I don't think she likes me,' she said. 'None of them do. Still, like I said, it's best that way. I must go. We don't want people talking, do we?' With that she disappeared in the direction of the buffet car.

Hal didn't know what to do. Should he go after her or not? He had been a married man, out of the game for years. He didn't understand the rules any more. Worse, he was not confident. It was this that made him decide to return to his carriage, wondering if he had just allowed another of life's opportunities to pass him by.

*

'Okay, okay. Look, you're supposed to be imagining I'm Hal, remember?' Mary suggested.

Belinda giggled, yet again.

'Look come on, this is serious. So, I'm Hal—'

'You're gorgeous, Hal,' Belinda said huskily, before giggling again.

'Thank you, I know I am. Out of curiosity, does he know he is?' Mary asked.

'No, I don't think he does, actually,' Belinda decided, as she gulped a little more wine.

'Good. So I'm Hal, and here we are, sitting at the dining-table. And you have the perfect teasing prop right in front of you.'

'Do I?'

'Yes. The glass of wine. I want you to rub your finger round the rim like this.' Mary demonstrated.

Belinda attempted to copy her.

Mary screwed up her face. 'How are you managing to do that?'

'What?'

'At worst it's supposed to produce a sweet high note. You're making a sound like someone scraping a finger-nail across a blackboard.'

'Sorry.'

'Never mind. Try this one. Pick up the glass. That's it. Now, gently run your tongue lightly over the rim, like so.'

Belinda tried.

'Oh, no.' Mary sighed.

'What?'

'You're supposed to be flicking your tongue sugges-tively around the rim. You look like you're using a scouring pad on the bottom of a saucepan. Look, even you can't cock this one up. Take the stem of your wine glass, Belinda. That is Hal's willy.'

'Oh I hope it's not,' Belinda stated, giggling again. 'I mean, I don't exactly want a "Jake the Peg", but there are limits.'

'You place your thumb behind, two fingers on the front of the glass, and move them up and down seductively.'

Belinda grasped the stem of the glass.

'For crying out loud, Belinda. You're supposed to be making him long for you to touch him. The only thing Hal could look forward to if he saw you grip a glass like that *is a trip to fucking Casualty*!'

'Can't I just tell him how much I love him and see what happens?' Belinda begged.

'You can't afford to leave anything to chance. Come on, let's head for the sofa.' Mary dragged her friend into the sitting room and they sat down.

'Now, imagine you're wearing sheer tights, and rub one foot over the other like this . . . or have a go at stroking your thighs. Remember, you're not supposed to be aware you're doing it.'

'Mary.'

'No! Imagine Hal's stroking them, don't rub them as if they were chapped.'

'I just can't,' Belinda said. 'All these old tricks are never going to work. Anyway, I'm not after a quick one. I want more than that.'

'Okay, I give up,' Mary said. 'Let's try it your way. So, I'm Hal. Look me in the eyes and tell me you love me.'

'I love you,' Belinda said unconvincingly.

'Okay, try again. Tilt your head to one side. That's good. Now look out from under your eyelids. That's brilliant,' Mary said encouragingly. 'Now go for it.'

'I love you, Hal.'

'Do you?'

'Yes I always have.'

'I didn't realise.'

'I'd do anything for you, Hal.'

'Really?'

Belinda nodded.

'Phwoarr, get your kit off, girl,' Mary yelled, and leapt on top of her.

They squealed and shrieked, then tumbled off the sofa. It was Belinda who reached for a cushion and struck the first blow.

12

Hal had expected to rehearse at the BBC rehearsal rooms, but found himself instead in a community-centre hall in Chalk Farm. The reason for this was that it was within spitting distance of Tony's favourite pub.

The location filming was in the can, but they still had to film the bulk of each episode in the studio in front of a live audience. Everyone had sat in a circle and read the script. Then the floor was marked with gaffer-tape, to represent the rooms and doors of the set, and Hal walked through his scenes, writing his directions on to his script. It was a simple day.

Just one thing was bothering him. Jessica had sat six feet behind the desk from which Tony was directing operations. She had observed the action, while remaining aloof. She had behaved exactly as she had said she always behaved around the rest of the cast. Which was fine. Except she hadn't once caught Hal's eye. It was as if he didn't exist. Hal was confused. During a break for coffee and biscuits, he could take it no longer. Just as he had decided to cross the floor and talk to her, Sebastian tugged at his sleeve. 'I've got an interview with the *Daily Express* this afternoon,' he crowed.

'Have you? That's nice.'

'It happens,' Sebastian said cockily. 'It's about how

we're coping after losing Ian. Would you like me to say something nice about you?'

Sebastian was playing games with him, and Hal knew it. 'If you feel you can,' he said noncommittally.

'Em?' Sebastian screwed up his face. 'Don't worry. I'll make something up.'

'How kind.'

'Okay, can we have Hal, Penny and Edwin for scene thirteen, please?' barked Patrick, the floor manager, a thick-set man with curly hair, a cheery personality and a deep, resonant laugh.

Hal glanced at Jessica as he made his way on to the floor. No response. Maybe she had had a change of heart.

He shrugged his shoulders, and tried to concentrate on the work at hand.

Hal mooched towards Chalk Farm tube station through the drizzle. He was startled by the loud tooting of a car horn. It had come from a vehicle with tinted windows. The passenger door opened, and Jessica peered out. 'Get in, quickly,' she barked.

Hal was not about to argue.

'Sorry. I didn't mean to be bossy,' she said, as he clambered in and shut the door. 'I just don't want us to be seen.'

'Why?' Hal asked.

'I'll explain in a minute,' she said, pulling away from the kerb.

She drove off in the direction of Belsize Park, and eventually parked in a suburban street behind a white Ford Mondeo. Then she turned to face him. 'I thought I'd better explain. I owe you that. I'm not playing games, Hal,' she blurted out. 'I meant what I said. I can't stop thinking about you. It's been years since I was so instantly attracted to anyone. I feel like a schoolgirl.'

'Oh, Jessica—' Hal was delighted.

'I really want to see you, but I can't,' she stated bluntly.

'Why not?'

'It's Sebastian.'

'Where is he?'

'With Tony. The two of them are doing an interview this afternoon. Tony's bringing him back later. He's going to stay for supper.'

'I'm jealous,' Hal confessed.

'Don't be silly, it's nothing like that. It's Sebastian's career. That's the problem. Since his father left, I've done everything I can to make his life a success. He's famous, Hal. But there's nothing the newspapers like more than to take a star and tear him to shreds.'

'Not an eight-year-old, surely?' Hal argued.

'I can't take the risk. Can you imagine if you and I . . . Can't you just see the headlines in the *News of the World*? "The Nation's Poppet's Mother in Torrid Affair with Actor Playing Screen Dad".'

Hal could have lived with the scandal. Especially if it meant a torrid affair.

'I can't let that happen. His father let him down, and I vowed I wouldn't.'

'Couldn't we keep it secret?' Hal asked.

'Oh, I'd have to trust you an awful lot, and I'm not sure I could ever again trust a man.' Tears were forming in Jessica's eyes.

'Oh, please, don't cry. Look, it's all right. I understand. These things happen. I really like you, but if it's not meant to be then—'

'Oh, Hal—' Jessica buried her head in his shoulders. Then she turned her face to his and kissed him. Her passion took Hal by surprise. It was breathtaking, the sort of kiss you sink into irretrievably. The sort of kiss that excites you and warns you that you are in trouble

125

at the same time. Hal hadn't felt like this for a long time.

Then suddenly it was over. Jessica pulled away abruptly. 'No. I'm sorry. I can't do this.' She sat up, straightened her hair and wiped her eyes. 'I'll take you back to the station,' she said coldly.

'Jessica, we can't leave it like this. You're confusing me. Can't we meet up again, talk things through?'

She shook her head, started the car and drove off.

When they arrived at the station, she put on the handbrake, and Hal turned to her. 'There's another reason why we can't get together,' she told him.

'What's that?'

'I can't tell you. You'd hate me. You'll just have to believe me.'

'You can't leave it like that,' Hal begged.

She stared directly ahead.

Hal sighed and opened the door.

'Hal?'

'Yes?'

'You won't tell anyone about all this, will you?' she asked.

'If that's what you want.'

'Promise?'

'Yes. You don't have to worry.'

Within seconds, Jessica had driven away.

'What the fuck was all that about?' Hal muttered, and walked dejectedly into the tube station.

When he arrived back at his flat he checked his post. Two bills, one black, one red, a double-glazing brochure, and an envelope stuck to a wrapped bin-liner from a charity asking for clothes, bedding, furniture, and bits of unwanted jewellery. There was also a postcard from Jake.

Dear boy, For some bizarre reason, we have gone away to a disused youth hostel somewhere in the region of Bodmin Moor to rehearse this Shakespeare. Something to do with bonding as a company. The cast that lives together are at each other's throats before bedtime the first night, or some such drivel. I will contact again with details of my opening afternoon, and you can come along to some ghastly comp at Elephant and Castle and sit among gum chewing, mini-skirted nubiles, and be reminded of the fumblings of your youth. Ever yours, Jake.

He went into the sitting room, and checked his answering-machine. There were two messages. The first was from Pippa, his agent. 'Hi, Hal. Got your message about the extra hours you worked. I shall make sure I invoice the swines on your behalf. Talk soon.' The second was from Belinda. 'Hiya, Hal, it's me. Listen, I'm sure you must be back by now. How about coming over tomorrow for a bite of supper? I'm dying to hear how the location stuff went. Give me a ring and let me know if you can make it.'

Hal considered Belinda's invitation as he headed into the kitchen in search of coffee.

Belinda stood back and admired her handiwork. The dining-table looked magnificent: lace tablecloth, blue napkins, best cutlery, and crystal glasses.

She had had such fun shopping with Mary the previous night. They had gone to almost every clothes shop in central London and she had tried on the most extra-ordinary outfits, everything from geisha kimonos to see-through chiffon blouses.

She had eventually bought a simple, black, wrap-around dress, new underwear, sheer tights, and a crip-plingly expensive pair of high heels. She felt good, if a little nervous. Tonight was important to her. She had thought endlessly about what she should say, and even more about what she shouldn't. She had to tell Hal she loved him, but she didn't want to frighten him. She wanted to give him the chance to fall in love with her.

Her tummy fluttered.

Hal had arrived with a bottle of her favourite wine, after-dinner mints, and a carefully chosen bunch of flowers. First, he apologised for his behaviour on their previous get-together, which wrong-footed her, and it took her a while to recover her equilibrium. However, Hal had kept the conversation going by asking lots of questions about her work. This endeared him to her even more: she knew he must be dying to tell her about his own adventures.

By the time they had finished the pudding, Belinda had begun to talk to him about life on location. She had consumed just enough wine to be brave, though not enough to make her feel calmer. She tried to remember some of Mary's tips.

'So Sebastian really gave you a hard time about forgetting your lines?' she asked, toying seductively with her hair.

'Yes. Why are you pulling your hair out? You got nits, or something?' Hal asked, laughing.

'Sorry, I didn't realise I was. Carry on.'

'Then he tells me he never forgets his lines. Oh, and he also said I wasn't very good.'

'How awful,' Belinda sympathised, and dipped her finger into her wine glass. She rubbed it round the rim.

'Then I had dinner with Penny, the woman playing my ex-wife. She's dreadful. What a moaner. Not a good word to say about anyone. Can you stop that? You're setting my teeth on edge.' Hal requested.

This was not the effect Mary had predicted and

Belinda felt increasingly nervous. Now Hal was saying something about having an extra scene thrown at him. Something about fingers grappling with his—

'Oh, bugger!' Hal exclaimed, as Belinda's wine glass tipped over spilling its contents into his lap.

'Oh, Hal, I'm so sorry,' Belinda exclaimed.

'It's easily done,' Hal said. 'Most of it's gone on the floor, anyway. Good job it wasn't in the sitting-room over your cream carpet. I'll grab a cloth.'

'Oh, leave it.' Belinda waved a hand. 'I'll wipe it up in the morning. Shall we go into the sitting room and perch on a sofa?'

'Good idea,' Hal agreed. 'I'll bring the wine?'

'Do,' Belinda stood up and led the way.

Hal followed her and, to Belinda's delight, sat on the same sofa as she did.

'Anyway, as I was saying,' Hal said, 'he pulled my swimming trunks down in front of everybody.'

'Sorry, who did?' Belinda was pretending to stroke her thighs absentmindedly.

'Em . . .' Hal said, watching her.

The old trick seemed to be working, Belinda noticed.

'Em . . .' he said again, but Belinda wasn't listening: she was rehearsing her speech. Phrases like 'I love you' . . . 'Don't worry, you don't have to say anything' . . . 'I love you' . . . 'I don't want to frighten you away . . .'

'Sebastian. It was all hanging out. And the worst thing was it was in front of . . .'

I love you . . . I always have . . .

The moment arrived. Desire and courage collided and she said, 'Listen, I've got something I want to tell you.'

And so did Hal.

Belinda's heart skipped a beat. 'Gosh, that's weird,' she said.

'Isn't it?' Hal laughed. 'So, after you.'

'No,' Belinda replied, suddenly coy. 'After you.'

'I don't know if I can, actually,' Hal confessed.

'Of course you can.'

'I don't know. It feels a bit funny telling you.'

Belinda grabbed his hand. 'It's okay. I understand.'

Hal looked directly into her eyes. 'Perhaps I'd better leave it.'

'Please don't, Hal. You can say anything to me. Anything you want,' Belinda urged.

'Well,' Hal began, 'it's like this . . .' He stared at the floor sheepishly. He looked embarrassed, vulnerable, and Belinda loved him more than ever. Felt certain she could make him happy.

'The reason I was particularly embarrassed was . . . that it all happened in front of Jessica.'

Belinda felt disorientated.

'Who?'

'Jessica. Sebastian's mother.'

To Belinda, the atmosphere in the room changed from a balmy summer's evening to a grey winter's night. 'I don't understand. What difference did that make?'

'Jessica is the most fascinating, gorgeous, sexy woman I have ever met in my life.'

Instinctively Belinda tucked her feet under her and folded her arms about her knees. 'Oh. Really?' she asked, on automatic pilot.

'Belinda, you should see her. Beautiful red hair, hypnotic brown eyes, and what a body! Sex on legs or what?'

Belinda wanted to run away and hide. 'Her husband's a lucky man,' she whispered.

'No husband. At least, not any more. Just the brat of a son.'

'That's okay, then, isn't it?' Belinda asked, in a small voice.

'It's not as simple as that. You see, the first time I saw her . . .' And Hal recounted the story. The meeting in the corridor. The cigarette outside her room. Breakfast. The train journey back to London. The kiss in the car.

With every instalment, Belinda crumbled a little more.

'. . . then she changes her mind again. Dumps me back at the station. Oh, Belinda, I really like this woman. What should I do?'

'Do you really need someone like her, Hal? She doesn't sound very straightforward. I mean, after Amy and everything?' Belinda had pressed the professional switch.

'I know.'

'And there's your job to consider. I mean, she's Sebastian's mother, and if he doesn't like you . . . I must admit it's a strange reason to give for not having a relationship. Then again, you're in a strange profession.'

'She said there was something else as well.'

'What?'

'She wouldn't tell me.'

Belinda sighed. 'Don't you think you should ask her?'

'How can I when she's avoiding me?'

'It doesn't sound very hopeful, Hal. Maybe it's best left—'

'Yes, but I just can't stop thinking about her. Today she just dropped Sebastian off, then picked him up at the end of rehearsals. She didn't even stay. The way she looked at me . . . I know she feels the same.'

Belinda rested her chin on her knees. 'Have you told her how you feel?'

Hal paused. 'Not exactly.'

'Then perhaps you should.'

'Should I?'

'If she means so much to you she has a right to know. If she turns you down, at least you'll know. You don't want to waste time pining for what might have been.'

Hal sighed. 'You're right. I should have seen it myself. Oh, Belinda, what would I do without you?' Hal pulled her into his arms and hugged her, his face buried in her neck.

She wanted to melt into those arms, wanted the lips to plant kisses on her neck. Instead she tensed.

Hal pulled away. 'Shit, look at the time. I must be off. I've got work tomorrow. And you've no idea how good it is for an actor to be able to say that.'

She followed him to the front door, and waited as he put on his coat.

He opened the door and turned to her. 'You okay?' he asked.

'Just tired.'

'My fault. I've kept you up past your bedtime. I'll call soon. Dinner out. My treat.' He planted a kiss on her forehead, then skipped off into the night.

Belinda closed the door, walked into the sitting room and switched off the lights. Then she took off her dress, her tights and her knickers, and put them in the kitchen bin.

Then she went to her bedroom, threw herself on to the bed, buried her head in the pillows and sobbed.

13

Hal was a little late in arriving at the community centre, but for once, congestion on the tubes gave him a lucky break: Jessica was in the doorway smoking a cigarette.

As he approached she glanced over her shoulder. 'Don't say anything, please, Hal,' she whispered.

'I have to, Jessica. This is driving me crazy.'

'I've already explained—'

'Yes, you have. But I haven't felt like this in years.'

'*Keep your voice down!*'

'I can't stop thinking about you. I know it won't be easy, Jessica, but I have to see you. I can't sleep, eat, concentrate on the work. All I think about is you, remembering that kiss, what it felt like, what it meant—'

'Hal, stop!' she begged.

'Tell me you don't think about me. Jessica?'

She looked at the floor. 'I can't.'

'Then I have to see you. At least let's talk—'

Edwin appeared. 'Hello, Hal. I was beginning to think you weren't going to show today.'

Jessica slipped inside.

Edwin's gaze followed her. 'Smoking again, was she?' Edwin asked.

'What? Yes,' Hal answered distractedly.

'Doesn't like to smoke in front of the boy. Quite right too, if you ask me.'

'Glad you've arrived. Got another little teaser for you.'

Hal pushed past him, and nodded good morning to the others as his eyes scanned the room. She was behind Tony's desk. Sebastian was beside her. He stuck out his tongue.

The rehearsal went well for Hal, until the break, perhaps because he didn't have a scene with Sebastian. As tea was poured he saw Tony take the boy aside for one of their little chats.

Jessica dipped her hand into her handbag, fished out her cigarettes and headed for the door.

Hal waited until he was sure no one was looking at him, then followed her.

When he appeared at her side Jessica jumped. 'Hal, go back in.'

'When can I see you?'

'You can't.'

'I must.'

'Okay.' Jessica softened. 'We'll talk.'

'When?'

'Hal, please!'

'Tonight,' he pressed. 'Tonight. Or I'm going to kiss you now.'

Jessica's eyes widened. 'Okay, tonight.'

'Where?'

'I'll find you.' Before he could ask any more, Jessica dropped her cigarette on the ground and slipped back inside.

Hal worked hard to keep his mind on his acting until the rehearsal ended at lunch-time. He watched Jessica cross to Tony and Sebastian. Then Edwin came up to him. 'Fancy a pint?' he asked.

'No, thanks, I've got things to do.'

'Suit yourself. But before you go, will you give me another of your educated guesses for this ruddy clue?'

'Edwin . . . I'll try.'

' "Lear's man knows true value of glittering promise." '

'Eh? Fool something,' Hal suggested.

'What?'

'Well, Lear's man. The fool, as in *King Lear*.'

'Of course!' Edwin exclaimed. 'True value of glittering promise. Fool's gold. Imagine! *King Lear* – and me an actor. I couldn't see it for looking.' Edwin chuckled.

Hal scanned the room. Jessica had vanished. 'Listen, I'll catch you tomorrow, Edwin.' Hal grabbed his rucksack and sprinted out of the door.

Jessica wasn't in the car park either.

He sighed. He kicked a stone across the concrete. Maybe Belinda had been wrong. Perhaps he should have kept his feelings to himself.

'So he hasn't had her yet?' Mary asked.

'Keep your voice down,' Belinda begged.

'Belinda, we're in a busy pub. Nobody's listening to us.' Mary placed their drinks on a table in the Highgate Village pub and they sat down. Belinda had recounted the events of the previous night on the walk there.

'So, have they done it yet or not?'

'No, I told you. She's blowing hot and cold. One minute she's all over him, the next she's telling him she doesn't want him.'

Mary took a sip of her wine. 'Oh, she's playing that game, is she? Treat 'em mean, keep 'em keen. It doesn't work, just pisses blokes off.'

'What does it matter?' Belinda said. 'He's in love with her.'

'He's in *lust* with her. Not everybody needs to be in love to want to go to bed with someone.'

'You should have seen the way he looked when he talked about her. She's hooked him,' Belinda said, sadly.

'I wouldn't give up hope yet.' Mary gulped at her drink.

'What?' Belinda exclaimed. Picking up her bottled beer. 'Don't be ridiculous. Of course I'm giving up,' she said, taking a depressed swig.

'Belinda, if I gave up every time I came up against a bit of competition from a woman who was better looking than me, I'd never have a feller.'

'Don't be silly, Mary. You're a lovely looking girl,' Belinda reassured her.

'And you're a crap liar. I'm taller than a lot of men, I have a nose like a small growth, shoulders like an Olympic swimmer, feet like flippers, and at Christmas I use my thighs to crack the brazil nuts no one else can get into.'

For the first time since Hal had left her flat, Belinda laughed.

'Oh, Mary.'

'It's true. The difference between you and I is, that I don't care about my deficiencies. Sex appeal is about confidence and wanting someone badly enough,' Mary informed her.

'That's the trouble. I didn't have much confidence to begin with. And now . . .'

'If you love him you should put up a fight.'

'How?'

Mary pondered. 'She might blow him out, of course, but let's suppose she doesn't. I reckon it'll fizzle out. Especially if she dotes on this kid, and he's as big a brat as Hal says he is. You're going to have to hang in there, and bide your time.'

'I can't. I don't think I even want to see Hal right now.'

'Don't be daft. You must. You didn't get round to telling him how you felt, did you?'

'No, thankfully.'

'So he's none the wiser. He sees you as a friend again, which suits our purposes perfectly.'

Belinda's mouth fell open in disbelief. 'It does?'

'You've got to pretend you're still just a friend. Encourage Hal to talk to you about her. Interrogate him – subtly, mind. Get him to tell you all the gory details.'

'Oh, Mary, I don't think I could bear that.'

'You must. You're in the perfect position to glean all the inside information. That way, you'll know exactly when things are going wrong.'

'Mary—'

'You'll just have to trust me on this one. We'll get Hal back for you. Just do what I tell you, when I tell you. Same again?'

Belinda sighed. 'Why not?'

'Don't go away.'

I've nowhere to go, Belinda thought, as Mary headed off to the bar.

Hal sat on his sofa watching the nine o'clock news. It was as depressing as ever: wars, murders, economic gloom.

He'd had a miserable evening. He knew his lines by heart for episode one, so it had taken only ten minutes to run through them. Now a long evening lay ahead – a long evening of thinking about Jessica. He tried to think of her as just a prick-tease, but he didn't believe it. He was sure she felt something for him too.

Nine twenty-five. He thought about going to bed early, but he wasn't tired. He needed someone to talk to, but Jake was away, and none of his other male friends had grown out of the school playground where matters of the heart were concerned.

He considered ringing Belinda. She had been so

helpful the night before, incisive, constructive and sweet. He wondered why no man had snapped her up. She was attractive, bright, kind, funny, and had a nice figure. Perhaps she was ultra-choosy.

The doorbell rang.

He hoped it wasn't someone looking for Mrs Worrel. She was away visiting relatives.

It rang again.

He got up, went downstairs and opened the front door.

Jessica stood before him.

'Hi,' Hal said. He felt a mixture of excitement and fear, anticipation and dread. 'You'd better come in.' She stepped over the threshold and he closed the door behind her. 'Up the stairs,' he murmured. He couldn't take his eyes off her shapely legs as he followed her upstairs.

As he closed the flat door behind them Jessica was walking into the sitting room.

'I didn't think you'd come,' he said.

'I said I'd find you,' she reminded him. 'It took time to make arrangements for Sebastian.'

She stood before him in a tight-fitting burgundy jumper and a short black skirt. Her hair was pulled into a pony-tail, enhancing the perfection of her cheek bones. Her mouth was quivering and she was wringing her hands. 'I shouldn't be here, really,' she said.

'Listen, Jessica, I didn't mean to pressure you, and I don't want to upset you, but I can't stop thinking about you and it's driving me mad.'

'I've thought of nothing but you since I saw you outside Penny's room in the hotel in Bournemouth. I'm almost convinced I lo—' she stopped.

Hal could hardly believe what he was hearing. 'Then why—'

'Oh, Hal, can we have a secret affair? Can we begin something—'

'Does it *have* to be secret?'

'Yes! I thought I'd explained that.' She looked desperate. 'This was a bad idea. I must go.'

Hal caught her arm. 'Please don't. I don't want to lose you. I'll do whatever you want—'

'I have to. I must.'

'Why, for heaven's sake?'

'Remember I told you there was something else? Well, if I tell you, will you promise to keep it to yourself?'

'Of course.'

'I'm still married.'

Hal dropped her arm.

'See? You've no trouble in letting me go now, have you?' she said, and left him.

He was still frozen to the spot when he heard the door slam behind her.

After a sleepless night, Hal realised he had to talk to Jessica again. Find out just how 'still married' she was. He was the first person to arrive at rehearsal the next morning. Jessica appeared with Sebastian, hugged him and left without glancing at Hal.

The rehearsal room was buzzing. Situation comedy, Hal discovered, is filmed using several cameras at once, all covering different angles. Today's rehearsal was for the benefit of the camera crew, and the cast performed the episode straight through as if it were a play.

Throughout it all Hal kept looking between shoulders, or through legs to see if Jessica had returned.

At the end he sat and waited as cast and crew slowly disappeared. Still there was no sign of her. At last, only Sebastian and Tony remained. 'No home to go to, Hal?' Tony enquired, as he put on his coat.

'I'm on my way. I was just killing time before I meet someone,' Hal lied.

'Someone, Hal? Very cryptic. In my experience "meeting someone" usually means a romantic liaison.' Tony chuckled.

Hal glanced at Sebastian and blushed. 'Your mother not coming for you, Sebastian?' he asked.

'Doesn't look like it, does it?' Sebastian snarled.

'Jessica's away on business until the weekend so Margery, my wife, and I will have the pleasure of Sebastian's company until then.'

Friday's rehearsal was an oasis for Hal: he knew Jessica would not be there and he could concentrate on his work.

But Saturday morning was purgatory. It was the weekend and he had expected her back but, once again, he found himself alone in the dusty rehearsal room, waving goodbye to Tony and the Nation's Poppet.

He was almost at the station when a car horn sounded behind him.

'Get in,' Jessica called, through the open window.

'It's all right, I know the routine,' Hal said as he clambered into the passenger seat.

Once again she drove around the back-streets before parking.

'Where have you been? I've been worried about you,' Hal said.

'That's nice.'

'Not for me, it wasn't. Tony said you were away on business.'

'He doesn't know I'm back yet. I wanted to see you before I collected Sebastian. I had to go away because there was a problem at one of the shops.'

'Shops?'

'I own a couple on the coast.'

'Really?'

'Don't sound so surprised. You didn't think I lived off Sebastian's earnings, did you?'

'Of course not.'

'That's something else I never tell anyone. I'm not sure why I keep telling you all my secrets.'

'I just needed to talk to you. I mean, after that last little bombshell you dropped I—'

'I'm so sorry about that, Hal,' she interrupted, taking his hand. 'I shouldn't have blurted it out and run away like that but I was scared. You'd said your ex had had an affair and how you didn't believe in such things and I thought when I told you I was still married you'd hate me.'

'I don't hate you. I was just stunned.'

'It's not quite what it seems. Will you let me explain?'

Hal nodded.

'Sebastian's father was a waster. He never did a day's work in his life, just bled me dry. When he found out I was pregnant with Sebastian he went ballistic. He wanted me to get rid of the baby. When I refused, he upped and left. He told me he would only come back if I did as he asked.'

'That's terrible!'

'He said he wasn't going to pay for a child he didn't want. After Sebastian was born, he stopped getting in touch. Told me he was moving to Manchester. He just disappeared out of our lives. I haven't spoken to him or heard from him in almost eight years. I don't even know where he is.'

'Are you saying Sebastian has never met his father?'

'That's right.'

Hal ran his hands through his hair. 'Haven't you tried to divorce him?'

'No.'

'Why not, for heaven's sake?'

Jessica sighed. 'Money, really. At least at first. I'd worked hard to build up my business, and I knew he was broke, and I was scared he'd try to claim a stake in it. Then, as the years went on, I just didn't bother. I didn't need to. I never wanted to marry again, I wasn't even interested in having a relationship with a man . . . until now.'

'I don't know, Jessica, I'm confused . . .'

'Hal, I really want to start seeing you, but I have to think of Sebastian. "The Nation's Poppet's Mother Has Affair with Screen Dad" is one thing. Add "While Still Married to Previous Husband" to it and it's a disaster.'

'But surely this will always be so unless you divorce him.'

'Well, I probably will. But it's a big step, and I'd rather wait a little, see how things . . . develop between us before I put myself or Sebastian through all that unpleasantness. Besides, I've got to find him to divorce him.' Jessica squeezed Hal's hand. 'I just never believed the day would come when I felt I might be able to trust someone again.'

'You can trust me,' Hal promised.

'I want you to go home and think about it, Hal. Please don't tell anyone what I've—'

'I won't.'

'Please. Not your friends or your landlady.'

'My landlady's still away and I won't telephone any of my friends.'

'If it's all too weird for you, I'll understand.' Jessica leaned over and kissed him lightly on the lips. 'I'll drive you to the station,' she said.

Two hours later Hal was in his flat, still thinking when

the doorbell rang. Cursing, he ran downstairs in a state of extreme agitation.

When he opened the door, Jessica brushed past him and climbed the stairs to his flat. 'I know I shouldn't be here. I couldn't keep away. I should have given you longer – days, if need be. But . . . have you thought about things?'

'I've thought of nothing else.'

Jessica took a deep breath. 'And?'

'I think we should give it a try and if things become serious—'

Suddenly she was in his arms and they were kissing hungrily.

'Oh, God, I haven't made love in so long,' Jessica murmured, 'but is this wrong? I want you, Hal, like I've never wanted any man.'

'Ssh,' Hal replied, kissing her again, tenderly stoking her cheeks.

She pulled away briefly, and removed her sweater. She placed Hal's hands on her naked breasts. 'Oh touch me, please, just touch me,' she demanded.

Hal caressed her breasts gently and she shivered.

Then she removed his hands and pressed herself against him. She kissed his face, his lips, his neck, as she lowered her hands and undid the belt of his jeans. Buttons were wrenched apart and her soft hand slid into his underwear and stroked him.

'Jessica . . .'

'On the floor. Now.' She put her hands on his shoulders, and pushed him down on to his back.

She removed her shoes, her tights and her underwear in one swift motion, but left her skirt on. Then she crouched over him, covering his neck, and chest and mouth in kisses.

'You're so beautiful,' he whispered.

'Oh, Hal . . . So are you. So are you,' she told him before feeding a breast into his mouth. He kissed, tenderly, yet with desire.

'Oh God,' she moaned.

She sat up. 'I'm sorry, I can't wait any longer . . . I'm so sorry,' she said, and Hal could see tears in her eyes.

She slid her frame downwards until Hal could feel her rubbing her sex along his length.

'I need you, I need you,' she whispered softly.

And then he was inside her . . .

She placed his hands upon her breasts and she rode him with a passion and an intensity he had never known before.

Her beauty rose and fell before him. Never in all his life had he felt such passion, such desire from a woman for her man.

'Oh, God, Hal. Oh God You're going to make me come.'

Tears were falling down her cheeks, and yet she was smiling. There was an air of wonderment behind the water and mist that glazed over the deep brown of her eyes. Her body shuddered, and her breathing became erratic, and she cried out. And he joined her in this moment, unable to contain himself any more, the intensity of it almost made him want to pass out.

Jessica collapsed on top of him, still shaking.

'Sssh,' he whispered. 'It's all right. I'm here. I'm here for you,' he told her.

Later, she kissed him lingeringly, then nuzzled her head into his neck.

'Oh, Hal, I'm in love with you. I fell in love with you in Bournemouth. I'm sorry. I know it's going to be difficult—'

'It's okay,' Hal interrupted her. 'It's okay. We'll do whatever you want. I just don't want you to worry.'

'I love you. I'm sorry but I love you,' she said.

Hal cradled her in his arms. 'I could be wrong,' he said, 'but I think I love you too.'

14

It was Sunday, and they were to record the first episode at Television Centre. Hal was shown to his dressing room by one of the floor assistants. She was armed with a walkie-talkie, and talked continually to the studio floor and the gallery, where the producer and technicians controlled the recording, as she led him along a never-ending series of corridors. He had been grateful for her guidance. Television Centre is one large circle, awash with corridors and stairs. To Hal, it was like a maze. It was colour coded as a rough guide, blue section, red section, etc. but this made little difference to Hal's sense of disorientation. He decided he would not wander any further than from the dressing-room, down to studio three where the show would be taped. Otherwise, without the aid of an Indian scout and a compass, he could be lost for days.

Hal had dreamed for years of working at the BBC, and now he was. He felt excited.

The dressing room was basic, though not as bad as he had been led to believe by other actors who had worked here. The decor was dingy, and took 'bland' to a new level, but it was no worse than his flat. There was a chair, a sort of single divan bed, that was harder than those found in casualty departments up and down the country, a washbasin in one corner, and a toilet off. There was a mirror, with lights, and on one corner of the dressing-room, there was a portable television set, showing the airing BBC programme, with the sound switched off.

Through a speaker in the ceiling, he could hear muffled conversation and noise, presumably coming from Studio Three, where other members of the cast were already working. This was one of the happiest moments of Hal's life.

He and Jessica had made a pact to keep their distance in public. When they had parted Hal promised to leave the details of their next meeting to her. He had felt like a naughty teenager seeing an older woman, and had even begun to think he might enjoy the secrecy.

Twenty minutes after she had left him the previous afternoon Hal was surprised to hear Beethoven's Fifth emanating from somewhere in his flat. It seemed to be coming from behind a sofa cushion. He investigated and discovered a mobile phone tucked behind it. He had put it to his ear and pressed a button. 'Hello?' he said, tentatively.

'How do you like my little present?'

'When did you manage to hide it?' he had asked.

'When you went into the kitchen to make the coffee. It's my old one, and I can contact you any time I want.'

'You were confident of a successful seduction, weren't you?'

Jessica laughed, mischievously. 'I lived in hope. I hope you noticed it has a red face. I thought it might help you remember your lines tomorrow night,' Jessica teased. 'Now I know you'll want to give the number to all and sundry, but don't, not even to your agent. I want it saved for me.' Then she had told him how much she loved him. Again and again and again.

Hal flopped down on the bed, and put his arms behind his head. Life was good. He had it all: a beautiful girlfriend, money coming in, a fantastic job, a big career ahead of him.

He stared up at the ceiling and a smile of sheer joy spread across his face.

When Hal first arrived on set, nobody spoke to him, which was just as well, because he wanted to enjoy the moment. As he looked around the sets for *Bringing Up Ralph*, he felt a tingle down his spine. They were simple enough – a kitchen, a sitting room, a bedroom and a pub, all of which looked half the size they appeared to be on screen – nothing fancy or expensive-looking, but to Hal they were magical. He remembered the first time he had been on a stage set, for a local youth-theatre production of *Oh! What A Lovely War*, made of old timber reclaimed from a disused quarry. To Hal it had been like stepping into another world, and he felt the same sense of excitement now.

'Morning, Hal, how are you today?' Tony asked.

'Fine,' Hal replied.

'Good. Bit boring this morning, all very technical, so don't worry about performing. It's basically for me and my boys. Make sure I don't cock up my camera angles. It'll be tiring and stop-start.' Then he walked away.

It was eleven o'clock. At eight o'clock that evening Hal knew they would be recording in front of a live studio audience.

His body tensed as the thought entered his head.

By the time they broke for lunch, they were behind schedule. It was Hal's first trip to the BBC canteen, and he was overjoyed to discover that the food was as bad as it was reputed to be. He tried hard not to stare at the famous faces around him as he ate with Penny and Edwin.

Penny was complaining. 'Why can't Tony do his job properly for once? Wasting time sorting out all the camera positions he marked down wrong at the rehearsals. We'll end up with barely enough time to rush through a dress rehearsal before they start letting the punters in.'

'What sort of people come to watch a recording?' Hal nibbled at a bread roll.

'The dregs, dear,' Penny told him. 'At one end of the scale you get busloads of blue-rinse pensioners, who can't hear a word you're saying, and at the other, herds of schoolkids who giggle at every mistake and stare vacantly when you want them to laugh.'

'Not all audiences are like that, Penny,' Edwin insisted.

'True. Some must be shipped in from the mortuary, they're so dead. Honestly, Hal, getting laughs out of them with this script will be like trying to take a urine sample from a gnat. Difficult, requiring great expertise.'

'Oh, stop it, Penny. You're depressing the boy,' Edwin chided her.

'I'm only telling him how it is. I wished someone had warned me when I started.' She looked at her watch. 'Better be getting back before the Ayatollah sends one of his supporters to chase us,' she said.

'We'll catch you up,' Edwin told her.

'Suit yourselves, darlings.' She walked quickly towards the exit.

'Don't take any notice of her. She was born to complain. She's divorced, you know. Three times. Can't say I'm surprised.'

Hal laughed.

'Jessica's looking sexy today, don't you think?' Edwin said unexpectedly.

'I haven't seen her,' Hal replied nonchalantly.

He had, of course, but not clearly. He had spent most of the morning on set, and she had been in the auditorium, towards the back where he could make out little more than her outline.

'T-shirt, and jeans so tight she'll have to take them off with a wallpaper scraper. Lovely bum, though.'

You're not wrong there, Hal thought.

'Pity she's such a snooty bitch,' Edwin went on, and Hal bristled protectively.

Then Edwin leaned towards Hal and lowered his voice. 'Just remember that warning I gave you. Watch what you say within her earshot. That goes double today. Remember, there are mikes all over the set, feeding up to the dressing rooms and the gallery. You'll be personally miked-up too. So be careful.'

'Thanks for the warning,' Hal replied.

'I mean it,' Edwin said. 'Even Penny's not stupid enough to open her mouth around the studio. Come on. Time to show our faces.'

Hal followed him out of the canteen. He would be extra careful about what he said – but his opinion of Sebastian was not the secret he mustn't give away.

Everything went fairly smoothly after lunch until scene twelve, when nothing was right and tempers frayed, especially on the technical side.

Eventually they decided to move on.

Hal had done his last scene in the episode so he wandered off the set. 'What do I do now?' he asked the assistant, who had shown him to his dressing room.

'Wait there,' she said, and crossed to the floor manager to confer.

Satisfied, she came back to Hal. 'We've finished with you for now, so it's up to you. You're welcome to stay and watch, or you can go to your dressing room and relax. We'll come and get you when we need you.'

'I'll be in my dressing room then,' Hal said, as another angry voice roared in the background.

'I don't blame you.' She rolled her eyes.

'This is my first telly job,' Hal confessed, then asked, 'What happens next?'

'When we've finished this there'll be a tech-run. You won't be in costume for that but you will be miked and you'll treat it like a performance, although the run may be stopped for technical reasons. Then, fingers crossed, there'll be a full dress rehearsal, you'll be given notes, then break for a meal – if you can eat before a show. Then costume, makeup, out from the trenches and over the top we go,' she finished cheerfully. 'Good luck for tonight.'

Hal glanced towards where Jessica sat reading. She did not look up from her book.

Sighing, he trotted off to his dressing room. He felt drained, and there was a long way to go yet.

An hour later Hal was called for the tech-run and miked up. This was the first time they had gone through the whole piece since they had left the rehearsal room.

'You look awful,' Sebastian told him, as Hal paced around the set.

'I'm nervous, okay?'

'But it's only the tech-run.'

'I know, I know – I'm being daft.'

'You're not going to puke, are you?'

'No. At least, I don't think so.'

'Don't chuck on the set, will you?' Sebastian said. 'Someone might skid in it. Yuck!'

'Could be worse. I might have thrown up in the swimming-pool the other day,' Hal remarked.

'You're disgusting!'

'And you're . . .' Hal counted to ten. '. . . such a tease.' Hal forced a grin.

'And you're a pig.'

The technical rehearsal went okay. Hal remembered his lines and didn't bump into the furniture. The dress rehearsal was reasonably smooth, but although Hal didn't forget his lines, he stumbled over his words.

Afterwards the cast assembled in the audience seats. Tony sat in one of the front rows facing them. 'Okay, I've loads of notes on that run, but there isn't time to give them all to you. We're running seriously late.'

'Just for a change,' Penny whispered to Hal.

'I'll dish out the most important ones. Generally,' he said, snapping his fingers, 'pace, pace, pace. We overran by a minute. If that happens tonight I'll have to chop it in the edit, and I'd rather not. I know we're all tired, but let's make it snappier. Penny?'

'Yes, Tony.'

'Make sure you put the kettle down on the right mark, otherwise we can't see Sebastian in the background behind you, going through your handbag for the mobile, and we need to before we go to his mid-shot.'

'Sorry, darling.'

'Edwin? I'm sure your mind was on one across, but could you try to remember that Hal's character is called Michael, not Malcolm. You called him Malcolm three times.'

'Did I really? How stupid of me.'

'Try not to do it tonight as we'll have to retake. Well done to Hal for carrying on regardless.'

The praise cheered Hal no end. 'Thanks, Tony,' he said.

'You haven't heard what else I've got to say yet, Hal. First, diction, diction, diction. Second, you don't have to

152

project. You're miked, the set is miked, and we have a boom mike. You're not in the theatre, Hal, and I want you to take your whole performance down a peg or two.'

Hal felt as deflated as he had been elated just seconds earlier.

'If you don't, your performance will look over the top. That's particularly important to remember tonight when a studio audience is in these seats. You'll be tempted to play to them. Don't. Keep your performance for the cameras, and for the ten million or so viewers who will be watching this at home.'

'Okay.'

'I'm not being hard on you, it's for your own good. Sebastian?'

'Yes, Tony,' the child's voice chirruped.

'Great work in the handbag-rifling scene.'

I might have known wonder-boy would be praised to the skies, Hal thought bitterly.

'Only take your time with it. I don't want it thrown away. If we run over, I'll chop one of these buggers' lines, not that moment. Okay?'

'Yes, Tony.'

Hal was aware of a shared company bristle.

'Those who want to eat had better go now, but check your makeup call first. We've not got long till kick-off. Good luck, everyone.'

People began to disperse, but Hal didn't move.

'Are you going to sit there all night?'

It was Sebastian and Hal stopped staring into space. 'No, of course not.'

'It's just pretend, really. Why don't you just pretend?' Sebastian asked.

'That's not bad advice, I suppose,' Hal thought aloud.

'You'll be okay. You've been quite good so far.'

Hal was speechless.

'Come on, Sebastian. Let's go and get you ready.'

Jessica was standing at the bottom of the steps that ran down the aisles between the seats. Hal wanted to put his arms around her for comfort, reassurance . . . love?

Sebastian went to join her, and she led him away.

Still Hal remained motionless. He kept hearing Tony's voice saying, 'Ten million viewers.'

15

Hal was pacing back and forth in his dressing room. He could hear the audience gathering in the studio. There was an air of excitement about them that reminded him of the theatre. 'Play to the camera, not the audience,' he was repeating to himself.

He decided to warm his voice, to relieve the tension. He made a few A and Oo sounds – he had a tendency to sound them through his nose, reminiscent of Kenneth Williams with a head cold. He did a few horse buzzes, blowing his lips, then placed his hands on his thighs and E-buzzed on a sliding scaled Ee, up and down his vocal range, from bass to soprano and back again.

There was a knock on his dressing-room door. He opened it to find Peter. 'Come in,' Hal said.

'Sounded as if there was a cow in labour in here with you,' Peter quipped.

'Very funny.'

'I came to see if you wanted help dressing.' Peter clapped his hands together. 'Thought you might be a bit nervous. But you're all ready to rock and roll.'

Hal blew out his breath. 'Well, I'm dressed anyway.'

'Now, don't be silly. You're going to be fine. Wardrobe have been keeping a close eye on you, and the verdict is you're talented. You're also the sweetest person on the show, so don't worry, we'll be cheering you on. Stardom awaits. Just go out there and blossom.'

Hal was touched. 'Thanks, Peter. That's nice.'

'All part of the service.' He smiled and left the room.

Hal sat in the makeup room, foundation on his face. The television monitor was blank, but the sound from the studio was filtering through its speakers. He could hear the warm-up man talking to the audience.

'Is that your missus, sir? She'll have to take that hat off before the show starts. Bloke behind her thinks she's got two heads. One on top of the other.'

The laughter that ensued made Hal's nerves jingle a little more.

'You okay?'

Edwin was staring down at him.

'Fine.'

'I just wanted to say, have a good one.'

'Thanks.'

'By the end of the evening, you'll wonder what all the fuss was about.' Edwin patted his shoulder, then took his place in a makeup chair.

Hal could hear the warm-up man saying, 'Occasionally thespians . . . I said thespians, missus, don't get over-excited . . . From time to time, our actors make mistakes. If this happens, we'll have to shoot the scene again. This is where you come in. If we have to go for a retake, you lot have to remember where you laughed the first time, and laugh twice as hard when you see it the second time. Do you think you can remember that?'

'*Yes!*'

'And you promise to laugh on the second take?'

'*Yes!*'

'And the third, fourth, fifth, sixth . . .'

More hilarity.

Hal hoped he wouldn't be responsible for such an event tonight.

'Good luck, darling.' Penny swooped down on Hal and planted a kiss on his cheek.

'Thanks.'

The television monitor sprang into life and the opening credits rolled. This startled Hal. 'Bloody hell!' he shouted.

'Don't panic, sweetie. It's just a rehearsal for the plebs,' Penny reassured him.

'Okay, everyone, can we have you out around the back ready for the introductions?' Patrick, the floor manager, barked.

'Introductions?' Hal quavered.

'Didn't anyone bother to tell you?' Penny asked. 'We have to be introduced to the audience one at a time. I'm usually called first so I have to stand there cringing while everyone else makes their little bow.'

'And today, children, we're going to enter through the kitchen door,' Patrick announced.

Hal caught up with him. 'Nobody's told me about this.'

'You don't have to do anything,' Patrick said. 'Just go on and take a bow.'

'Who do I follow?'

'Just listen for your name. You're not in the first scene, are you?'

'No.'

'Sebastian goes on last. Just remember, when first positions are called you come straight back here. Don't hang about on the set.'

'Right. Got you.'

'Okay, it's time to meet the cast,' the warm-up man announced. 'First up, a fine actress whom many of you will have seen in the West End over the years, not to mention the National Theatre, the Royal Shakespeare Company and too many television series to mention, playing Barbara Thompson, our hero's mother. A big hand, please, for the lovely Penny Davenport!'

Penny slipped through the entrance and out on to the studio floor to warm applause.

'Now, we have a newcomer for you,' the warm-up man went on, and Hal's palms sweated. 'I'm sure most of you have read about the tragic death of Ian Wilson.'

Hal's heart leaped into his mouth. He'd forgotten the added pressure of taking over from a popular actor. What if the audience didn't take to him?

'We all miss him and, in many ways, things won't be the same without him.'

Thanks a bunch, pal, Hal thought.

'Having said that, the producer has found a smashing lad to take his place. He's a great actor too. Right now, he's probably shaking with nerves, so give an extra-warm welcome to the very talented Hal Morrisey.'

Someone pushed Hal on to the set.

The audience's reaction was generous and sympathetic. They clapped and cheered, and he took his bow, wishing he was bowing at the end of the performance, not the beginning.

When Sebastian was announced, Hal thought the roof was going to fly off the building.

'First positions,' Patrick whispered.

'Okay, everyone, the actors will take their places on the set now, and in a few moments' time the opening credits will roll. We all know what we have to do then, don't we?'

'*Yes!*' the crowd roared.

'Okay, ladies and gentlemen, my name's Dan Jones, thank you for your time.'

Hal heard the applause as he made his way to the

makeup room. Most people gathered there when they were not on set: they could follow the show on the monitor, and it was conveniently close. When he went in the opening titles were rolling.

He felt sick. He wished someone was in the audience supporting him.

He heard dialogue. The first scene had begun. He could see the shots on the monitor as they were recorded.

Three scenes to be filmed before he went on.

Three retakes for scene one. Just one for scene two. And they had just finished a second take for scene three. He didn't know why. Nothing had appeared to go wrong.

'Okay,' he heard Patrick call. 'Moving on to scene four. Positions, please.'

This was it. Hal went icy cold. Somehow he dragged himself out of his seat, and made his way to the back of the set.

Patrick was there to greet him, and Hal took his position.

'Good luck,' Patrick whispered.

'And . . . we have action,' Patrick informed him quietly.

Hal heard Penny and Sebastian begin the scene. He wanted to die. He took a deep breath and gritted his teeth. He gave himself a pep talk. This was the moment he had been waiting for all his career. This was a chance. And he could not blow it.

Hal's cue to enter was not a verbal one. It followed Sebastian's rifling of Penny's handbag. He looked at Patrick and waited for his signal. Patrick was waiting for instructions from Tony in the gallery. The floor manager raised his arm, kept it there for what seemed to Hal like for ever, then brought it down and Hal entered. In character.

It seemed unbelievably surreal. He knew he was acting, but it was almost as if it were on automatic pilot. He could see Sebastian and Penny, knew they were reciting the lines he had heard a hundred times in rehearsal, yet their voices seemed far away. It passed quickly. The scene was virtually over.

And there was one sound he still had not heard. Not after the delivery of a single one of his lines.

Laughter.

He panicked as if he was doing something wrong. He wanted the scene to end. Felt desperate to get off the set.

It ended in an argument with Penny. Hal had to exit in a temper, leaving her to deliver the final line.

He crossed to the door. He was almost safe. He began to relax.

He delivered his final line. 'I've told the boy. Daddy knows best,' then grabbed the door handle.

Which came off in his hand.

Now he heard laughter, so loud it made his ears pop.

The audience were in hysterics. They hadn't laughed at his lines, but they were busting their guts at his misfortune.

He looked across at Penny and Sebastian. They were helpless, and Penny was almost crying.

Then the evening changed for the better. Because Hal began to laugh. He looked at the door handle in his hand, and instinct took over. He offered it to Penny, then to Sebastian. They refused it. He pretended to think about putting it in his pocket.

Finally, he slapped it down on the fake kitchen work surface next to the door and said, 'That's what you get when you hire cheap carpenters.'

Uproar. Mass applause.

Penny clapped. Sebastian glared, then giggled again.

When things died down Patrick said, 'I think we'll be retaking that one, ladies and gentlemen.'

More laughter.

'I'm good with props, me,' Hal said, to more tittering. 'Sorry, Tony,' he added, looking up in the direction of the gallery.

A chippie arrived to replace the door handle.

'First positions,' Patrick called.

'Can we see your qualifications?' Hal asked, as the chippie passed. 'Don't let him touch the plumbing,' he added, as he left the set.

Patrick was waiting for him. 'Brilliant, Hal,' he said.

For the rest of the night, Hal had the audience in the palm of his hand.

And he remembered to play to the camera.

In the makeup room after the recording everybody was congratulating him – Patrick, the floor assistants, the makeup girls, Penny and Edwin. Even Sebastian tugged at his sleeve. 'Well done, pig,' he said quietly.

'Thanks,' Hal whispered back. He rushed up to his dressing room, took off his costume and rushed to the sink to remove his makeup.

As he dried himself there was a knock on the door and Peter strolled in. 'I've come to take your clothes off,' he said, and gathered up Hal's costume from the floor.

'Oh, aren't I the lucky one to see you strutting around in your boxers?'

'Behave yourself!' Hal laughed.

'When that show goes out, they'll all want a piece of that. You'll get fan mail from straights and queens alike, all wanting pictures of you with your shirt off,' Peter told him.

'Don't be daft.'

'Wait and see. A star is born.'

'Bit of an exaggeration.'

'I don't think so. You were superb. And your public awaits you in the BBC bar. I'll have a large gin and tonic waiting for you when you get there. Didn't I tell you it would be all right?'

Hal blushed. 'You did. Thanks for everything, Peter.'

'No trouble. Now I must dash. I've two more costumes to collect and I'm dying of thirst.'

'Oh, Peter, wait! I don't know how to get to the bar.'

'Ask anyone you pass, they'll point you in the right direction.' With that he was gone.

Hal closed the door and clenched his fist. '*Yes!* The boy has arrived. Woo-hoo!'

Then he got down to the serious business of trying to find his socks.

It took him ages, and by the time he left his dressing room everyone else had already shipped out. He wandered aimlessly until he bumped into a man sporting a ponytail, who gave him directions.

As he turned the corner to the bar he saw Jessica. And she was alone.

'Jessica,' he called, in a stage whisper, and ran towards her. 'I'm so glad I've caught you alone,' he said.

'Hal—'

'Wasn't it fantastic tonight?' He threw his arms round her.

'Hal, no,' Jessica said, and he felt her hands on his chest, pushing him away.

Then Hal saw Sebastian. He hadn't noticed him walking in front of his mother. The child fixed him with an icy stare. Hal was unnerved and released Jessica. 'Hi, Sebastian. I didn't see you there,' he said weakly.

'Come on, Sebastian,' Jessica said. 'Let's go and find Tony.'

Hal followed them into the bar, but stood just inside the doorway and watched. A few feet in front of him, he saw Jessica bend down to talk to her son. Sebastian glanced at Hal, still glaring, then returned his gaze to his mother.

Jessica straightened, and Sebastian walked back across the room towards him. Jessica was shuffling nervously.

Sebastian reached him. 'Mummy's made me promise not to tell anybody,' he said, flatly, 'so I won't.'

Before Hal could respond, Sebastian walked away. Then he turned back to Hal. 'You're a dead man,' he said, and hurried back to his mother.

'You look as if you've seen a ghost, Chuckle.' It was Peter. 'Exhausted, are we? Drained after giving your all for the sake of your public?'

'Something like that.'

'Well, you come with me, I've a large drinkie-poos just itching to slide over your tonsils.'

Hal followed him to the bar, trying not to look in Jessica's direction.

Belinda looked at the clock on the mantelpiece. Five more minutes, and she could return to the bathroom, then go to bed.

The doorbell rang.

Belinda glanced back at the clock. Twenty-five to twelve. Mary had threatened to call round – she had been out on a hen night. She dreaded to think what state her friend would be in. However, she went to the front door, and opened it.

'Hi. Sorry, I know it's late. You're not cross with me, are you?'

It was Hal.

Belinda gaped. 'No, of course not,' she managed eventually.

'Can I come in?' Hal asked. 'I don't want to be any bother. I can go away if it's too inconvenient,' he added, staring at her rather oddly.

'No, come in. It's lovely to see you,' Belinda assured him.

She stepped back into the hallway and Hal closed the door.

'You going off to war?' Hal asked. 'Or are you auditioning for Queen Boadicea?'

Suddenly Belinda remembered she had yet to remove her face-pack. 'Oh how embarrassing. Look, go into the sitting room and I'll be right back,' she said, and sprinted into the bathroom.

Hurriedly she washed her face. Without makeup she felt instantly old and wrinkly. She dipped into her makeup bag for lipstick, mascara, eye liner, anything. Then she told herself that she was being silly. There was no time for that. She ruffled her hair, trying to make it look tousled and sexy, then kicked off her slippers, wishing she was not wearing her pink pyjamas with the teddy-bear motif on the pocket. She undid a couple of buttons, which didn't help: she looked like Shirley Temple trying to impersonate Britney Spears now.

Sighing, she gave up and went resignedly to the sitting room.

Hal was slumped on one of the sofas so Belinda sat opposite.

'Sorry about that,' she said. 'Do you want a coffee?'

'No, thanks.'

'To what do I owe this unexpected pleasure?'

Hal rubbed his hands over his face. 'I've got problems. I didn't know who else to talk to. No, that's not true. I wanted to talk to *you*,' Hal corrected himself.

Belinda felt encouraged. 'Hey, problems are my

speciality. I make a living out of listening to people's problems,' she quipped.

'I've hit a bit of a snag tonight. Actually, that's an understatement. I've had a major disaster.'

'Tonight was your first recording, wasn't it?'

'Yes.'

'Did it go wrong?'

'No,' Hal replied. 'In fact, after a shaky beginning, it was a triumph. Everyone was delighted with me, I think.'

'Oh, Hal, I'm so pleased.'

'It was after the recording when I messed up. I made a boo-boo with Jessica.'

Belinda's hackles rose. She felt angry, jealous and sick all at the same time. 'Go on,' she said.

And Hal recounted the tale. As he did so, Belinda kept hearing Mary's advice. Hang in there. Wait for it to go wrong. Remain a friend. Be ready to pick up the pieces – and seize the opportunity.

'Can you believe he actually said I was a dead man? You should have seen his face, Belinda. It was scary.'

'I think you've watched *The Exorcist* a few too many times,' she joked.

'And that was it. She left without saying a word. I don't know what to do.'

Belinda stared at him.

'Sorry – I shouldn't have turned up so late and laid all this shit on your shoulders,' Hal said, apologetically. 'But what should I do?'

Belinda had been waiting for this question. It was decision time.

She took a deep breath, and crossed her fingers. 'I think you should do nothing,' she said.

'That can't be right, surely,' Hal expostulated. 'I should speak to her, shouldn't I?'

'Under normal circumstances, perhaps. However, this

165

is different. There's lots to consider. Your career for a start. You don't want to blow that.'

'I know, but Jessica—'

'Remember the warning the rest of the cast gave you about her? How she doted on her son? You've upset Sebastian, Hal. You might find Jessica's attitude changes towards you.'

Hal looked crestfallen, and Belinda almost relented. 'Hal, you're skating on thin ice. They could have you sacked from *Bringing Up Ralph*. You don't want that, not after having worked so hard to get there.'

'I suppose not. It's just—'

'You had to keep your affair secret . . . I presume it is an affair now?'

Hal nodded, and Belinda died inwardly.

'You had to keep the affair a secret, so it didn't attract adverse publicity for her son.'

'Yes, that, and . . .' Hal decided not to mention that Jessica was still technically married.

'She told you that Sebastian and his career came first,' Belinda continued. 'You don't want it to be at the expense of yours, do you?'

'What are you suggesting?'

'Sit back. Do nothing. Say nothing. If she wants to pretend it never happened, and Sebastian is happy to play along with that, perhaps that's the best possible outcome.'

'Shit, Belinda, that's going to be tough.'

'I know,' Belinda said softly. 'If she wants to speak to you, fine. You'll just have to leave it to her to make the move.'

'What if she doesn't?'

'She's given you a mobile phone, so she can ring you if she chooses. Just keep your head down, Hal, and see what happens.'

Hal sighed. 'I suppose you're right.'

'I think so.'

'Thanks, Belinda. You've been a real help.'

Her conscience pricked. 'You look exhausted,' she told him.

'I am,' he admitted.

'Do you want that coffee now?' she asked.

'No, but I don't think I can face the journey home at this time of night. I couldn't kip down in your spare room, could I?'

Belinda's heart pounded. She had never stayed under the same roof as Hal without Amy being there too.

'Of course.' She stood up, crossed to him, took his hands and pulled him to his feet. 'Come on, before you fall asleep on the sofa. I'll show you to your quarters.' She led him by the hand to the spare room. 'What about some hot chocolate?'

'Go on, then.'

'Get into bed, and I'll bring it to you.'

Five minutes later she crept into Hal's room with a mug.

He was fast asleep.

She placed the mug on the bedside cabinet, then reached out a hand and stroked his hair. She bent down, and kissed his forehead.

Hal opened his eyes, and found himself staring down the front of Belinda's pyjamas at her breasts. Then he looked into her calm, green eyes, which met his own.

But they weren't Jessica's eyes. And Hal was not the sort of man to love more than one woman at a time. He let the moment pass, and allowed himself to slip into sleep.

Belinda stood upright. Shaken, she turned to leave the room. Reaching the door she turned for one last look at him.

At that moment, Hal turned over, taking the duvet with him, the appearance of buttocks showing he was naked.

Belinda wanted to climb in next to him. Hold him. Comfort him. Had she seen something in his eyes?

She turned again and left the room to spend the night alone. A restless night, filled with guilt, hope and desire.

16

For Hal two days of nervous-breakdown territory had followed. He sat by the mobile phone Jessica had given him for almost the entire twenty-four hours of his rest day. He had attended the next day's rehearsal in a state of anxiety. Tony had made a nice little speech, saying how pleased he was with the previous recording, and singling out Hal for praise. A dream come true, under normal circumstances. But Jessica had sat behind Tony's desk, and not looked at him once. She had not even slipped out for a cigarette.

Even more unnerving, Sebastian had ignored him too. He had blocked the moves of the scenes he had with Hal, without raising his eyes from his script.

Hal had expected some reaction from the boy – a scowl, a criticism – but there had been nothing.

The moment the rehearsal finished Jessica and Sebastian had left.

The call came at seven o'clock that evening.

'Hal?'

'You were expecting somebody else?' he replied, trying to remain detached.

'Please, don't be like that,' Jessica pleaded.

'I'm sorry. I didn't mean to be horrible.'

'Sebastian and I would like you to come to dinner tonight,' she said unexpectedly.

After he had taken down details – time, place, directions – and switched off the phone, he had slumped on to his sofa. '*Sebastian* and I would like you to come to dinner.'

What the hell did that mean?

He decided to ring Belinda for advice.

'Damn it! Bloody answering-machine,' he cursed, then left a message. He looked at his watch. He'd have to get a move on. There was no time to hang around in case she called back.

Belinda was on the sofa next to Mary, who had come for supper.

She had recounted the story of Sunday evening within ten minutes of Mary crossing her threshold. 'Good girl. Good girl!' Mary kept saying.

'Yes, but then I felt guilty—'

'Ah, ah, ah, no relapses. You did brilliantly. Played the right hand. You've gotta fight fire with fire for the man you love.'

Belinda nodded. 'I know, but it was hardly fair.'

'Fair be buggered.'

'But—'

'No buts. Concentrate on the positive. Hal was naked in your spare bed. Weren't you tempted to whip the rest of the duvet off and have a good gander at his willy?' Mary asked.

'No, I wasn't!'

'You bloody liar!' Mary yelled, as the telephone rang.

'Oh, damn!' Belinda exclaimed.

'Let the answering machine get it. I want to know how tempted you were to slip into the bed and grab yourself a nice juicy handful?' Mary persisted as the answering machine kicked in.

Belinda put her hands over her face. 'Very!' she confessed, then heard Hal's voice. 'It's him!' she screeched. The beep signalled the end of the call and Belinda rushed to the machine and pressed play.

'Belinda? Bugger, it's the machine. Quickly, then. I did everything you told me to do, and they behaved exactly as you said they would. It was as if I didn't exist.'

'Yes!' Belinda whispered victoriously.

'Then, a few minutes ago, I get a call on the mobile. It's Jessica saying she and Sebastian would like to invite me to dinner. And Sebastian? What do I read into that? What do I do? Listen can you call me when—' Beep!

'Oh, fuck it!' Belinda exclaimed.

'My, my! The girl swears! There's hope for you yet, Belinda,' Mary declared.

'I really believed . . . When I heard the first part of that message I got all excited.' Belinda flopped onto the sofa. 'Shall I call him back?'

'Best not. You've not had time to consider your response.'

'Well, that's it. It's all over. I might just as well give up. He's going to dinner with Jessica. It'll be mad passionate love-making the minute the crème brûlée has slipped down their throats. I don't even want to think about it.'

'You didn't listen to the message.'

'Yes, I did. He's going to dinner with Jessica.'

'And Sebastian,' Mary reminded her.

'What difference does that make?'

'*Every* difference. The child hates Hal. The mother loves the child. The child is the star of the flipping television series. Hal needs the job. Yes, Jessica's invited him to dinner, and the kid is going to be right in the middle of it.'

Belinda stared at Mary. 'So?'

'So, it's got disaster written all over it. All you need to do is sit back and let it happen.'

It was a nice, large basement flat, in Kensington, plainly decorated with inoffensive pastel colours, and sparsely furnished. 'Minimalist' leaped into Hal's mind. In his experience that usually meant the mortgage was costing so much there was no money left to put anything inside it.

Jessica answered the door. She smiled, but there was no kiss. 'Come through,' was all she said.

Hal followed her past one bedroom, down the hall and into a large living area, with an almost equally large kitchen area off it. 'Lovely flat,' he said.

'It belongs to Jeremy, Sebastian's agent, one of three properties he owns in Kensington. I think he inherited two. He lets us stay here.'

'That's very sweet of him.'

'Yes.'

An awkward silence followed.

Then Hal realised that there was no sign of the diminutive saboteur. 'Jessica, what's been happening? I've—'

'Hi, Sebastian,' Jessica interrupted.

Hal turned round. Perfect timing from the child, as always. There he stood, smartly dressed, hair brushed, cheeks rosy, wearing that expression of innocence for which the British public had come to know and adore him.

'Hello, Hal,' Sebastian said, his smile hinting that he was holding a large hammer behind his back.

'Hello, Sebastian. Nice to see you. Thanks for the invite.'

'It was Mummy's idea,' Sebastian said pointedly.

'Oh, right. Well, thank *you*, then,' Hal said, turning to Jessica.

'Don't be silly. It was a joint decision. We thought it was a nice idea, didn't we, Sebastian?' Jessica prompted.

'Yes,' Sebastian's mouth replied, but his eyes said, 'In your dreams, pal.'

'Well, I'm grateful anyway. A small contribution.' Hal handed a bottle of wine to Jessica. 'And these are for you,' he told Sebastian, as he handed him a paper bag.

Sebastian pulled out two packets of sweets. 'Nerds?' he said. 'You trying to be funny?' Sebastian glared, and Hal felt stupid and embarrassed.

There was the sound of a cork being pulled out of a bottle in the kitchen area.

'Come on, Sebastian, Hal tried his best,' Jessica said, filling two glasses. 'He's not used to buying things for an eight-year-old.'

'Pokémon,' Sebastian blurted.

'What?'

'You could have got me anything to do with Pokémon,' Sebastian said.

'Poker Man? Is he some sort of caped crusader? When the fire's in danger of fizzling out, Poker Man swoops down and gives it a good old stoking?'

Jessica laughed.

'It's a cartoon,' Sebastian said, and he wasn't laughing.

Hal sensed he'd made another wrong move.

'It's a dreadful foreign import of a cartoon,' Jessica enlightened Hal, handing him a glass. 'And they've made a fortune by marketing cards and toys that cost a fortune.'

'Thanks,' Hal said, acknowledging the wine. 'And I'll remember, Pokémon,' he promised Sebastian.

'Shall we sit down?' Jessica suggested, and planted herself on one of the cream, two-seater sofas.

Hal sat next to her.

Sebastian squeezed himself between them.

Jessica put her arm round her son, and Sebastian turned to Hal and grinned. 'This is cosy, isn't it?'

'Bordering on claustrophobic,' Hal retorted.

'Why are you shaking?' Sebastian asked.

'Sorry. I suppose I feel a bit nervous,' Hal confessed.

'Why? Mummy's a good cook.'

'I never said she wasn't.'

'Then why are you nervous about dinner?' Sebastian's eyes hardened.

'Don't know, really,' Hal mumbled.

'You're weird,' Sebastian growled.

'Now, that's not nice, Sebastian. Hal is our guest. Is everyone hungry? Shall we eat?'

'Great idea,' Hal agreed, desperate to get off the sofa.

'I'm afraid the dining room is downstairs. Sebastian will show you where it is. I'll bring the starters in a minute,' Jessica said, and headed for the kitchen.

'This way,' Sebastian barked.

Hal dutifully followed. They walked back up the corridor, past the bedroom Hal had noticed on the way in. Jessica's room. Sheets and pillows of white lace, masses of cushions piled high on the bed.

They descended a set of stairs on the right, and passed another room with the door tight shut, which Hal presumed was Sebastian's. A few steps further and they were in the dining room, covered in the same cream carpet, painted in a variation of other pastel shades. Hal assumed this must once have been the cellar of the house in its glory days, before developers moved in, drawn by the scent of money.

'Sit down,' Sebastian ordered.

'Where?' Hal asked.

'At the table, dummy.'

'No, I mean in which seat?'

'Any seat,' Sebastian replied.

Hal picked one and began to sit.

'Except that one,' Sebastian said, when Hal's backside was inches away from landing.

Hal sighed, and moved to the next chair.

'Or that one,' Sebastian repeated, almost causing Hal to lose his balance.

'Sebastian?'

'I'm only playing,' Sebastian snapped.

Hal bit his tongue.

'Of course you are. And I fell for it. Well done.'

Jessica arrived with a full tray. 'Here we are. Sit up straight, Sebastian. I'll just pop back for the wine.'

'Do you need a hand?' Hal asked.

'No, no. You two stay there and chat,' she said.

They listened to her footsteps going up the stairs.

'So,' Hal began awkwardly, 'how did you think the recording went on Sunday?'

'Fine.'

'The audience were good, weren't they?'

'Yeah.'

'You were on top form, I thought.'

'S'pose.'

When in doubt, flatter an actor, Hal thought. 'You were, seriously. All your scenes—'

'Mummy doesn't need you,' Sebastian said.

Hal was dumbfounded.

'*We* don't need you. We're okay now. We're fine.' Sebastian's face was granite hard, and his eyes clouded with anger.

'Sebastian—'

'You two getting on okay?' Jessica asked, as she walked into the dining room armed with two bottles of wine and a corkscrew.

'Fine. Isn't that right, Hal?' Sebastian stared at him.

'Sure,' Hal lied, following the rules Sebastian had laid down.

The evening was a nightmare for Hal. Sebastian made jokes about his clothes, table manners and drinking habits. Jessica laughed, so Hal felt he had to add to his own humiliation by laughing too. Jessica looked beautiful, and the more Hal drank the more radiant she looked. Her hair was piled high on her head, her black halter-neck top fitted tightly over her breasts, and her matching trousers hugged her hips. He wanted to touch her. And all she did was ruffle Sebastian's hair, touch his cheek, and tell the little rat how 'sweet' he was.

Hal realised that Belinda had been right. Sebastian *was* the light of Jessica's life. And he was jealous of an eight-year-old boy.

Hal made a big effort. He oozed charm, sympathy, understanding in Sebastian's direction, and gained little or nothing in return.

Eventually he needed respite. 'At the risk of being impolite,' he said, 'may I be excused? I need to visit the little boys' room.'

Sebastain grinned at him. A look passed between them. Hal was too slaughtered to read it precisely.

'Oh, Mummy, I need to go first. I'm bursting. Please, Mummy? Please, Hal?' Sebastian begged.

'Go on, then,' his mother conceded, 'but be quick about it.'

Sebastian sprinted out.

Jessica stared into Hal's eyes, with something resembling affection for the first time that evening. 'You okay?' she asked.

'Fine.'

'Thank you,' she whispered.

'What for?' Hal asked.

'Making the effort. It means a lot to me.'

Hal wanted to respond verbally. The best he could manage was a smile.

Jessica leaned across the table, took Hal's face between her hands and kissed him.

The sound of tiny feet clomping down the stairs broke the moment.

Jessica rolled her eyes.

'Right,' Hal said, as Sebastian sat down. 'My turn. Where is—'

'Up the stairs,' Jessica said, 'past the bedroom, and it's on the right-hand side before you get to the sitting room.'

Hal clawed his way up the stairs, hunted out the bathroom, closed the door behind him, and slumped on the edge of the bath. Sanctuary. Then he stood up and approached the wash-basin. It was a lovely bathroom: white porcelain, the basin sunk into a white marble surround, with gold taps. Hal leaned against the stand for support, turned on the cold tap, and splashed water over his face. The cold brought the world back into focus temporarily. He gazed into the mirror. 'I look surprisingly human,' he said aloud.

Then he noticed. A huge wet patch was stretched across the most personal section of his trousers. Had he been wearing jeans, he might have got away with it. In grey chinos he looked like a teenager who might have watched a particularly raunchy episode of *Biker Grove*.

Hal wanted to disappear in a cloud of smoke. He grabbed a towel and began to rub at the offending area. It made no difference.

And then it struck him.

Sebastian had used the bathroom first. Had the little swine set a booby-trap for him? Surely not.

He flushed the loo, to give a sense of normality to the proceedings, and left the bathroom.

Slowly, he made his way down the corridor, his eyes on his nether regions. As he passed the bedroom he glanced in and, as luck would have it, spied the technological cavalry coming over the horizon. There, lying on the floor by a tall free-standing mirror on the left of the bed, was a hair-dryer.

Hal went in and closed the door behind him. He picked up the hair-dryer, switched it on and waved it over his crotch. He prayed the sound would not carry downstairs into the dining room. 'Come on, come on,' he muttered. Soon, fuzzy as his vision was, he could see that his trousers were drying. 'Come on, come on,' he urged.

Frantically Hal rubbed the hair-dryer back and forth over the drying patch.

'Come on, Come ON!' he yelled without realising.

'Don't let me down, don't let me down. You can do it. You can do it for me. Come on baby!'

'*What on earth are you doing?*'

He froze.

'Hal?!'

He turned his head slowly and looked into Jessica's disbelieving eyes. 'It's not what it looks like,' he said.

'What? Turn that thing off.'

Hal did as he was asked.

Jessica held Sebastian protectively against her.

'What do you think you're playing at?' she asked.

'It's not what it seems, it's—'

'I think perhaps you've had a bit too much to drink,' she snapped.

'But, Jess—'

'We need some coffee,' she announced, pointedly. 'It's sitting on the dining room table going cold. Run along downstairs,' she said to Sebastian, 'You can pour it, if you like.'

Her withering glance at Hal all but broke his heart.

He caught her at the top of the stairs. 'Please, Jessica—'

'What the hell were you doing?' she whispered hoarsely. 'In my bedroom, rubbing a hair-dryer over your goolies half-way through dinner! With my son in the house.'

'I wasn't—'

'What were you doing in my bedroom, anyway? I suppose I'm lucky not to have caught you sniffing around my knicker drawer!'

'Jessica, please listen—'

'Just get downstairs, and drink some coffee. Oh, Hal, I worked so hard for tonight, and it was all going so well,' Jessica said sadly.

'I'm sorry, but let me explain—'

'Some other time. Maybe.' Jessica swept down the stairs.

Sebastian knelt on his chair, carefully pouring coffee from the jug into the mugs.

'I just leaned against the wash-basin, stepped back, and there was this huge soggy patch—'

'Did you wet yourself?' Sebastian interrupted, gleefully.

'*No!*'

Hal stared hard at the boy. For a second, he was met with a stern glare, and then the cherubic features broke into a smile.

'Sugar?' Sebastian asked.

'Four,' Hal replied. 'I have a sweet tooth.' He needed coffee, and plenty of it. He had to sober up if he was to have any chance of persuading Jessica that he hadn't set out to ruin the evening.

'One, two,' Sebastian counted, 'three, four, five – oops! Sorry.'

'Doesn't matter. I'll drink it,' Hal said. 'Thanks, Sebastian.' He opened his mouth and gulped down the coffee in one. He gagged.

'Are you all right?' Jessica asked, disdainfully.

'No . . . I feel a bit – Excuse me.' Hal raced upstairs into the bathroom and threw up.

The little shit had poured salt into it.

Between retches, Hal realised he had encountered an opponent who would prove difficult to beat.

17

On Saturday afternoon Belinda and Hal were in a crowded pub in Crouch End. It was crowded and smoky, its dark wooden floors and furniture giving it a brooding atmosphere. Jazz filtered up from the basement club beneath it.

Hal had kept a low profile since his dinner at Jessica's: pride had prevented him calling Belinda – he hadn't felt in the mood for an I-told-you-so speech. As the days passed, though, he had felt the need to talk to her, so he had telephoned her sheepishly.

'Can you believe an eight-year-old is capable of all that?' he asked

'It sounds a bit far-fetched,' she admitted. 'I mean, it could have been an accident, couldn't it, giving you salt instead of sugar? Especially if, as you say, they were in similar pots.'

'I suppose.'

'And he acknowledged his mistake to you and his mother.'

'But what about the bathroom incident?'

'He's only eight. Little boys aren't the tidiest people in bathrooms, are they? It's a bit of a leap to say he made it all wet on purpose.'

'What about the snide comments and the insults? He might be a child but you grow up fast in this business. He's eight going on forty-seven.' Hal sipped his beer.

'Actually, Hal, I'm more worried about the little speech he gave you.'

'The we-don't-need-you soliloquy?'

'Exactly. It sounds like he's formed a close protective bond with his mother. He must know his father left her?'

'I believe so.'

'Well, maybe she's told him Daddy wasn't very nice. Especially to Mummy. Sebastian may have a thing about men because of it. Maybe he doesn't want his mummy to get too close to someone in case they make her unhappy.'

'You might have a point there.'

'How has Sebastian been behaving at rehearsals?' Belinda asked.

'Savagely. Yet with great subtlety.'

Belinda looked confused. 'How do you mean?'

'He's been difficult about our scenes together. There's always a problem. He always wants to rehearse them again.'

'Could it be that he just wants to get them right?'

'I don't think so. It's not that he's actually blaming me for getting them wrong. It's just implied. And, of course, he breezes through his scenes with the rest of the cast.'

Belinda baited her hook, and fished for a little more information. 'Have you spoken to Jessica since the dinner?'

'All the time. Only on the mobile, of course. She rang to apologise about the salt, accepted my explanation for the hair-dryer fiasco.'

'Has she mentioned seeing you again?'

'Oh, all the time, but she never shows up. Sebastian's homework, Sebastian's had a nightmare, it's always something to do with the kid.'

'It's tricky, Hal, even without the career problems it

might cause. Another man's child, who doesn't like you, and an over-protective mother? Are you sure you should get into this?' Belinda probed.

Hal finished his pint. 'So what should I do?'

Belinda smiled. 'I'm a psychiatrist, Hal. I don't give the answers. They come from you. I just ask the relevant questions.'

'And they pay you for that?' Hal queried.

'They do. But I'll say one thing. Sometimes the answer to your prayers is right under your nose.'

'Another drink?' he asked.

'Please,' Belinda replied.

She watched him move to the bar. 'Where's there's light, there's hope,' she said to herself. 'Even if it's only a tiny chink at the end of a very long tunnel.'

Sunday. The recording of episode two. Hal stood behind the set, sweating. Take seven. Take *seven*! Hal had dried six times. He could scarcely believe it. This was his funniest scene. Perhaps the best chance he had to shine in all six episodes. He loved this scene. It was the best piece of writing, perhaps the only good piece, he had been handed in the entire series. For once he wasn't just a feed for the established characters or to make the star look good. Yet he was failing miserably.

Asking an audience to laugh at a scene twice, was risky enough. Three times meant severe pushing of luck. But seven times? They were bored and embarrassed.

He took his cue and entered again.

Hal: 'Hello, son. You're mother's not about, is she?'

Sebastian: 'No Daddy, she's on the toilet.'

Hal: 'Now listen, you know your daddy knows best . . . er . . . knows best . . . she . . . em . . . em . . . That's nice for her . . . em . . . em . . .'

'Hold it!' Patrick, the floor manager screamed. 'Okay we go again,' Patrick announced.

Hal almost felt the audience groan. He could sense they were tasting his tension. Sensed vast numbers of them were looking at their feet with embarrassment.

He walked disconsolately off the set. He talked to himself, backstage. Slapped his thighs. Balled his fists. He had to get this right.

'Psst,' a voice whispered. 'Hal.'

Hal looked round. Edwin's concerned face was gazing into his.

'Hi.' Hal acknowledged him in a daze.

'He's feeding you the wrong cues.'

'What?'

'Sebastian. He's feeding you bum cues. That's why you're drying. It's not you, it's Sebastian.'

Hal's brain raced. 'Are you sure?'

'Yes,' Edwin assured him. 'Have you pissed him off?'

'Not that I'm aware of. What do I do?'

'Concentrate. Remember your own lines in sequence. That's your best shot. Don't let him put you off. It's a great scene.'

'Thanks, Edwin. I'll try.'

'You'll be fine.' Edwin smiled briefly. 'And I didn't say anything. Okay?'

'Of course.'

'And don't blame anything on Sebastian, whatever you do. Right?'

Hal felt calmer. He knew his own lines. Rock solid. As he heard his cue and entered, he made a silent vow never to lose patience with Edwin's cryptic clues, ever again.

Afterwards Tony approached Hal in the bar. 'Could I have a word?' he asked.

The word 'bollocking' leaped into the minds of Penny,

Edwin, Patrick, the guest actors for episode two and the crew with whom Hal was drinking.

'A bit concerned about scene six tonight, Hal,' Tony said.

'Yeah, me too,' Hal admitted.

'Don't get me wrong,' Tony continued. 'I'm not a fool. I know the script. I accept Sebastian was a little wayward with the cues. But having said that, we must remember he's a child, playing a child, being a child. I happen to think he'll grow up to be a great actor, don't you?'

'Yes.' What else could Hal say?

'But he isn't yet. He relies on our support. It's up to the older actors to carry the heavy burden of profession- alism, yes?' Tony asked, in a manner that left no room for debate.

'Sure.'

'Look, Hal,' Tony softened, 'I know you're new to television and have more than enough on your plate dealing with that, but you have to admit that a few pages of dialogue is pitiful compared with the amount you've had to carry in your memory for the theatre.'

Hal nodded.

'Good. I'm glad we're agreed. Learn your scenes thoroughly. Then if the young chap has a wobble, it won't matter.'

'Fair enough.' Hal was smarting.

Tony coughed. 'One more thing. The young fellow is a bit upset. Convinced himself that tonight was all his fault. Got it a bit out of perspective. You remember what it was like when you were his age?'

'Of course.'

'To tell the truth, he's in floods of tears. It mightn't be a bad idea if you came over and apologised. Took the rap, as it were. Otherwise I fear poor Jessica's in for a hell of a night of it.'

Hal shuddered. There were times when he hated being an actor. He had never been comfortable with kowtowing, schmoozing or grovelling. He was aware that this had held him back in his career. Other, less talented actors had built significant careers on such skills.

As he agreed to the humiliation, he asked himself why. Was it for Jessica's sake, or for the benefit of his career? Either way, it sucked. 'Okay,' he told Tony.

'Good man,' Tony patted his shoulder and steered him across the bar to the corner table where Sebastian and Jessica were sitting.

As he neared their table, Hal looked at Sebastian. Who wouldn't be moved by his tears? Jessica was holding his hand, stroking it.

Hal didn't wait for Tony to prompt him. He already knew the lines he had to recite. 'Sebastian?'

The child looked up into his eyes.

Oh, he was good. Tony was right. There were the makings of a fine actor there.

'Tony tells me you're blaming yourself for the big cock-up on scene six tonight.'

Sobs. Quivering lips.

Protective squeezing of a child's hand, by a loving mother.

Hal hardened. What the hell? See it through. Fuck it!

'Well, you mustn't. It was my fault. I had a mental block. It happens as you get older, especially under pressure. The memory isn't as sharp as it might be.'

A snivelled response.

'You didn't have any problems with the other scenes, did you?'

Sebastian shook his head, his chest still heaving.

'Well, there you are, then. My mistake. All mine,' Hal recited.

He looked at Jessica. Was that a blush? Had she

186

recognised that Hal was genuinely angry? Was she worth it?

'Th-th-thank you.' Sebastian gulped.

'Don't mention it,' Hal replied, impassive. 'I'll leave you three friends to enjoy your drink.' He turned and walked away.

Vaguely Hal heard the telephone ring. He fought hard to go back to his dream of being interviewed by Michael Parkinson, but gave up. He threw back the duvet, sloped out of his bedroom, pattered into the kitchenette, filled the kettle, then stumbled into the sitting room and pressed play on the answering-machine. He congratulated himself on having done all this without fully opening his eyes.

'Ah, dear boy,' the message began, 'I have been touring those bastions of British theatre, the assembly hall, the playground and the school gymnasium. This week I find myself interred in a community centre in the heart of Elephant and Castle for three days. I wondered if you would care to spend an hour or two watching an old friend struggle to prove that there is more to the English language than finishing a sentence with "That's cool, innit"? I will be grateful for your support. Performances are at ten o'clock in the morning, or at the more civilised time of two p.m. The address is . . .'

Hal laughed. Here was he being all self-pitying when his old friend was slogging his guts out on a schools tour. He'd go to the afternoon performance. It would be good to see Jake and cheer him on, think about someone else for a change.

He heard the click of the kettle, and set about the task of making himself feel more human.

The community centre was on one of *those* estates. Park

your car and return to find it propped on bricks. The sort of estate that made you walk quickly, glancing over your shoulder while attempting to exude an air of casual confidence.

Hal walked into the centre. An elderly woman was taking ticket money on the door for those who were not pre-booked with a school. Teenage louts swept past her. Hal paid for his ticket and, clutching his programme, entered the hall.

There were between twenty-five and thirty-five rows of hard wooden seats, and teachers lined the walls like prison officers. 'Blind eye' appeared to be their maxim for the day: children were climbing, fighting, snogging and generally running riot.

Hal decided to sit in the front row. Needless to say, this was the most unoccupied stretch of seating. The set consisted of a couple of large polystyrene pillars, a few gauze drapes, a *chaise-longue*, a wooden table with two silver goblets, and a dagger.

It was going to be a traditional production then, even if it did look like the set of *Julius Caesar* rather than *Romeo and Juliet*: all fairly standard low-budget Shakespeare props. Hal knew what that meant and his heart went out to the cast. To Jake.

The stage manager appeared from behind the screens that hid the cast from their aggressors. The hisses, wolf-whistles and caterwauling increased. He held up his hands, and waited as long as he could for some semblance of silence. 'Good afternoon, boys and girls,' he began.

First mistake. Hal thought. He'd be lucky to escape without being lynched for calling them 'boys and girls'.

'Today we're going to perform a play that most of you are studying.'

Boos.

'It is one of the finest love stories ever written.'

Wolf-whistles. Cat-calls. Boys shouting, 'Romeo, Romeo, wherefore art thou, you dozy twat?'

Girls shouting, 'Do we see him give her one, then?'

'It is a love story about two people your age. Younger, perhaps.'

'Is she on the Pill?' a boy shouted.

'Sadly,' the stage manager persevered, 'it is a love story with tragic consequences, as you will see.' His face wore a resigned look. Clearly he was used to the audience forcing him to go through the motions. 'The first speech will tell you exactly what the play is about, and make the rest easier to follow.'

Oh, thought Hal, so that's why he's out there. A plea for silence.

As far as Hal could tell, he had more chance of negotiating peace in the Middle East than he had of silencing this rabble.

'Okay,' the stage manager declared, 'let the play begin.'

There was no lighting to be lowered, but a drumroll played through a rather poor sound system.

'Funky!' screamed a girl.

Some ill-chosen oboe music played as an actor walked on stage to deliver the prologue.

More wolf-whistles, whoops, and cries. 'Oo, get 'im, ducky!'

'Look at that lunch-box, Linford!'

'Nice codpiece, mate!'

The actor sighed and began his speech. 'Two house-holds, both alike in dignity—'

'Show us your bum!'

'Bender!'

'—from ancient grudge, lead to new mutiny—'

'Get off!'

'Bring on the strippers!'

And so it continued. How Jake suffered. He was playing old Capulet, Juliet's father, and the actress playing Juliet was not much younger than he was. She must run the company, Hal thought. Romeo, on the other hand, was a fresh-faced boy, probably chasing his Equity card. This made the love story look vaguely perverse, illegal even. The production wouldn't have stood a chance in front of a civilised audience, but in front of this mob it was doomed.

Jake's personal humiliation began modestly enough. In Capulet's first scene with Paris, the louts concentrated mostly on his headwear, which was enormously tall, designed, Hal supposed, to give the character an air of authority.

'Where did you get that hat, where did you get that hat!' sang a small instantly formed chorus.

'Oi mate! Does your head go to the top of your hat!'

'Woss that geezer doin' wearin' a giant condom on his bonce?'

At this stage, Hal was proud of Jake, whether he was doing it for pride, or because of Hal's presence he was unsure. But somehow, he was managing to hold on to some semblance of a performance.

Needless to say Jake reappeared for his next scene, no longer looking to win a prize at Ascot. The 'titfer' had been ditched.

Then the heckling became more personal—

'Who's this old fart?'

'He's not her dad. He's too old to get it up.'

'Boring!'

'Not the first time you've worn a dress, is it you old faggot—?'

'Granddad, granddad, you're lovely,' the singers chorused again.

Jake deteriorated as the play wore on. He looked confused, wounded. Several times he looked at Hal, pain in his eyes. His distress made him fumble over lines. His delivery doubled in speed. He seemed desperate to get off the stage, for this public humiliation to be over.

The only time the pupils were anything near appreciative was during the brawls, fights and deaths.

One piece of choreographed violence struck a chord that even Hal would not have predicted. It came during Capulet's best scene, when Juliet refuses to marry Paris, enraging her father. Jake seemed to recover. The power of the scene helped him to ignore his surroundings and the acting took over.

The director had gone for uncontrolled aggression from Capulet to gain the maximum shock value.

Hal recognised stage fighting when he saw it. He knew that when Jake appeared to slap Juliet's face, it was the palm of her hand, placed deliberately by her chin that he struck to give the realistic cracking sound.

However, for one, tall, muscular girl, three rows behind Hal, it proved too realistic. 'Leave her alone, you slag!' she screamed. 'No dad should slap his daughter, all right?'

The scene stopped. Jake and the other actors on stage looked shocked.

'Just because your old man—'

'Fuck off, Willis!' the girl yelled. She picked up her chair and hurled it at the offending youth. Other chairs scattered as people took cover.

The distraction gave the girl time. She was on top of the actors before anyone could react. She brushed past the nurse and Lady Capulet, heading for Jake. She balled her fist as she stepped over Juliet, who was lying prone on the floor.

Jake tried to move out of the way of the blow, but the girl caught him on the side of the head, and he went down.

Hal leaped out of his seat and ran towards his friend.

A teacher was dragging the girl away. 'It's okay, Linda, it's just a play. Calm down,' he told her.

Hal bent down to Jake as the rest of the cast gathered round him.

'Jake, are you okay?'

'Ah, dear boy. Pity, really, I was doing quite well. I think I lost it in the fourth round,' he said.

'Silly old bugger. I told you to take a dive.'

Jake smiled. Then he began to weep.

18

Mary showed up around lunch-time on Saturday.

'I didn't think I'd see you today,' Belinda said, as she let her in.

'Nor did I,' Mary said.

'Weren't you supposed to be having a night of passion with the new doctor?'

'The man should be in computers, not medicine,' Mary stated.

'Why?' Belinda asked following her.

'Why? It's a three-and-a-half-inch floppy, that's why,' Mary moaned.

Belinda tried not to laugh. 'So size does matter?'

'Of course it does!' Mary exclaimed. 'I mean look at the size of me! It was like putting a size three foot into a size eleven wellington boot. If it could have talked there would have been an echo.'

Belinda laughed. 'Oh Mary, I'm sorry.'

'Liar! At least it was brief. Dr Song makes love like Superman. Faster than a speeding bullet.'

'Never mind.'

Mary sighed. 'Maybe you're right, Belinda. Maybe I should be a bit more fussy. Maybe I should wait until I'm in love, instead of just shagging around.'

'Blimey!' Belinda said, sitting down in mild shock. 'It must have been bad last night.'

'It did feel a bit . . . empty.' Mary sighed. 'Oh well, hey-ho. What's done is done and all that. Have you heard from Hal?'

Belinda shook her head, sadly.

'Ring him,' Mary instructed.

'I don't know. What excuse do I give this time?'

'You're friends. Do you need one?' Mary asked.

Belinda shrugged.

'Sit-coms are done in front of a live audience, aren't they?'

'So.'

'Isn't it about time you went along to one. Cheer Hal on, like?'

'Well—'

'Come on,' Mary interrupted standing. 'You can buy me a drink while you think about it. I'm depressed,' she said as she exited the sitting-room.

'Yes, boss,' Belinda mumbled, as she picked up her handbag and followed Mary to the door.

It was Saturday, the final rehearsal day before the recording of episode three tomorrow. Hal was worrying about Jake: he hadn't heard from him for several days.

It was exactly a week since the day of the play, which had been abandoned. He and Jake had returned to Jake's bedsit, and Jake had refused to see a doctor. The only medicine he was prepared to take was the fermented fruit of the vine. The room was scattered with empty wine bottles and empty foil take-away boxes. Jake's distress at how low his career had sunk was apparent. He was tired and wanted to go to bed. He refused Hal's offer to cook for him, clean the flat or stay until he woke.

Hal made his friend promise to telephone him the minute he came to, which he had, but there had been nothing since.

He sighed. For him the week had been mixed. Sebastian, to his surprise, had not made his life particularly difficult. He had not asked to re-rehearse Hal's scenes. Instead he had walked through them, reciting his lines parrot fashion. Otherwise he had contented himself with pulling faces at him.

His mother, however, was a different matter. She had been icy, and perfunctory in their telephone conversations. Maybe she was still blaming him for the failed dinner party. They had not seen each other outside the rehearsal room.

When Hal heard his name called, he shook himself out of his reflections and strode into the centre of the room to rehearse the scene.

Hal had a major speech in scene three of episode three in which Michael, his character, was supposed to be drunk. At the climax of the scene, he had to get onto the coffee-table in the sitting room and rant incoherently. It was his scene, with the occasional reaction shot from Sebastian and Penny. Consequently, Tony's attention was focused on him. However, every time Hal was standing unsteadily on the rickety table, Sebastian did his best to put him off.

Tony didn't see what the boy was doing, and everyone else ignored it, as they generally did where Sebastian was concerned.

After another rubber-faced performance, Hal went to talk to Edwin. 'Did you see that?'

'See what?' Edwin asked. 'Oh, you mean our little friend's antics. Of course.'

'Why does everyone ignore it?'

'None so blind as those who do not wish to see,' Edwin replied.

'That doesn't answer my question.'

'Why do you ignore it?' Edwin asked.

'Well . . . I'm new, aren't I?'

'It's your call, Hal.'

'Has he ever played games with you?'

'No.'

'Penny?'

'Not to my knowledge.'

'What about my illustrious predecessor, Ian Wilson?'

Edwin sighed. 'He was always rather fond of Ian, as I remember.'

'Really? Is that why he messes me around?'

Edwin rustled the paper. 'It's a possibility, I suppose. He is only an eight-year-old boy. They can be difficult enough, but he's also the star of a major television series. That's a dangerous combination.'

'I know, but—'

'If I were you, I wouldn't take it so seriously. It could be worse. They might introduce a trained Labrador to upstage us in the next series.'

Hal chuckled. 'He's actually been quite reasonable today, by his standards.'

'Well, there you are, then. Now, ten across. "Tempestuous fermentation." Two words. Five and seven letters respectively. First word is something T, something R, something?'

Hal thought. 'Something T? Hold on,' he said, counting on his fingers. 'Storm brewing.'

Edwin looked at the paper. 'Of course. Now, why didn't I think of that? I really must try to get out of comedy and into serious drama.'

'Keep heading the way you are, Edwin, and it'll be never-ending guest spots on *Blankety Blank* for you, my friend.'

Everyone was having a quick coffee before the final run-through, and Hal was in a corner with Penny and Edwin. 'My mother's back for next week's episode,' Penny informed Hal.

'Your mother?'

'Elizabeth Sage, Hal, not my real mother. Hadn't you noticed she was missing this week?'

'Well, actually—'

'What a treat we're all in for,' Penny went on. 'Rehearsals will take four times as long, because she can't even remember who she's supposed to be talking to, let alone her lines. They've given her yet another new boyfriend in this series, but if Tony's cast someone as addled as Elizabeth, it's going to be a strain on us all.'

'She's not that bad,' Hal argued.

'Yes she is, dear. Lord knows why Tony cast her,' Penny grumbled on.

'I heard a rumour that Jessica had something to do with it,' Edwin whispered.

'Really?' Hal asked.

'Don't be silly, Edwin. That cow gets people fired not hired,' Penny mouthed.

'Carla's in next week as well, isn't she?' Edwin said.

'She plays your best friend, doesn't she, Penny?' Hal asked.

'Yes – and be careful, Hal, or she'll have you performing little playlets to the Sunday school she runs.'

'I'm surprised they've not been in more episodes,' Hal said.

'Actually,' Edwin revealed, 'they're usually only in about three apiece per series.'

'Okay, positions please. Let's run it!' came the cry.

Hal put his coffee cup on a convenient windowsill. When he turned he saw that Sebastian was staring at him. Then he smiled evilly. He raised his thumb, then turned it upside-down. A quick glance around the room told Hal that he was the only one to notice.

The run-through went at a cracking pace. Hal was in the first four scenes, and the first two went beautifully. There was a crispness about them that had been lacking earlier.

Scene three began well. Both Penny and Sebastian were on top form, and Hal was happy with his drunk acting.

Then he leaped onto the coffee table, and began to deliver his lines. Penny looked aghast, as her character was meant to. But Sebastian didn't.

The evil smile had returned to his face.

Hal reached the climax: 'Daddy knows best!' and at that moment the table collapsed. Hal fell and the back of his head hit the floor, then the rest of him. He lay there, winded, his head pounding, his hair moist with blood, straining for breath.

At first he was only vaguely aware of people swarming around him, of his head being raised on to someone's lap, the scent of panic.

'Fuck!' He groaned, and ran his hands through his hair in search of the seat of the pain. He felt dampness. 'Shite! I'm bleeding to death.'

'Sorry to disappoint you, but it's not that bad. I don't think it's even going to be a stitches-for-the-sake-of-my art job.' Edwin was gazing down at him.

'Are you all right?' Tony was flustered, as crimson as beetroot juice. 'How the fuck did that happen?' he shouted. 'Sorry, Hal, we should have got you something more solid to rehearse with.'

'Time for me to share the secret of my diet with you, sweetie.' Penny squeezed his hand.

'I don't think the leg just snapped,' Hal heard Patrick, the floor manager say. 'It's the wing-nuts.'

'I want to sit up.' Hal was feeling cramped and claustrophobic.

Someone helped him into a sitting position. His head throbbed. He was directly in line with Sebastian's gaze. At first the boy looked almost concerned. Then that smile returned.

'One of the wing-nuts had worked loose and the leg gave way under Hal's weight,' Patrick stated.

Hal knew who was to blame.

'Of course the wing-nut had been loosened,' Hal shouted, staring at Sebastian. 'And I know exactly how that happened, don't I?'

From nowhere Jessica appeared, her arms engulfing her son.

'Steady, Hal,' said Tony. 'I know it's tempting to think of suing, but it was just a bump—'

'How do you think it happened, sweetie?' Penny interrupted.

Hal stared into Jessica's eyes. He witnessed the anxiety. He couldn't do it. 'Wear and tear,' he lied. 'It must have been working loose all week. Someone should have checked it.'

General agreement, with awkward blushes from the crew.

'Right. Let's get you to a doctor, have you checked out,' Tony suggested.

'I'm okay,' Hal snapped.

'Nonsense. Can't risk anything untoward happening to one of our stars, can we?' Tony fawned, uncharacteristically.

Hal looked directly at Sebastian, who had changed once again. Now Hal was looking into the innocent eyes of a child.

19

Jessica did not telephone that night, as Hal had hoped she would. He needed looking after. By Jessica, the woman he adored. He wanted to know that, just occasionally, he came before her son.

But the next day she came to him in his dressing room. It was Sunday, recording day.

Hal was in the first four scenes of episode three. Then he had a long break while the rest of the cast discussed and reacted to his character's drunken behaviour.

He came back in the last scene, for what he hoped would be one beautifully delivered 'curtain line' to wrap up the episode.

'I wanted to see you sooner,' she said. 'Forgive me, my love, it was just—'

Then she had made love to him. 'I was so worried,' she said. She held him as if she never wanted to let him go. 'I love you so much.'

Afterwards she dressed quickly. Before she left she said, 'I grilled him. He didn't do it, Hal. I know my son. It wasn't his fault.'

'Jessica—'

'You mustn't worry about Sebastian. He's had a difficult time. He's not used to being around men, that's all. I've not been with anyone since his father. He'll come round.'

'I'm not sure—'

'Sssh.' Jessica stopped his mouth with a kiss. 'I shouldn't be here. I must go. I'll be missed if I don't.'

Within seconds, she had gone.

Everybody was *so* kind to Hal. Especially Tony who, for some reason, couldn't pay him enough compliments.

The recording went smoothly and without incident.

In the bar afterwards Hal had just ordered a drink when a voice from behind said, 'I'll get that.' It was Tony.

'Thanks very much,' Hal said.

'My pleasure. How are you feeling?'

'Fine.'

'Sure?'

'Yeah.'

'Good.' He ordered himself a double whisky. 'I'll be frank, Hal,' Tony began, as they collected their drinks from the bar and stepped away, 'the suits were nervous. I think they thought you might make a fuss. Call in the union rep. I told them you weren't that sort of a chap. In fact, I told them how reasonable you were about it.'

Suddenly Hal realised why he had been so well treated that day. Maybe he should make a fuss? But he knew that if he did he'd never work at the BBC again. 'Tell them to stop panicking. I'm all right,' he said.

'Good. You did well tonight, coming off the back of an injury. Very professional. I think you're beginning to get the hang of this television malarkey.'

Hal wished the compliment was genuine.

A silence followed.

Tony sighed. 'I've got a slight problem with the next two episodes.'

'Oh?'

'Yes,' Tony continued, looking over Hal's shoulder for

more exciting company. 'I hired this old fart of an actor I know – known him donkey's years actually. Anyway, I hired him to play Elizabeth Sage's boyfriend.'

'I know,' Hal put in.

'Well, I hired him for the next two episodes, and now the silly bugger's gone and caught chicken-pox off one of his grandchildren, so I'll have to spend tomorrow trawling through *Spotlight* and ringing agents to find a replacement.'

Hal's brain clicked into overdrive. 'How old is this character supposed to be?' he asked.

'Oh, sixties, pushing seventy. It's only a small part. Couple of lines and a grunt or two, really.'

'I know an old guy who'd be perfect.'

Suddenly he had Tony's attention. 'Really?'

'Yep.'

'Vouch for him, can you?'

'Oh, yes.'

'Much telly experience?'

'Enough for a role of that size. Bloody good actor.'

Tony made his decision.

'I was told that once before on this show and I've been regretting it ever since. Oh, what the hell? I trust you. Save me working my socks off tomorrow.' He took out a pen and a small pad. 'What's his name, and who's his agent?'

'He's just left his agent, actually,' Hal admitted.

'He doesn't have an agent?' Tony's face fell.

'He's just *changing* agents,' Hal snapped. 'It's a toss-up between three. Funnily enough, I was trying to help him choose over a bottle of wine the other night.'

'Hmmm.' Tony wasn't convinced.

'They're all quite worthy, really, but I couldn't decide,' Hal continued. 'Perhaps if you get a chance, and I know how busy you are, he could pick your brains about it?

You're probably in a better position than we are to know who's good and who isn't.'

Hal saw the light shine in Tony's eyes. Got him. Ego, ego, ego. What a business.

'Well,' Tony puffed out his chest, 'I do know a bit about these things. Of course I'd be happy to help if I can as he's your friend. All right, keep him away from anybody infectious and drag him along on Tuesday. You won't let me down on this, will you, Hal?'

'He'll be there.'

'Great. That's sorted, then. Now, if you'll excuse me, I must mingle,' and Tony departed.

Hal felt a small glow inside. He'd been worried about Jake, and now he'd got his mate a job. It was a nice feeling. Almost worth the headache that was invading his battered skull again.

Hal woke early – well, at nine-thirty, which was early for a working actor on his day off. After a quick shower, coffee and a bacon sandwich, he was out of the door and heading for Jake's bedsit.

It was probably no more than two or three minutes that he spent on the doorstep ringing Jake's bell but it felt like twenty. As luck would have it, another inmate of the house came out while he was there, allowing Hal to go in and climb the stairs to Jake's room.

He banged on the door. Eventually it opened and Jake's bald pate came into view. 'I gather you wish to gain entrance,' he said.

'Whatever gave you that idea?' Hal replied. 'Truth be told, I only came round to practise my karate on this fine piece of plywood here,' he said, stroking Jake's door.

Jake stared at him hard, as if fighting for focus. 'Do you know any death blows? I've been contemplating suicide. Trouble is, I find myself lacking in courage. I have been singularly unable to think up a quick enough method. Except for suffocating between the copious breasts of Iris McCready. Sadly, I lost her telephone number in nineteen fifty-seven.'

Hal froze at the mention of suicide, unsure how seriously to take it.

'Have you tried ringing Directory Enquiries?' he found himself saying.

'To no avail. Apparently she no longer resides with her parents in Walthamstow. Father was a vicar with missionary ambitions, you see.'

'So you might as well soldier on, then, eh?' Hal suggested.

Jake did not reply.

'Can I come in? I didn't come round to sing a Christmas carol, though I do bring glad tidings.'

At last a spark of recognition appeared in Jake's eyes. 'Oh, dear boy. I'm forgetting my manners. Age, you see. The old grey cells are melting faster than ice-cream in a microwave. Do enter my little den of iniquity. At your own risk, of course,' he added. 'Glass of wine, my young friend?' Jake asked, brandishing a half-empty bottle.

'At this time in the morning? It's only half past ten, Jake. You're turning into an alcoholic.'

Jake sighed. 'Who cares?'

'I do.'

'How touching. The big television star actually cares about this sad old relic of the forgotten age of theatre.'

'What do you mean by that?'

'I was merely pointing out how nice it was that someone who has risen to the dizzy heights of situation-comedy stardom can remain humble enough to spare a thought for those of us who have spent years paying our dues in repertory companies, fringe shows and number-two tours just waiting for such an opportunity.'

'Wait a minute—'

'Those of us who have spent over forty years in the profession to end up scrubbing around doing schools tours for adolescent thugs.'

'That's not my fault, Jake. Shit, I've been there. I've waited over fifteen years for this chance. Until now I've spent my working life in crap jobs for no money, the same as you have.'

'But you're not *still there*, are you?' Jake ground out.

'And you'll never be there again. But I'll be there until I shuffle off this mortal coil, dear boy. That is all I have left to look forward to.'

'You sound so bitter.'

Jake slumped on to a kitchen chair. 'I am bitter! It is the one solace I have left.'

'Don't turn it against me, Jake. I'm your friend.'

'Are you?' Jake mumbled, and slugged back more wine.

Hal's anger rose. 'What was I supposed to do? Turn it down so I could remain one of the boys? Is that what you wanted me to do, Jake? Is that what friendship is all about? Sharing failure?'

Jake remained silent.

'You encouraged me. You were the one who said I had talent, that my chance would come.'

'It doesn't matter! I hate you for your success. The way I've hated everyone who has been luckier than I. The way you would be hating me, dear boy, if I were the one who was about to climb above the massed ranks of nobodies and strugglers.'

'I couldn't hate you, Jake, no matter how successful you became. Even if I was still struggling. Even if I'd given up. I was full of rough edges when I met you. You taught me how to act, how to apply everything I'd learned. I've always been grateful. And, frankly, it pisses me off that you can't be happy for me that a bit of good luck finally came my way. If it wasn't for you, I'd never have got this far.'

Tears welled in the old man's eyes. 'You've shamed me,' he muttered.

'I should bloody well think I have, you old bastard.' Hal picked up his rucksack, took out the two scripts and hurled them across the room at Jake. The first flew over his left shoulder, the second hit him full in the face. 'There. You'd better look at those.'

Jake picked up the second script. 'What, pray, is this?'

'It's an episode of *Bringing Up Ralph*. So is the other,' Hal informed him.

'I don't under—'

'It's your lucky day, Jake. Some other old git has had to cry off sick. I talked the producer into not re-auditioning. There's a small part in the next two episodes for you. Spit-and-cough stuff, but it's something.'

'You mean—'

'Yes,' Hal interrupted. 'The part's yours. It's sorted. Two weeks' work starting tomorrow.'

Silence followed.

'Dear boy. I don't know what to say.'

'I don't want thanks. I'd like to think you'd do the same for me. This isn't going to make you a superstar. It's just a foot – maybe just a toe – in the door. However, I've told this producer you're a good actor. I did not tell him you were a piss-head who was losing his grip. So you, my friend, are going to go and get into the bath. I'll make you some strong coffee to help you sober up and I'll buy you a cooked breakfast somewhere cheap. Then you can look at the script and tell me if you want to do it or not.'

Jake was shaking. 'Hal – son – of course I'll do it.'

'Quite right,' Hal said. 'I promised this guy you'd

show up tomorrow. Have a bath, Jake. Clean yourself up. I'll fill you in over breakfast about the people you're going to be working with.'

'Hal—'

'Not now, Jake, there's no time. I'll put the kettle on.'

Jake stood up unsteadily. 'One hopes the communal bathroom is free,' he said, and slowly made his way towards the door. 'If I'm not back in twenty minutes, come and rescue me. I may have gone down with my rubber duck.'

'If you're not back here in ten minutes, I'll come and drown you. Is that clear?'

Hal looked around the room and let out a sigh. He crossed to the kitchen area, filled the kettle and put it on. Then he ferreted around under the sink until he found a dustpan and brush. 'Where do I start?' he muttered.

A woman and child were ringing the doorbell as Mrs Worrel squeezed through her garden gate. She carried a bag of shopping in each hand, and the cigarette in her mouth was making her eyes sting.

'Looking for His Nibs, are you?' she asked.

'We're looking for Hal, actually,' the woman replied, in husky, well-rounded tones.

'He's never in, these days, now he's come up in the world. Time was when he'd always find a minute to have a cup of tea with me. Not any more, he don't.'

'Well, if you're sure he's not at home, we won't trouble you any further,' the woman said.

Mrs Worrel dropped her shopping bags, took a last drag of her cigarette, then threw it on to the pavement. 'Tell you what,' she said, wheezing, 'he's a lazy git. He might be loafing in bed, ignoring his bell. Why don't I let us in? I've got a spare key to his door. We can shout up, see if he's about.'

'Oh, no, we don't want to be—'

'Do us a favour, love. Pick those up and carry them in for me, will yer?' Mrs Worrel asked. 'Take them through to the kitchen for me, dearie, and I'll get the key.'

The woman did as she was asked while Mrs Worrel retrieved the spare set of keys to Hal's flat from the broom cupboard under the stairs. She opened the door at the bottom of the stairs and bellowed, 'Oi, Mr Morrisey, you up there? You got visitors. One of 'em's a very pretty girl.' She listened for a reply, then shook her head. 'Nah, you're out of luck, dearie. If that didn't bring him running, nothing would.' She shut the door. 'He shouldn't be long. Why don't you stay and have a cup of tea with me? See if he turns up?'

'Oh, no—'

'Nonsense. I insist. Give 'im 'alf an hour. If he 'asn't the good sense to turn up by then, it'll be his loss.'

'Actually, Mrs . . .'

'Worrel, love.'

'Mrs Worrel, we wouldn't want to trouble you.'

'Don't be daft. If I didn't drag the odd stranger off the street I wouldn't talk to no one from one month to the next. Except family, of course, and you can't count on them, can you?' she said, brushing past them into the kitchen.

They stood in the doorway, looking uncomfortable.

'Well, come in, then,' Mrs Worrel urged. 'Don't just stand there 'oppin' from one foot to the other like you're in the queue for the ladies' toilet in Debenham's.'

The woman led the boy into the kitchen.

The child smiled sweetly, but he huddled close to his mother.

'What's your name, then?' Mrs Worrel asked.

Sebastian looked at his mother. It had been a long time since anyone had failed to recognise him. 'Sebastian,' he replied.

208

'That's a nice name. Very unusual.'

'Thank you.'

'Now, then, would yer like an orange squash? Or a cup of tea, dearie?'

'Tea, of course. I'm not a baby.' Sebastian pouted.

'Of course you're not. You're a bloke after me own 'eart. Tea all round, then. Sit yourselves down at the table. It's not self-service.' Mrs Worrel put the kettle on to boil and scooped the tea-leaves into the pot.

'So, have you two known Mr Morrisey long, then?' she enquired.

Mother and son exchanged glances.

'Not very long, no.'

'He's a nice feller, though, don't you think?'

'Yes, he is. A lovely man,' Jessica replied.

Sebastian remained silent.

Mrs Worrel poured boiling water into the teapot. 'For an actor, I mean. Mind you, he's got a bit above himself since he landed that telly thing.'

'The comedy, you mean?' Jessica asked.

'Yes, so I'm told. I never watch comedies, see. Soaps and documentaries, me.'

'I see.' Jessica stifled a smile.

'Do you two know many actors?' Mrs Worrel asked.

'My dad was one,' Sebastian replied.

'Was one, dearie?'

'How many actors do *you* know, Mrs Worrel?' Jessica asked.

'Only Mr Morrisey, and one or two of his friends. They strike me as a lonely bunch. His Majesty's been by himself for over a year now. His marriage went down the pan.' She put the teapot on the table. 'Mind you, that weren't his fault. She was an old tom.'

'Really?' Jessica glanced at Sebastian in an exaggerated fashion.

Mrs Worrel picked up the signal. 'Sorry, love. Shouldn't talk like that in front of the boy. Would you like a biscuit, sonny?'

'Yes, please,' Sebastian replied politely.

'He's been on his own too long,' Mrs Worrel resumed. 'Nice girls don't like actors, you see. Too fly-by-night.'

'I know what you mean,' Jessica said.

'He wants to get himself a proper job, and find a nice girl.' She took down the biscuit tin from the shelf. 'Like that friend of his. The one he talks about.'

Jessica blurted. 'Which one's that?'

Mrs Worrel put some biscuits on to a plate. 'Oh, Gawd! Now you're asking. I've met her a couple of times. What's her name? Melissa? Dorinda? Something with an A at the end.' She poured the tea. 'Help yourself to a biscuit, sonny Jim, no need to stand on ceremony,' she told Sebastian.

'You were saying?' Jessica said, trying to get Mrs Worrel back on track.

'What was I saying?' Mrs Worrel asked. 'Oh, yes, dearie. Nice girl. Good job. Nurse, or doctor, or solicitor, or something. Can't quite remember. Linda! That's her name, I think.'

'So she's been here, this Linda?' Jessica fished.

'Yes, dearie, once or twice, Come to think of it, Hal wasn't in that time either.'

'Well, I'm afraid we can't wait for him any longer. Finish your tea, Sebastian. Then we must go.'

Sebastian took a couple of swift gulps, and coughed. 'Sorry,' he said. 'It's got bits in it.'

'Those are tea-leaves,' Jessica told him as she stood up. 'Mrs Worrel makes tea properly, not with teabags.'

Sebastian stood up and wiped his mouth on his sleeve.

'It was nice meeting you,' Jessica said, offering her hand for Mrs Worrel to shake.

'Nice chatting to you too, dear. And you, young feller-me-lad.' The old woman ruffled Sebastain's hair.

When they reached the door Mrs Worrel asked, 'Do you want me to say you've called when His Majesty comes home?'

'No, it's okay. I'll telephone him. Thanks for your hospitality. Say goodbye, Sebastian.'

'Goodbye, and thank you, Mrs Worrel,' Sebastian said.

Mrs Worrel waved as they disappeared out of the front gate. Then she closed the door and shivered. It was cold. She might have to bite the financial bullet and put the heating on earlier than usual.

It was later that same evening, after she had eaten a meal, that Mrs Worrel did the washing-up, dishes first, then cutlery, then the teapot, and finally the cups and saucers.

She had to look. She couldn't resist. So she stared hard into the cup. 'Oh, my dear God,' she whispered.

It still wasn't crystal clear. Once again she saw it had something to do with being a father. Yet the child looked so innocent.

Suddenly she felt dizzy and sat down at the kitchen table. She held her shaking hand to her mouth. She would have to tell him, no matter what he thought. He must know. She decided she would wait up for him. She had to speak to Hal the moment he stepped through the door.

By ten o'clock, Mrs Worrel was exhausted. She felt tired, drained, and the dizziness hadn't cleared. She also felt hot, and she was sweating. She hoped she wasn't in for a bout of flu. Otherwise she was going to tell that doctor where he could stick his jabs next year.

Hal had not returned. She made a decision. She would

tell him first thing tomorrow morning. Set the alarm as back-up in case she overslept, which she never did.

She stood up. She felt a little unsteady. She'd be better for a good night's sleep, she thought.

Hal returned home at eleven o'clock. He was knackered. Jake had been hard work.

He climbed his stairs, took off his clothes, and crawled under the duvet. He set his alarm a little earlier than usual as he had agreed to meet Jake so that they would arrive at the rehearsal together.

Next morning, as soon as the alarm went off, he showered and dressed. Then he went into the kitchen, put the kettle on and opened the fridge. 'Damn. No milk.'

He picked up his wallet and keys, threw on a jacket and sprinted down the stairs.

In the hall, he could hear an alarm clock ringing, which was odd. He couldn't remember his landlady using one before. She must have an important appointment today, he thought.

A few minutes later he returned from the corner shop, armed with a pint of milk, a newspaper and a Mars Bar. He was about to open his door, when he realised the alarm clock was still ringing.

Something was wrong.

'Mrs Worrel?' he called.

No reply.

He put his purchases on the floor and walked apprehensively down the hall. 'Mrs Worrel?' he called again, when he reached the kitchen.

He noticed that there were unwashed cups and saucers by the kitchen sink, and his unease grew.

He followed the sound of the alarm to her bedroom door, which was ajar, took a deep breath and opened it.

She was lying on the floor next to the bed. Her eyes were closed. The alarm clock was also on the floor, a few inches from her left hand.

20

Hal ran into the car park next to the rehearsal room. He was late. Unable to gain a response from Mrs Worrel, he had rung for an ambulance. Next he had telephoned her niece. Mrs Worrel had once waffled on to him about being 'an old duffer', and had told him her niece's number was on the pin-board in her kitchen should she ever 'have an accident'.

Next he had contacted Jake, explained the situation, and told him to go to the rehearsal ahead of him. He asked Jake to explain his late arrival. Jake wasn't happy: he was nervous about arriving by himself.

Hal waited for the ambulance to take Mrs Worrel to hospital. Then he let her niece know which hospital the old lady was going to. The niece promised to ring Hal later to let him know how Mrs Worrel was.

Then he headed off to the rehearsal.

They were finishing the reading of episode four when Hal crept through the door.

Edwin waved, secretly, but nobody else acknowledged his arrival, not even Jake, whose face was sculpted in concentration.

Jessica sat in a corner, reading a book. She did not look up.

The reading finished, people relaxed, and Patrick gave the timing. They were running two minutes over.

'Right. A five-minute break, then we'll block the first scene,' Tony announced. He rose from his chair, and walked over to Hal. 'It is very important that you turn up on time for rehearsals, Hal,' he said.

'I know that. I'm sorry. It was unavoidable. Didn't Jake explain?'

'That's another thing. The poor man had to arrive on his own. Nobody knew who the hell he was. He's supposed to be your friend. You were supposed to make the introductions.'

'I intended to. I'd arranged for us to arrive together. Did he not tell you what happened?'

'He said something. Your landlady's sick? Hardly an excuse for letting your fellow professionals down. Patrick had to read your part.'

'Tony, we're not talking tummy-bug, here. She's an old lady. I found her collapsed on the floor. I thought she was dead.'

'And is she?'

'No—'

'Well, there you are, then.'

'She's not far off it, though,' Hal countered. 'I had to wait till the ambulance arrived. The paramedics think she's had a stroke. What was I supposed to do? Step over her as if nothing had happened?'

'Wasn't there anyone else who could have dealt with it? A relation or a neighbour?' Tony asked.

'No. I didn't have any choice.'

'Very well. But I don't expect it to happen again. You have a duty to everybody here. In future, we must come first. Now, I suggest you go and talk to Jack—'

'Jake.'

'Introduce him to people. Help him calm down.'

'Of course. How did he read?' Hal asked.

'He was fine. Let's face it, what he's being asked to do

215

isn't difficult. A trained chimp could probably manage it.' Tony walked away in a huff.

Sometimes Hal hated the business. The staggering selfishness of it all infuriated him. Death, illness, decapitation, the bloody show must go on.

He had been in a play the day his mother had died. He went on that night. What's more, it had been expected. Hal could think of no other profession that would ask as much.

He shook himself and found that Jake was grinning beside him. 'Ah, dear boy, how are you?'

'Just fine and dandy,' Hal replied, through gritted teeth.

'I saw you talking to our esteemed producer. What did he say about me?'

Hal sighed despondently. 'He said you were very good.'

'Really?' Jake beamed.

'What did you say to him, Jake, about why I was late?'

'Exactly what you told me to say, dear boy.'

'So how come he just bawled me out for my late arrival?'

'I've no idea.'

'What did he say when you told him?'

'Nothing, really. I repeated your words perfectly. No paraphrasing. No omissions. Not even an attempt to edit out your appalling grammar, or embellish your unimaginative use of the English language.'

Hal chuckled. 'Come on, you old swine, let's introduce you to a few people. See who else you can irritate.'

'You're too kind,' Jake responded. 'May I make a request?' he added. 'Don't bother introducing me to Elizabeth. We've already conversed. Sadly, her mind wanders as freely as a flea on an untreated cat. She started off by saying I reminded her of someone.'

'Well, perhaps you do.'

'And for a while I thought I had met her before. Then she became convinced I was her local priest. Kept calling me "Father". Which, when you consider her age, I found insulting.'

'Oh dear.' Hal led Jake in the safer direction of Edwin and *The Times* crossword.

After rehearsal, Hal and Jake avoided the pub, much to Jake's disgust. Instead they found a coffee shop, and ordered cappuccinos.

'Well,' Hal asked, 'what did you think?'

'Of whom?' Jake replied.

'Everyone.'

'Starting with?'

'Tony.'

'Our esteemed producer-director. Clueless, dear boy. Devoid of talent, lacking in communication skills, ignorant of the needs of actors, and almost drowning in a sense of self-importance. In short, a typical director. I found it a great relief that he shared the same level of incompetence as the average theatre producer. It was familiar – and comforting, in a masochistic way.'

'Edwin?'

'Dangling towards the dull, but a competent actor, and a nice enough chap. If he applied the level of concentration to his acting that he utilises in the pursuit of solving puzzles, he might rise to the dizzy heights of quite good.'

Hal sipped his coffee. 'Carla, the best friend?'

'Solid enough actress, but rather mouselike. Also, she's really rather Christian for a thespian. I wouldn't be at all surprised if she were to enter this café dressed in a claret and black uniform, and sing "The old rugged cross", while banging a tambourine and rattling a collection box under our noses.'

'What about Elizabeth, your girlfriend?'

'Barking mad. Next.'

'Penny?'

'Oh, *your* girlfriend,' Jake retorted.

'*Touché.*'

'Neurotic, hyper, turns complaining into an art form, yet somewhat sensual.'

Hal was surprised. 'Really?'

'Indeed. Nice figure, but it's the voice, that deep, husky tone, that I find so alluring. I've always had a thing for that type of overt sexuality in a woman's voice. I hear a woman with a deep voice and I instantly think everything "deep". Deep, as in "complex" which appeals to me, and deep as in "mysterious", which teases me. Mostly, of course, I think deep as in "throat".'

'And what about our star?'

'Oh, spoilt, precocious, obnoxious. Typical child, really.'

'Do you think so?' Hal asked. 'Just an average kid?'

'Certainly. A far from average mother, though. Another who is easy on the eye.'

'She's so quiet I hardly notice her,' lied Hal.

'Have you been wandering around with your eyes shut, dear boy? After all I taught you about the importance of observation!'

'Sorry,' Hal apologised. But he was panicking. If anyone could see through him, it was Jake.

'She's highly curvaceous. Full lips, long legs, and large breasts. Reminds me of someone, actually. Somebody famous, perchance? The woman who used to be married to that good-looking American dwarf. Surname something to do with ships.'

'Oh, Nicole Kidman?'

'Yes, indeed.'

Hal wanted to tell Jake everything, ask his opinion, but

he couldn't. Jake was on the show now, and it was too risky. He'd have to bluff it out.

His mobile phone bleated inside his rucksack. For a moment he contemplated ignoring it but the temptation was too great. 'Excuse me,' he muttered to Jake. 'Hello?'

'Can you talk?' Jessica asked.

'Not really, no.'

'Sebastian's agent is taking him to the cinema, and then on for an early dinner. I can be at your flat in half an hour. How about you?'

Hal checked his watch. 'Probably more like three-quarters.'

'Get there faster or I might have to start taking my clothes off on your doorstep. I've missed you so much.'

'You too. Right, okay. If you're sure it's that important, I'm on my way.' He smiled awkwardly at Jake. 'Sorry about that. Something's come up,' he stated. 'That was Pippa, my agent. She wants me to go to her office right away. She has someone with her whom I have to meet apparently.'

'Ah,' Jake sighed, 'the snowball of stardom doth run down the hill gathering mass with each full revolution.'

'What?'

'Nothing, dear boy. I shall see you on the morrow.'

'Cheers, Jake.'

Jake picked up his coffee cup, drank what remained, then set off in search of the nearest bar.

Jessica and Hal spent a blissful afternoon together. Two minutes after she left, the telephone rang. It was Mrs Worrel's niece. The old woman had suffered a major stroke. It was touch and go, but she was putting up a fight. Early indications were that the clot had flooded the left side of her brain. She had regained consciousness briefly but had been unable to speak. Hal said how sorry he was, and offered to set up a standing order for his rent to go directly into Mrs Worrel's bank account. The niece told him that such matters should be attended to later. Hal offered to visit. The niece asked him to stay away until her aunt was stronger.

Hal was upset: he was fond of his landlady. He decided that when she came out of hospital, he would buy Mrs Worrel a new tea-set, complete with pot.

'He's a friend of yours. That's why he's playing the part. Not because he's any good.'

It was the coffee break. They had spent most of Wednesday morning rehearsing the first four scenes, and it had been heavy going for a variety of reasons, mostly because Elizabeth kept forgetting her lines.

The minute the break had been called, Sebastian had found Hal and gone on the attack.

'That's partly true. Tony needed a replacement actor in a hurry and I knew—'

'He stinks of beer,' Sebastian added.

'I doubt it. He doesn't drink beer.'

'Whisky, then.'

'Sebastian.'

'I could have him sacked, you know.'

'*What?* Why? Just because he's a friend of mine?'

'Stop seeing Mummy then. I told you, we don't need you. If you stop seeing her I won't get him sacked.'

This time Sebastian had pushed him too far. 'Maybe we should go and talk to Tony about this,' Hal suggested. 'Tell him why you want Jake off the show.'

Sebastian glanced over his shoulder. 'Tell him what you like. I'm not stupid, pig. I never said anything about it,' he snarled, then marched off in Tony's direction, the charming smile back in place.

Hal looked desperately around for Jake. And finally located him. He was talking to Jessica.

He broke the cardinal rule and approached his lover. 'Excuse me, Jessica, sorry to disturb you . . .' He thought he saw her turn pale. 'I wondered if I might drag Jake away. I need to talk to him about the scene he just rehearsed.'

'Can't it wait, dear boy?' Jake asked.

'Afraid not,' Hal said, and pulled him away by the arm.

Half a dozen steps later Jake said, 'Is there any reason why you are frog-marching me around like a recently arrested animal-rights protestor at a fox-hunt?'

'What did you say to her?'

'Who?' Jake replied, at full volume.

'Sssh. Jessica!'

'Not a great deal.'

'Did you say anything about Sebastian?'

'I did not.'

'Are you sure?'

'Yes. Why? Should I have?'

'Absolutely not.'

'Why?'

Hal thought fast. 'Because rumour has it that she's had people sacked for making comments about her son.'

'Why didn't you tell me?'

'I forgot. Didn't Edwin or Penny warn you? They both told me.'

'They did not.'

'Apparently she sits there listening, and if anyone—'

'This is nonsense, surely?'

'Why risk it? Look, she doesn't like being spoken to. She keeps herself to herself.'

'But I never received an answer to my question.'

'What question?'

'Don't look so worried, dear boy. It was perfectly innocuous,' Jake assured him.

'Then you can live without receiving your perfectly innocuous answer, can't you? Besides, Sebastian doesn't like anyone speaking to his mother either.'

Jakes eyes widened. 'Why not?'

'I don't know. I don't have all the answers,' Hal retorted, frustrated.

'How very Greek. Our star has a touch of Oedipus about him, does he?'

'Maybe. Anyway, he doesn't like you as it is, so I suggest—'

'He doesn't like me?' Jake interrupted. 'He told you that?'

The more Hal said to make things better the deeper into the mire he sank. 'No . . . not in so many words . . . Okay, maybe he did, just a little.'

Jake looked wounded. 'I don't understand it. I have been nothing but warm, friendly, bordering on paternal to the child.'

'I don't know why he doesn't like you. Maybe it's because—'

'He's a little prick?' Jake suggested.

'Could have something to do with it. Or it could be that you've been breathing alcohol all over him. Have you been drinking this morning?'

'Certainly not.'

'Jake?'

'I had half a glass of port before I left home. Just to oil the old larynx, you understand. Get the golden throat fully operational.'

'Well, don't do it again,' Hal warned him. 'Use honey and lemon.'

'So, I mustn't drink, I mustn't talk to anyone, and I am already despised. Working in television would not appear to be all it's cracked up to be,' Jake mused.

'Just keep your head down and steer clear of trouble.'

'Very well. May I have a cup of coffee? Or is Nescafé on the banned list as well?'

'Of course you can. I'll join you.'

'No, thank you, dear boy. I shall sup alone, if you don't mind. I wouldn't want you telling tales to one of the various spies in the room.' Jake strode off towards the kettle.

Hal spent the rest of the week in a state of high tension. Jake had stayed dry – at least, Hal thought so – though he had spent the rehearsal period smelling like a giant polo mint which Hal found suspicious.

Sebastian had showed no sign of carrying out his threat to have Jake sacked, but he stared at him pointedly, then smirked at Hal.

Just before Hal was about to leave home for the final rehearsal on Saturday morning, his telephone rang. 'Hi, Belinda. Sorry I haven't been in touch. Things have been a bit hectic. In fact, I'm just on my way to rehearsal now.'

'It's okay.' Belinda was flustered. 'I shan't keep you. I was just wondering . . . I mean I'd quite like to . . . if that's all right with you?'

'Like to what, Belinda?'

'Oh, sorry. I'd like to come and see a recording. Cheer you on.'

'Great. Come to next week's episode. It's a better one for me than the current one.'

'Lovely.' Belinda perked up.

'Actually, Belinda, I could use a chat. Things have been getting a bit weird. Tell you what, can I call you back? If I don't leave now, I'll be late.'

'Yes, of course. Any time you like.'

'Thanks. 'Bye,' Hal said, put down the phone and rushed out of his door.

Belinda replaced the receiver.

'Well? What did he say?' Mary asked.

'Next week. He said something about popping round for a chat before then.'

'Well, there you are.'

'Hal's chats are about – *her*.'

'Look on the bright side,' Mary suggested. 'In just over a week, you can meet her face to face.'

'I can't wait.'

'You could always poison her gin and tonic in the bar.'

'Mary!'

'All right. Let's kidnap her and shave off her hair. Not many men like poking a baldy.' Mary got up, walked across to her friend and gave her a hug. 'If Hal does pop round for a chat, just tell him. Get it out in the open. Say you love him, and hang the consequences. I can't stand to see this eating you up any more.'

Belinda smiled half-heartedly.

'Come on, then, dust down your credit card. Let's go get ourselves some retail therapy,' Mary suggested.

'Actually, Mary, I don't think I'm in the mood for it.'

'Suit yourself. I'll pop round tomorrow. Catch you later.' Mary strode out.

Belinda gathered up her newspaper and flopped on to the sofa. A headline screamed, 'Why So Many Over-Thirty-Fives Are Left on the Shelf.'

'Cheer me up, why don't you?' she muttered, before turning to the relevant page.

21

On Sunday afternoon Hal was awakened from his day-dream by the sound of familiar dialogue filtering through the Tannoy. Shit, he thought. They're setting up my next scene. I'd better go. He sprang off the bed, opened the dressing-room door and almost fell over Sebastian. 'Argh!

'What's the matter with you, stupid?' Sebastian asked.

'Nothing,' Hal snapped. 'I wasn't expecting you to be there.'

'Shouldn't you be in the studio?'

'Shouldn't you?'

'I'm not in the next scene. Well? Aren't you going downstairs?'

'Yes, of course I am. I'm on my way . . . And why are you carrying an empty plastic bag around with you?' he asked suspiciously.

'It's a present,' Sebastian replied.

'A carrier-bag?'

'What was in the bag was a present.'

'For whom?'

Sebastian smiled from ear to ear. 'A friend of mine.' They stared at each other for a moment. Then Sebastian said, 'So, pig, aren't you going down? They'll be getting cross with you soon.'

Hal didn't reply, but began to make his way down the

corridor. The boy worried him. It wasn't long since the incident with the coffee table and he couldn't help wondering if Sebastian had another surprise in store for him.

It wasn't until just before the dress rehearsal that Hal noticed he had hardly seen Jake all day. Admittedly he was only in one scene, and that was early in the episode. When he did appear, he blanked Hal.

'Jake, where've you been, mate?'

Jake didn't reply. Instead he stared into Hal's eyes and said, 'Judas.'

'What?'

'Prince Hal turns his back on old Falstaff, eh?'

Before Hal could ask any more, first positions were called, and Jake disappeared again.

The warm-up man came and went. The introductions, the opening titles, the first two scenes. Hal was nervous. He checked with the girls in Makeup. Jake had been first in the chair. He had been fine, but quiet.

Eventually Jake appeared in the makeup room half-way through the first take of scene two. He sat down near to the monitor.

Hal slid his chair along until he was next to his friend. 'About time you came out of your hidey-hole. Where have you been?'

'Reclining in my dressing room,' he replied flatly.

'Funny. I knocked on your door and didn't get a reply.'

'I was not – not inclined to receive visitors . . .'

Warning bells rang in Hal's head. 'Well, your big moment's coming up. Are you nervous?'

'Big moment! Don't so bloody patronising. I only have lines three – three lines.'

'Jake, you're drunk.'

'I am not!' Jake insisted. 'How dare you?'

'I'd better get you a coffee.'

'I don't want a toffee. I'm perfectly sober. I may have imbibed a small tincture just to toosen my lonsils. But I do not need the shig-bot – big-shot actor with only half my theatrical experience treating me like a novice.'

'I'm not! I'm trying to save your arse. You cannot go out in front of a studio audience three sheets to the wind and expect to get away with it.'

'Oh, off . . . piss,' Jake said.

'Jake, what's Tony going to say? The rest of the cast? Sebastian?'

'D-d-don't . . .' Jake stuttered '. . . blacken that b-boy's name any more. Telling me he didn't like me, that he wanted me . . . show the off – you know what I mean. That child has treated me like a k-k-king today.'

'I bet he has.'

'He doesn't want me off the show,' Jake snapped, lucid now. 'You do.'

'That's madness. I got you the job in the first place.'

'That child told me you've given him a terrible time since you joined this series, telling tales to Tony, ruining his scenes. It's because you're jealous!'

'It's not true, Jake. It's been the other way round.'

'How come nobody else has a problem with him?'

'Keep your voice down.' Hal glanced at the makeup ladies.

'Positions for the start of scene three, please.' Patrick's voice came over the monitor.

'Damn!' Hal cried.

'Excuse me. I do believe that's my cue,' Jake stated, and climbed unsteadily to his feet. 'Mustn't keep my public waiting,' he declared, teetering towards the door.

There was nothing Hal could do.

He sat in front of the monitor, crossed his fingers and

prayed that Jake's years of experience would see him through.

On the monitor, he saw Patrick struggle to get Jake into position on the sofa, then talking into his microphone, evidently warning Tony that they had a problem.

Jake was clearly leaning on Elizabeth Sage for support. She was a frail old lady and Jake was a big man: she was wilting under the strain.

Patrick went over to have a word.

'Of course I'm all right,' Jake barked out.

The take began.

It was a simple scene: Elizabeth, playing Sebastian's grandmother, was arguing with Penny about hiring a nanny. Jake's character was barely introduced, except for a quick opening joke. Elizabeth's character turned up with a new boyfriend in every series. It was a running gag. Jake had just three lines.

Hal was sweating as the first drew near.

The gallery were calling different shots from the ones used at rehearsals. Jake had lost at least two close-up reaction shots, and one establishing mid-shot.

First line. Jake said, 'Don't speak to your mother like that.'

Hal breathed a sigh of relief. Elizabeth dried on her next line.

First line, second time round, and Jake said, 'Don't speak to your mother like that.'

Penny responded, 'Who asked you to butt in? You're just Mother's toy-boy.'

'No need to be nude. I mean, no need to be rude . . . Sorry did I say nude?' Jake fumbled.

The audience laughed with him and another take was ordered. Jake couldn't stop laughing. It took several minutes to calm him down.

Take three.

Jake: 'Don't speak to your mother like that.'

Penny: 'Who asked you to butt in? You're just Mother's toy-boy.'

Jake: 'No need to be . . . rude.'

Penny: 'Mother, I simply haven't found a suitable nanny.'

Jake: 'Haven't nound a fanny!'

The audience roared.

So did Jake. He lifted his legs in the air, and fell off the sofa, taking Elizabeth with him and landing on her.

It looked a nasty fall. The audience stopped laughing when Patrick rushed on to the set with some of his team to assist.

It took three of them to pull Jake off Elizabeth, who lay prone. They lifted her slowly to her feet. Her right arm was clearly hurting, and Hal thought he saw her limp as they helped her back to the sofa, but she agreed to continue.

Jake was pushing himself up. Someone went to lend a hand. 'I'm all right,' he shouted, and walked back towards the sofa, where Patrick met him and spoke to him.

'Sorry about that, ladies and gentlemen, and I'm sorry, my dear,' Jake said, as he plonked himself on to the sofa and patted Elizabeth's leg.

'Oh dear, oh dear,' Elizabeth said.

Hal could sense the audience's embarrassment.

'We're going again,' Patrick shouted.

Hal put his head in his hands. He couldn't bear to watch any more.

When the scene was finally finished several floor managers helped Jake off the set.

Hal didn't go to him. He couldn't, he was in the next scene. Frankly, he wasn't sure he could face seeing him, anyway.

Hal was in his dressing room, washing off his makeup, when Peter came in. 'Your chum put on a bit of a show tonight,' he said.

Hal groaned.

'I think poor Elizabeth is going to have to go into therapy, Chuckle. Talk about traumatised. She's daft as a pheasant during the shooting season anyway, but after this?'

'Yes, all right, Peter.'

'Don't get touchy, just take my advice. Don't take your chum to the bar. Rumour has it Tony's spitting blood.'

'He's not blaming me, is he?'

'Don't ask me, dear. I just do the frocks. I don't interfere with family quarrels.' Peter flounced out with Hal's costume.

As he left, Tony stormed in. 'Trustworthy, you said, Hal. Good actor. Reliable. Won't let you down. You left out the bit about Jake being a raving piss-head. Seventeen takes it took to get anything vaguely usable of scene three!'

'It wasn't all Jake. Elizabeth fluffed her lines too.'

'Elizabeth's memory might not be what it was but I don't think it helped to have sixteen stones of drunk drop on her head, do you?'

'No, but—'

'If it wasn't for the fact that his character appears in the next episode, I'd sack the bastard. In fact, I'd sack the pair of you. He doesn't have much to say, thank goodness, but it's important he's there. You get him to rehearsals on Monday, sober, and make sure he stays that way. Or else you'll find *yourself* written out of the next series, I'm telling you. I want him to apologise. I want him to eat humble fucking pie in front of everyone, you hear?'

'Yes, Tony.'

'Especially to Elizabeth. The poor woman's had to go to Casualty to see if her wrist is broken. Now I'm going to the bar to inform the writers that they may have to come up with a reason for Elizabeth's character to be in plaster next week. You are not going to the bar. You are going to get that prick out of the building and start sobering him up. Okay?'

Hal nodded.

'His door's open. He was on the floor when I last saw him. I would have bollocked him myself but I don't think he would have heard me.'

Hal pulled on his sweatshirt, and his boots, packed his rucksack, and headed along the corridor to Jake's room.

He found him slumped, comatose, in a chair in front of the mirror. 'Oi, you old bastard, wake up. I want a word with you.'

Three empty wine bottles were scattered on a table, and another stood in the waste-paper basket.

'Come on. Let's get you home.' Hal put his arms around Jake and tried to lift him, but he was too heavy.

'Is everything all right?' Jessica was in the doorway, Sebastian beside her.

'I've got to get Jake home and I can't lift him.'

'We'll help,' Jessica offered.

'Don't be daft. We'll be seen—'

'No, we won't, everyone's in the bar. Besides, this is different. This is us helping you get Jake out of here. If anyone sees, it's nothing to do with—'

'You and him,' Sebastian interrupted.

Hal looked at him. And something dropped into place. 'The carrier bag! You fed him all this booze. You got him drunk.'

Sebastian turned to his mother. 'I didn't make him

drink. I *didn't*. He's my new friend. I wouldn't hurt him, Mummy. I *wouldn't*!'

'Of course you wouldn't. You can't blame Sebastian, Hal. He's eight and Jake's a grown man. He must take responsibility for his actions. It's nobody's fault the man's an alcoholic.'

'I didn't, Mummy, I didn't.'

'All right, Sebastian. Look, this isn't getting us anywhere. Let us help.'

'We'll manage.'

Jessica snorted. 'Don't be so stubborn. You can't lift him by yourself, and you'll never get a taxi with him in that state. We have access to a BBC fleet car because of Sebastian's age. I'll sort it out. The driver's . . . fond of us.'

Jessica crossed to Hal and they got Jake on to his feet.

'Can I help?' Sebastian asked.

'You've helped enough already.'

'Please.'

Hal only had two arms. 'Carry his bag,' he said.

They loaded Jake into the back of the car, and Hal climbed in after him.

'Kensington as usual, Ms Taylor?' the driver asked.

'No. Our friend in the back isn't very well. He's on the show. We want you to give him a lift home first, I'm afraid.'

'Where to?'

'Tooting,' Hal told him.

'At this time of night?'

'Please, Bob,' Jessica begged. 'Then perhaps you could come back for us. I wouldn't ask if it weren't important.'

'Seeing as it's you and the boy asking, miss, I'll do it,' the driver said.

Sebastian's guilty eyes reflected in the headlights as the car turned the corner.

232

The next evening Hal walked into his flat and glanced at the clock. It was eight thirty. It had been a tough day. Jake had swung between contrite to aggressive, sometimes within seconds. There had been tears of shame, roars of anger and continual begging for drink.

Hal was worried. Jake was the professional's professional. *He* had taught *Hal* how to behave. He was the last person Hal would have expected to disgrace himself like this.

Through the course of the day Hal had discovered much. Jake was ill, lonely and frightened. He was feeling his age. He was scared of dying, and especially of dying alone as a failure. Extreme depression had made him turn to alcohol.

Hal didn't know how to help him. And how was he going to get Jake through the humiliation of a public apology at the next rehearsal, and keep him sober for a week?

Jake was clearly bitter about Hal's success. And, for the first time, Hal was angry with him: he had offered his friend a chance and Jake had thrown it back in his face. He felt let down.

But Jake was at his lowest ebb. And Sebastian had taken advantage of that. Jake had denied it at first, but had cracked under interrogation.

Hal felt guilty: part of him felt he should have stayed an extra night with Jake, made sure he turned up for work in the morning, that he didn't slope out to see John at Oddbins. But he hadn't been able to face it. Jake had begged to go to bed – he was tired, he had said, and needed to rest. He had promised faithfully to turn up in the morning.

Now Hal decided to give Belinda a ring and arrange to meet her.

He was in desperate need of advice.

To his disappointment, the answering-machine clicked in at the other end. He left a message, then went to bed.

The next day, Jake arrived sober, to Hal's relief, but he looked old and weary.

Thankfully, Elizabeth was not in plaster.

Before the reading Jake made his apology: 'Excuse me, everyone, and I mean everyone, friends, such as I have left, and colleagues. I sit before you wearing the damning cloak of shame. My behaviour on Sunday evening was unforgivable. You may choose to believe this or not, as you would wish, but that was the first time I have disgraced myself in over forty years in this industry. I have been trying to find a reason for this inexcusable lapse in professional behaviour. A reason you understand, not an excuse, for there can be no justification. I am a bitter, tired old man, coming to the end of his professional life. Remarkably, this is the first opportunity I have ever been given to appear on television. I must number among the few actors left in the country never to have been seen for an episode of *Casualty*. I arrived at the studio on Sunday, nervous, envious, and aware that such a day had arrived too late for me. I became resentful and depressed, and the rest . . . became a damning indictment of a sad career.

'I do not expect forgiveness. However, I feel it is essential that I apologise to my fellow cast members for embarrassing them so badly, to Elizabeth for crushing so delicate a flower, to Patrick, to whom I was rude beyond compare, to Tony, for the disgraceful way I repaid his kindness in casting me, and lastly to young Hal, for I fear I may have sullied his reputation among you all. I must stress that he was in no way connected to the incidents on

234

Sunday, and is not responsible for my actions. He merely thought he was doing an old friend a favour. The old Jake, the man he has known for many years, would not have let him down so badly. Please give him the respect his talent deserves.

'I am too old to adapt to this new medium of television. Too tired to start on the bottom rung. I shall honour my contract with you this week. There will be no repeat of Sunday night's débâcle. I apologise, most humbly, and in so doing I announce my retirement from the business. I thank you for your time.'

A brief silence followed, during which Hal sensed people's embarrassment, and witnessed his friend's tears of distress. He saw that Jake's apology had not been expected. And a smile of satisfaction on Sebastian's face.

It had come out of the blue. Hal had sloped home to his flat after another difficult day, during which Jake had refused to speak to him – 'I fear I am not the sort of brush with which you should be tarred, dear boy,' was all he had said.

They had shared one moment of eye contact. Hal had a scene in episode five in which his character had to become hysterical, as he did in most episodes. Hal's character was in such a fix that to demonstrate how desperate he was for help to Edwin's character, he took a kitchen knife from a drawer and ran it across his wrist, in a mock suicide attempt. It was quite a funny scene.

Rehearsing this, Hal had looked up for a second, and found Jake watching. After his emotional speech that morning a wry smile had passed between them, as if to say, 'I know how he feels'.

But that was it. After that, he had shut Hal out for the rest of the day. Today he behaved exactly the same.

However, although Jake had publicly absolved him,

the rest of the cast had treated him like a leper. Conversations had been polite, distant, interrupted by an excuse that forced them to 'dash off'. Even Edwin hadn't asked him to go for a pint. Sebastian had enjoyed every minute of it. And Jessica had not telephoned.

Hal dumped his rucksack in the middle of the sitting room, went in to the kitchen, and made himself a coffee.

The telephone rang.

Hal sprinted to his rucksack and searched for the phone, but it had stopped ringing. Then he found the plastic carrier bag. He pulled it out. He had no recollection of putting it in his rucksack. He opened it and fished out the contents, a piece of Plasticine. It had been shaped to resemble a man, as if a child had . . . Then Hal saw the needle stuck in the effigy's chest.

Hal looked inside the carrier bag again and found a piece of A4 paper. Glued to it were letters cut from a newspaper, a magazine, or possibly both. He read the message:

**NEXT TIME IT WILL BE REAL
I TOLD YOU. YOUR A DEAD MAN
PIG**

Hal felt faint. The carrier bag was of the same type that Sebastian had used to take wine to Jake. The boy was unstable, dangerous beyond his years. No one else would believe such a sweet, innocent child could harm a fly. But Hal knew different.

22

Hal sat on Belinda's sofa clutching a glass of wine. He had spent the last half-hour running through all that had happened since he had last seen her, including the latest shocking episode. 'I know it sounds crazy, but it all adds up. Don't you see?' he finished.

'Hal, please try to keep calm and sensible.'

'I'm telling you, Belinda, the little shit's got it in for me.'

'Are you sure it was Sebastian who put it into your bag?'

'Yes! Well, who else could it have been?' Hal asked.

'Might someone else have done this as some sort of joke? Have you talked to anyone else about your feud with Sebastian?'

'No. How could I? His mother would freak. No one else knows, apart from you. Look at the letter, Belinda. It could easily have been put together by a child. It's misspelled and there are no full stops.'

'Yes, but—'

' "You're a dead man." That's what Sebastian said to me the night he found out I was dating his mother.'

Belinda refilled his glass. 'Supposing it's true, that Sebastian is guilty. He hasn't physically hurt you, has he?'

'What about the incident with the coffee table? I could have broken something.'

'You did say it was unsteady.'

Hal drank more wine. 'The leg had been unscrewed. Patrick said as much. Look what he's done to poor Jake – he's all but finished his career. And he did that because Jake was my friend to warn me off seeing his mother.'

'Will you go to the police?'

'Hardly. What would I say? "I have a strong suspicion that the Nation's Poppet harbours homicidal tendencies"?'

'Hal! Get a grip. He's not a trained assassin. He's eight years old and you're ten times his size. What can he actually *do* to you?'

Hal sighed. 'You're right, I suppose. I've no idea what my next move should be. Any suggestions?'

'I'm a psychiatrist. I ask the questions and you give the answers, remember?'

'Brilliant!' Hal cried.

'What is?'

'You just said it yourself. You're a psychiatrist.'

'So?'

'Take a look at him for me.'

'Oh, no, no, *no*.'

'Why not?'

'Just no! Besides, how will you persuade his mother to let him come into the hospital for a session?'

'I couldn't. I'm not talking about anything so heavy. Just a chance meeting and a little chit-chat. Just enough to tell me whether or not you think he's . . . normal.'

'It's not as simple as that. I couldn't make a professional assessment on that basis,' she protested.

'A rough idea?'

'Without his mother's permission it would be unethical.'

'Please, Belinda.'

'And how are we supposed to just bump into each other?'

'I'll cook them a meal at my house, and you could—'

'No,' Belinda replied, 'I am not sitting through an entire dinner—'

'Okay. Be there when they arrive. Stay a few minutes then make your excuses and go.'

'Hal—'

'Please?'

It was no use. Belinda looked into Hal's eyes and her resolve melted. 'I wouldn't do this for anyone else, you know,' she told him.

'You're an angel.' Hal hurled his arms around her.

She buried her head in his chest for a few seconds. When she pulled away, their eyes met. The look between them lingered a little longer than usual.

'I'd better be going,' Hal said, and gathered the 'evidence' into a plastic bag. 'I'll call you as soon as I've made arrangements.' He made for the sitting-room door.

'One more thing before you go,' she said, and crossed her fingers.

'Yes?'

'I love you.'

A frightening silence followed. It was hard to tell who was the more surprised: Hal at what he had just been told, or Belinda because she had finally spoken the truth. 'Oh dear. I've done it now,' she said.

'Belinda, I—'

'It's all right, Hal. You don't have to say anything. I just thought it was time I told you.'

'No, no,' he stuttered. 'I want to. It's not that . . . I mean, it has occasionally crossed my mind—'

'Has it?'

'Yes, but . . . well, the timing . . . and there's Jessica,

not to mention our history, friendship – Amy.' Hal was hovering in the doorway.

'You don't still love Amy—'

'No, no, that's long gone.'

Belinda ran her fingers along the back of the blue sofa. 'I had to tell you because I couldn't keep it inside any more. Not after all these years.'

'*Years?*'

'I think so. But the other reason I told you was to be fair to you. You see, you keep coming to me for guidance. I can't honestly say that all the advice I give you about Sebastian and . . . Jessica is as professional as it should be. It may be a bit biased sometimes. I think you should know that.'

Hal's mouth opened and closed.

'Go home, Hal. Give Jake a ring and check he's all right. Call me when you've sorted out this chance meeting. If you still want me to come.'

A minute later, Hal was walking along the streets of Crouch End, and Belinda was sitting on one of her blue sofas gripping a glass of wine so tightly it might have shattered in her hand.

Hal had a torrid time at rehearsals. No one spoke to him, and his paranoia was rising. The one good thing was that Jessica had agreed to bring Sebastian for tea later that day, and he had set things up with Belinda. He had almost called off the whole thing, in the light of Belinda's declaration of love, but a day of being sent to Coventry, and Sebastian grinning mysteriously, had convinced him otherwise.

At coffee-break he was still being ignored. He crossed purposefully to Edwin and sat down next to him. 'Edwin, why isn't anyone talking to me? Are they still blaming me for Jake's behaviour? Or is there something else?'

'Three down. "Austral tree bites back aggression"?' Edwin said. 'Something "breaker". Three letters.' He did not look up from his paper.

Hal sighed. 'I haven't got a clue. Edwin, this is serious—'

'Austral tree. Three letters. Something "breaker".'

Hal supposed any conversation was better than none. He thought. 'Oh, I know. Axe. Axe-breaker is the name of the tree.'

Edwin raised his eyes from the paper and stared into the distance. 'Yes, that's it. Axe,' he said. 'Now I must grab a coffee before it's too late.' He stood up and walked away.

The tea was a disaster. Apparently Sebastian didn't like cheese or peanut-butter sandwiches. Neither did he like chocolate marshmallow tea-cakes, jelly, or Jammy Dodgers. He refused to talk, and Jessica was downbeat.

Hal had just watched the clock, waiting for Belinda's 'surprise' arrival.

'More lemonade, Sebastian?' he asked.

Sebastian shook his head.

'More tea, Jessica?'

'No, thank you.' She looked at Sebastian, who nodded.

'Hal . . .' Jessica began, and paused.

'Go on,' Sebastian urged.

'Hal. There's something I have to tell you. It's that—' Jessica was interrupted by the doorbell.

'I wonder who that could be?' Hal said.

'Don't answer it,' Jessica suggested.

'I'd better. It might be Mrs Worrel's niece. She said she'd drop in to give me an update.'

'How is she?'

'Conscious, last I heard,' Hal replied. 'She can't speak, though, and she's paralysed down her left side.'

The doorbell rang again.

'I'd better go.'

'No, don't,' Jessica urged. 'I've got something important to tell you, Hal.'

The doorbell rang a third time. Hal was frightened Belinda would scarper if he didn't hurry.

'It'll have to wait. I won't be a minute,' he said, ran down the stairs and opened the door. 'Oh, what a surprise! How nice to see you,' he yelled.

Belinda put two fingers into her mouth in disgust as she walked in.

'Why didn't you tell me you were coming!' Hal bellowed. He pushed Belinda up the stairs. 'Look who's here,' he said, as he shoved her into his flat. 'Let me introduce you to everyone. These are my friends Sebastian and Jessica.'

Belinda stared at the red-haired woman. She was beautiful and voluptuous. Belinda's self-confidence crumbled.

'This is Belinda,' Hal said, closing the door and Belinda's escape route.

'Oh, *you're* Belinda,' said Jessica. 'The doctor?'

'Psychiatrist, actually. How did you know my name?'

'Hal talks about you,' Jessica told her.

'Have a cup of tea, Belinda,' Hal said.

'Oh, no, I don't want to disturb you.'

'Please?' Hal asked, through gritted teeth.

'No, I only came to borrow that copy of *Equus* you said you'd lend me.'

'Excuse me, I must powder my nose,' Jessica announced, and headed for the bathroom.

Hal gestured to Belinda to sit down with Sebastian.

'Perhaps I will have that cup of tea,' Belinda said. 'I'm a big fan of yours, Sebastian.'

'Thank you,' he said, smiling.

Great start, Hal thought. Flatter the devious little swine. Lull him into a false sense of security, then drag the truth out of the little shit.

'It must be hard work, though, on the series?'

'Yes.'

'Tiring?'

'Yes.'

Just one-word answers. Accompanied by that famous smile.

'Tell me, what's the most difficult part of the job?'

'You're very pretty,' Sebastian said.

'Thank you,' Belinda replied, startled.

'Very pretty. Isn't she, Hal?'

'Yes, she is.'

'Much prettier than Mummy, don't you think?'

Hal was dumbfounded.

'Oh, Sebastian—' Belinda tried to protest.

'I think so. Don't you, Hal? She's much prettier than Mummy. Have you got a boyfriend?'

'Well, no, not exactly—'

'She should have a boyfriend, shouldn't she, Hal? Seeing as she's so much prettier than Mummy.'

At that moment Jessica emerged from the bathroom. She looked strangely at Belinda. Jealousy? Hal wondered.

'Sorry, everyone,' she said, 'I've just noticed the time. I'm afraid Sebastian and I must be going.' She collected their coats.

'Oh, don't rush off,' Hal begged.

'Please don't leave on my account,' Belinda chipped in.

'Do stay, I really must be going. It's getting late. Come along, Sebastian,' Jessica said.

As he put his jacket on, Sebastian looked at Hal and smiled. 'You don't know, do you?' he said. 'Nobody's told you yet, have they?'

'Told me what?'

'Not now, Sebastian. We're going. Thanks for a lovely tea, Hal. Sebastian will see you tomorrow. Bye-bye.'

'I'll walk you down,' Hal offered.

'We can see ourselves out.' They disappeared through Hal's door, closing it behind them.

'Bugger!' Hal cursed. 'Still, what did you think?'

'I thought she was gorgeous.'

'Not Jessica. The child.'

'She is lovely, though, isn't she?' Belinda persisted. 'She reminds me of someone.'

'Nicole Kidman, Jake says. Anyway, never mind all that, what did you make of Sebastian?'

'He seemed okay. I didn't have long enough to form an opinion.'

'Then give me a gut reaction.'

'He seemed okay.'

'Okay? Not you as well. Can't you see how devious he is?'

'Not from that conversation.'

Hal thumped the sofa in frustration. 'He's so manipulative. He had you wrapped around his little finger, that's for sure.'

'He did not!' Belinda said, indignantly.

'Not much. He's so clever. He can spot people's insecurities, weaknesses, and he plays on them.'

'And what weaknesses of mine did he wheedle out?' Belinda asked.

'Me. He used me. He can see you feel something for me. You should have seen his face when I agreed how pretty you were. Like a shark, smelling blood.'

'Oh, Hal,' Belinda exclaimed. 'That's not fair.'

Hal's telephone rang.

'I wouldn't upset you for the world. It's just . . . damn! I haven't got the answering-machine turned on. Just a second.' He leaped over and snatched up the receiver. 'Hello?' he barked.

Belinda watched the colour drain from his face.

'Why? What have they said?'

She couldn't make out the other half of the conversation. Just that it was bad news.

'So what happens now?'

Belinda watched Hal slump.

'That's it, then. Okay. Yes, sure. We'll talk soon.'

Hal put down the telephone. 'That was Pippa, my agent. They're not renewing my contract for *Bringing Up Ralph*.'

'What does that mean?' Belinda asked.

'I finish the next two episodes and I'm off the show. The little shit's got his way.'

23

Ten minutes later, Hal and Belinda were in the nearest pub.

'And what's really weird,' Hal said, 'is that if they're going to dump you, they usually wait until closer to the making of the next series before they tell you. Sometimes they don't bother telling you at all. They just wait for word to get round. Why tell me now?'

Belinda shrugged.

'Because Sebastian insisted.'

'It might not be his fault, Hal.'

'Come on, who else?'

'Your producer, perhaps?'

'Tony?'

'Who told your agent?' Belinda enquired.

'Some gink from the contracts department at the Beeb, or Jester Productions, I think. No clues there.'

'What reasons did they give?'

'Late arrival – Mrs Worrel's fault. Drying on set – Sebastian's fault. Bad atmosphere between cast members – Sebastian. The unsavoury incident with someone personally recommended for casting – Sebastian again. General misdemeanours since I joined the cast, or some such cobblers. You have to take your hat off to the child. He always gets his own way in the end,' Hal said.

'Does he? I thought what Sebastian wanted was for

you to stop seeing his mother,' Belinda reminded him. There was a pause. 'What will you do now?' she asked.

'What can I do? He's won. I'm off the show.'

Belinda swallowed. 'No. I mean, what will you do about Sebastian . . . and Jessica?'

'Any suggestions?'

'If you really believe that Sebastian is responsible for this, and for all the other incidents, I think you should take it up with Jessica.'

'Really?'

'That would be my advice. But I've warned you, it might be biased.'

'Look, I'll— em . . . get us another drink in, shall I?'

'That would be nice,' Belinda replied, forlornly.

Nothing was said at the rehearsal the next morning. Not even Tony found time to have a quiet word with Hal. Penny, Edwin, Elizabeth and Patrick ignored him and now Hal understood why: word had got out. Not for the first time was the victim the last to hear the bad news.

Sebastian had not gloated as Hal had expected. He had been civil when they rehearsed their scenes together and had worked hard. He had not smiled that smile once.

During the coffee-break, Hal sat next to Jake. 'You don't have to ignore me any more. I'm in the same boat. I've been sacked.'

'What?' Jake exclaimed.

'I've been dropped from the next series.'

'Oh, dear boy, I'm so sorry. That's my fault.'

'No, it isn't,' Hal replied firmly. 'It's Sebastian's.'

'Are you certain?'

'He did for me the same way he did for you.'

Jake didn't argue. 'Well, look on the bright side. At

247

least you'll be able to spend the rest of your time making life hell for the little bastard.'

Hal glanced at Jessica. 'I can't. At least, not yet anyway.'

'Why not?'

'I have my reasons.'

'I'm so sorry, Hal. Still, look at it like this. You've had six episodes' worth of exposure and you've been turning in a fine comedic performance. Casting agents, producers and directors will be throwing their knickers at you in an effort to entice you into their productions.'

'Maybe.'

'And did you really want to be stuck on this piece of manure for the rest of your career? You'll be telling me next that you always harboured a secret desire to appear on *Terry and June.*'

Hal smiled half-heartedly.

'Oh, well, Laurel and Hardy sail off into the sunset together once again.'

'Looks that way, my friend,' Hal said, resignedly.

After the rehearsal Hal called Belinda. 'I've got you a ticket for Sunday's recording,' he told her. 'Do you want to come?'

'I'd love to. How are things?'

'Jake and I are friends again.'

'Well, that's something. Have you spoken to Jessica about Sebastian?'

'Not yet. You'll come on Sunday, then?'

'You bet. Will I see you afterwards?'

'In the bar.' Hal gave her details of studios, ticket collection and how to get to the bar. He told her where to wait for him, and even gave her a description of Jake in case they missed each other. You couldn't miss Jake, Hal thought. He stood out in any room.

*

On the day of the recording Sebastian wouldn't stop talking to Hal. Every time there was a stoppage, he made banal conversation – as if nothing had happened.

He asked about Mrs Worrel, as if he cared. He asked whether Hal had eaten all the Jammy Dodgers he had bought for the tea, and he asked if Hal would like to see his collection of Pokémon cards.

They were rehearsing Hal's hysteria scene with Edwin when they had to stop yet again. Sebastian wandered on to the set of the kitchen. 'We've got a set of knives like that in our house,' he said, referring to the one Hal was holding.

'Why are you bothering me?'

'I'm just trying to be friendly.'

'Yes, and we all know why you're being friendly now, don't we, Sebastian? Don't push me too far. You might just get a taste of your own medicine.'

Hal noticed the silence. He doubted anyone had ever been rude to the Nation's Poppet on or off set.

Sebastian looked genuinely hurt, but he was a good actor. Hal had never doubted that.

'Positions, please,' Patrick called.

Hal stayed downstairs to watch Jake rehearse his scene. When it was finished, he walked on set to speak to his friend as the others departed. 'Well done, Jake. Very impressive. Maybe you should reconsider retirement.'

'Do you think so?' Jake smiled.

'Hal.'

He turned to see Sebastian staring up at him again.

'I just wanted to say sorry.'

'What?' Hal's nerves were taut. 'Why can't you just leave me alone?' he snapped, and headed for his dressing room.

'I strongly recommend you respect my friend's wishes,

and leave the poor man in peace,' Jake told Sebastian. 'Otherwise *I* shall personally defecate on the floor, and rub your nose in my excrement until I wipe that irksome grin off that cutesie little face of yours. Is that clear?'

Sebastian was speechless.

Jake lifted the lapel of his jacket, and spoke into the tiny microphone concealed beneath it. 'I do hope you got all that up in the gallery. I shall not be doing a retake.' Then he walked off the set, chuckling.

He did not see Jessica appear to comfort her dumbfounded son, or Tony descend from the gallery, panic spreading across his face.

In the early afternoon Jessica came to Hal's dressing room. 'Why the hell are you being so horrible to Sebastian?'

'Have I been?'

'Yes, and so has Jake. Have you gone mad? Aren't things difficult enough? Why were you so nasty to him?'

'Probably because he can't get me sacked twice.'

'Don't be ridiculous, Hal. Sebastian didn't get you fired.'

'Well, who did?'

'It was Tony.'

'Prompted by your son,' Hal insisted.

'No. Tony's not your biggest fan, I'm afraid, and the writer wants to get rid of your character and give Penny a new love interest. How could you think it was Sebastian? He's only eight.'

'And that blinds you to everything, doesn't it? He's eight years old and he's your precious son.'

'Hal, I've never seen you like this.'

'I've reached the limits of my patience. Think back,

Jessica, to when I first arrived – Sebastian's farting and blaming me, pulling my shorts down in the swimming-pool, criticising my acting. All harmless enough, I suppose. But think how it changed when he found out we were together.'

'Hal, you're exaggerating.'

'No, I'm not. I'm trying to make you understand. Remember the water on the washbasin? The salt in the coffee? Feeding me bum cues so that I dried in front of the audience time after time?'

'Hal—'

'What about the coffee-table? Who do you think unscrewed the leg?' Hal raged.

'You surely don't think—'

'Yes, I do. And there's more. Sebastian told me he would get Jake taken off the show if I didn't stop seeing you.'

'He wouldn't have!'

'He got Jake drunk, made the poor man screw up professionally for the first time in his life. All but bloody destroyed him.'

'Jake's a drunk, Hal. Face facts. You can hardly blame Sebastian for that.'

'Your child susses it and he made damn sure Jake didn't go short of the old *vino* when the time came.'

'Hal, that's outrageous!'

'Is it? Do you know how much wine you keep in your apartment? I should go home and count the bottles if I were you. And see if he's a couple of tubs of Plasticine short while you're at it.'

'This can't be true,' Jessica said.

'When I came to dinner at your place, Sebastian said that you two didn't need me in your lives. He warned me to stay away from you. When he first found out we were together, he told me I was a dead man.'

'No,' Jessica whispered.

'Yes, Jessica.'

Hal walked over to his bag. 'Look at that,' he said, handing her the effigy. 'It was placed in my rucksack with a needle stuck in its chest. This note came with it.'

He passed it to her. 'Pranks are one thing but this is serious stuff.'

Jessica sat on the bed. 'Have you shown this to anyone?'

'No,' Hal lied.

'Sebastian couldn't have sent this.'

'Have you listened to a word I've said? Read the note. Look at the words. Your son calls me "pig" behind your back.'

'Jake must have sent it.'

'*Jake?*'

'He's bitter and resentful, he said so himself—'

'Jake didn't send it, Jessica, Sebastian did. He hates the thought of us being together. That's why I'm sacked. He doesn't want anyone near you. The boy needs help, I'm convinced of it.'

'So that's why you brought your friend along, the psychiatrist. You brought her to your flat to see if my son's mad,' Jessica accused him. 'How dare you? Have you told her about all the things you've accused my son of doing to you?'

Hal was skating on thin ice. Belinda had said she was acting unethically. There were laws against malpractice. 'No,' he lied again. 'I just told her I was worried about him. I said he'd shown signs of strain. I asked her to take a quick look, tell me whether I should be concerned or not.'

'I bet you've told . . . Belinda all about us, haven't you? After I asked you to keep it a secret.'

'No, I haven't,' Hal lied for a third time. 'Ask her yourself. Anyway, what "us"? It's like we're having an affair. We have to sneak around in secret, we never go anywhere, we never see anyone, because of your son's precious career. Jessica, I have a right to be taken seriously in this relationship too. Your son is not perfect. He's got problems. And, frankly, I've just about had enough.'

'Give me a little time,' Jessica said. 'A day or two. No more, I promise. Let me talk to Sebastian. I can't do it now, not with the recording and everything. I have to tread carefully—'

'Oh, here we go,' Hal exclaimed.

'No. I mean if I'm to get to the truth. If you're right, and he has been up to all these terrible tricks, he's not going to want to admit it, is he?'

'You're just making excuses for him again! If it's always going to be about Sebastian and you then we might as well call it a day now.'

'No!' Jessica ran across the dressing room and threw herself into Hal's arms, weeping. 'Please don't leave me. I love you. I can't live without you.'

'You've a funny way of showing it.'

She pulled away from him, her eyes red with tears.

Hal felt himself weaken 'Look. Don't cry—'

'You can't leave me now, Hal, not when it's finally coming together.'

'What do you mean?'

'I've never liked "sneaking around", as you put it, either. They say every cloud has a silver lining. In just over a week you won't be working on the show any more.'

'Thanks for reminding me,' Hal responded bitterly.

'No, listen, it won't be as bad then. Of course I don't want to embarrass Sebastian, but neither do I want the guttersnipes to turn what we have into something sordid and tacky.'

'Excuses, excuses, and always Sebastian—'

'There's something else. I've found my ex-husband. I've tracked him down, Hal. He'd been living in Ireland for years, but now he's back in Liverpool. I've asked for a divorce and he's agreed.'

'Why didn't you tell me before?'

'I haven't had a chance. Hal, we only have to keep up this pretence for another week. Then you're off the show, I'll start divorce proceedings and we can slowly start being seen together. We can even say that's why you left the series. One more week, Hal, then all this nonsense is over.'

'I can't believe it.'

'It's true. Then we can start shouting from the rooftops. I promise.'

'Sebastian?' Hal challenged.

'I'll talk to him. Get to the bottom of all this. I won't let him come between us, Hal. I love you,' she told him, then kissed him passionately. 'I must go,' she said, breaking their embrace. 'Please tell me I haven't lost you? I couldn't bear that.'

'You haven't lost me,' Hal replied.

'Leave it with me, Hal. Everything's going to be all right.' She waved and left the room.

Ten minutes later and there was a knock on Hal's dressing room door. 'Come in,' he called.

Sebastian appeared.

Hal sighed. 'What do you want?'

'Can I come in?' he asked.

'Your mother's not here.'

'I know. She's in my dressing room. She's been crying.'

'Is that all you wanted to tell me?' Hal asked.

Sebastian nodded. 'Yes, but it's all right because I'm looking after her.'

'How reassuring.'

'We're going to be okay. You mustn't worry. We were okay before, and we'll be okay again.'

'I don't think I'm following this,' Hal confessed.

'You mustn't worry. I want you to be happy. We'll be all right.'

'So you keep saying, Sebastian, but I still don't—'

'Now that you and Mummy are finished we'll be okay. It doesn't matter. You can be happy.'

Hal's hackles rose. 'Is that what Mummy told you? That she and I were over?'

'You're leaving the show. You can't be together now. Everything can be normal again. It's okay.'

'It would be okay for you because that's what you want. What about me and, more importantly, your mother?'

'I don't understand.'

'What if she doesn't want us to be finished? What if she wants us to carry on? What if that would make her happy?'

Sebastian scowled. 'It wouldn't.'

'Have you asked her?'

'I don't need to.'

'Sebastian, the world doesn't revolve around you. People don't have to ruin their lives just to keep you happy.'

'I told you, we don't need you.'

'No, Sebastian.' Hal's temper flared. 'You don't need me, but your mother does. She told me so just a few minutes ago.'

'She didn't.'

'Yes, she did. She said she couldn't live without me, she needed me and she loved me.'

'*No!*'

'Yes. And she told me she wouldn't let anything stand in the way of our future. Not even you.'

'You're lying, pig!'

'No, I'm not. And, what's more, once I've finished on the show we won't be keeping our relationship secret any more. We won't be pretending it isn't happening, for your sake. And you won't be able to pretend it isn't happening either.'

'I've warned you. Haven't you got it, stupid? I've tried to warn you. Don't make me do things!'

'And don't you threaten me, Sebastian. What can you do to me? I'm a grown man. You're just a kid.'

'I warned you for your own good.'

'You just didn't want me to be with your mother. There's nothing more you can do to me. You've already got me sacked from the show and that's backfired on you because it's given your mother and me the opportunity to be together. The war between us is over, Sebastian. We might as well try to get along. I suggest you make an effort for your mother's sake. Now, if you don't mind, I'd like some time to go through my lines. We've a recording to do.'

Hal strode purposefully to the dressing room door and opened it.

Sebastian shuffled out then faced Hal. He looked sad. 'You're a dead man,' he whispered.

'Forget it, Sebastian,' Hal said, and closed the door.

During the dress rehearsal Hal's last words to Sebastian came back to haunt him. He was feeling strangely liberated. The tech run had gone well. Now, free of the worry of having to perform well to stay in the job, he was flying, enjoying the work for the work's sake. As they played their way through his hysterical scene, he was giving his emotions full vent.

HAL: If your daughter finds out it was me who set her up with Eddie the Elephant, she'll go mad. You mustn't tell her.

EDWIN: I can't lie for you again. Not this time. You've gone too far.

HAL: It was a joke.

EDWIN: She thought he was a dancer.

HAL: I know.

EDWIN: He's a male stripper.

HAL: I know.

EDWIN: Eddie the Elephant is his stage name. With some justification, so I'm told.

HAL: It was just a joke.

EDWIN: Setting your ex-wife up with a stripper is one thing. Organising him to attend her birthday celebrations as a stripper-gram is going too far, I tell you.

HAL: Bill. I'm desperate. (*Crosses to kitchen drawer and takes out knife.*) I might as well end it now. If you tell your daughter I'm responsible, I'm a dead man anyway. (*Makes a couple of exaggerated slashes at wrist with knife.*)

EDWIN: You can't make me feel sorry for you again. Not this time . . . Oh, God. Oh, God he's bleeding. Help, someone, he's bleeding!

There was a moment of stunned silence, before bedlam took over.

Hal stared at his bleeding wrist. He could make out some things that were being said. Cries for cloths, or towels. Hal thought they were worried about the set. He forgot all about compressing a bleeding wound. He heard someone question how a sharp knife had come to be on the set. Something about getting a car organised and hospital.

All the time Hal just kept staring at his wounds in disbelief.

A thought ran through his mind. He had spoken too soon.

The child could still frighten him. Though judging by the look of things, probably for the last time.

His knees buckled and he lost his fight to stay conscious.

24

A mixture of thoughts went through Hal's mind as he sat in Casualty having his wrist stitched. It was the third time this job had landed him in a hospital ward: Mr Warburton's head-butt, the coffee-table incident, and now this. Fortunately, each time the injury had turned out to be less serious than was first feared. His nose hadn't been broken, he hadn't been concussed, and now, thankfully, he wasn't going to bleed to death. However, four sutures seemed a paltry number compared to the amount of blood he thought he'd lost. Somehow he didn't think he'd be so lucky a fourth time. Mrs Worrel wasn't as batty as she seemed, with her tea-leaves and prophecies of doom. She had warned him not to take the job and now he knew why.

The doctor had told Hal to go home, that he was fine physically but that he was suffering from shock. Then, having administered an anti-tetanus injection, he disappeared. A minute later Tom, the assistant floor manager who had driven Hal to hospital, popped his head round the curtain. He held a mobile phone, and looked stressed. 'Listen, Hal, nobody wants to force you into anything, but do you want to do the recording now or not? I have to let Tony know – they've got to tell the studio audience as soon as possible if they have to cancel it.'

In no other profession would Hal have been asked to continue working and he wanted to say, 'Get stuffed.' But old habits die hard. 'I'll do it,' he said.

'Good man,' Tom said, and then, into the mobile phone, 'He's on. We're on our way.'

When he got back, everyone wanted to talk to him – except Sebastian – and be his friend again. Not because they were sympathetic, or concerned, Hal knew, but because he had shown up. He hadn't ruined the show.

Tony thanked him, said how brave he was, promised a full inquiry into what had happened, told him a car was available to take him home after the show.

Jake was genuinely worried. 'Dear boy, are you okay?'

'Yes.'

'You will sue the bastards, naturally?'

'I might.'

'Okay, what do you want? Hot strong tea? Or a large Scotch?'

'Both.'

'Your wish is my command, oh injured one.' He nursed Hal through the rest of the show.

In the end, the recording began only fifteen minutes late, and at the end Tony congratulated Hal, as did various members of the cast. Eventually Jake appeared in his dressing room, washed and changed. 'Time for a little more medicine of the grain variety,' he suggested. 'You can either drink it or pour it on to your wound. I shall leave the choice to you.'

'You go ahead of me,' Hal told him. 'I'll join you in the bar shortly.'

'Is it wise for me to leave you alone?'

'Please, Jake.'

'Very well. Anything else I can do for you?'

'Yes. Find my friend Belinda for me. Look after her until I get there, will you?'

'Certainly. How will I know what she looks like?'

'I've told her to stand just inside the entrance. She'll find you, probably. I've told her what you look like and, anyway, she saw you in the show.'

'I hope my uniquely distinguished features are as impressive in the flesh. Don't be long.'

'I won't,' Hal promised.

Then he was alone. The adrenaline that had pumped around his body to see him through the recording drained away. He began to shake uncontrollably.

Belinda was waiting in the bar when Jessica came in with Sebastian. They walked right past her without acknowledging her. Again Belinda was struck by something vaguely familiar about the woman. To her surprise, Belinda found that she was snarling under her breath.

Jake found Belinda just inside the doorway to the bar, just as Hal had said. She recognised him instantly.

The warm-up man had announced that Hal wasn't well and Belinda had spent the whole recording worrying. She asked Jake what had happened, and turned pale as he filled in the details. 'So it wasn't the same knife?'

'The prop-knife had been specially blunted. Looks like some idiot lackey cocked up and put the wrong knife in the drawer.'

'Or Sebastian did. Hal's convinced the child's got it in for him.'

'I know, my dear. And he may be right. There's some evidence to suggest he had Hal removed from the series. But this? Hal might have been killed. Yet he's off the show so why would Sebastian want to harm him?'

Perhaps it was panic that made her betray Hal's

confidence. 'Because Hal's been having a secret affair with Sebastian's mother.'

Jake's jaw dropped.

'And Sebastian is obsessively against it.'

'So that's why he warned me off speaking to her,' Jake said.

'Did he?'

'Yes. I only had a couple of brief chats. I thought I recognised her, you see.'

'So did I. Don't you think she looks a bit like Nicole Kidman or someone?'

'At first I did. But I think it goes much further back. I think I knew her father, when he and I were starting out. Lived down on the east coast somewhere.'

'Jessica's obsessed with her son's career. Look, Hal will be here any minute – would you mind if I telephoned you? I've been a bit sceptical about all this and I'm a psychiatrist.'

'I would willingly lie down on your couch and unburden myself at the slightest encouragement.'

Belinda chuckled. 'I don't mean to be dramatic, but when knives are involved . . . I might want to pick your brains. After all, you've been around the set, while I'm only hearing things second-hand.'

'Of course, dear girl.' He took out a pen and notebook, wrote down his number, tore the page from the pad and handed it to her.

Belinda tucked it into her pocket. Before either of them could say any more, Hal walked into the bar and straight to them.

'Jake told me what happened,' Belinda said, and hugged him.

'It's okay,' he said, but the haunted look in his eyes told a different story.

Jake handed him a Scotch. He downed it in one.

'Listen, Belinda, I'm going to go home in a minute, if you don't mind.'

'No, of course not,' Belinda replied.

'They've laid a car on for me. Does either of you want a lift?'

Jake saw the concern in Belinda's eyes. And something else. Time for him to step aside, he thought. 'No, thank you, dear boy. I've been on my best behaviour for over a week now. I feel the need to drink a little of the grape, and insult a few more people before I make my exit.'

Hal didn't have the strength to argue.

'I'll call you tomorrow, dear boy.'

'I'll take you up on the lift,' Belinda said.

'Okay. Give me a minute – there's something I have to ask someone before I go,' he told her, and scanned the room. Jessica was in the corner where she and Sebastian always sat. Hal headed towards her. Every step frightened him because the child was there too, where he always was, joined to her hip, as if he was protecting her.

He gazed at Sebastian as he neared the table. The child looked manic.

Then he turned to Jessica. 'Is it true?'

'Hal, not here. We agreed, one more week,' she whispered.

'Is it true? The prop-knife. He told me,' he said, pointing to Sebastian. 'Has something else gone missing from your flat other than wine and food?'

'Hal, please, I don't understand.'

'The prop-knife. Do you have a set of knives like it in your house? I want to know.'

Jessica put her arm protectively around her son. 'No,' she said, 'we don't.'

'You fucking liar!' Hal spat, and stalked away.

25

He sat in the back of the car with Belinda. It was the same driver who had driven him to Jake's house. 'Tooting again, is it, mate?' he asked.

'No,' Belinda replied. 'Crouch End.'

Hal stared at her.

'You're in no fit state to be by yourself tonight. You'll just have to let me look after you,' she told him.

Later, Hal sat on the blue sofa, still shaking, 'Ouch!' he said.

'What's wrong?'

'The painkillers must be wearing off. My bloody wrist's killing me.'

'Let me see,' she said, lifting up his arm. 'This feels too tight. Wait there.'

She returned a few minutes later with a bowl of water, some cotton wool, scissors, a towel and a clean bandage. 'I'll sort you out,' she told him.

'You'd better be careful. I might bleed all over your carpet.'

'You'd better not.' Belinda smiled. 'Brace yourself.' When she had finished, Hal smiled at her. 'What would I do without you?' he said, and ruffled her hair with his good hand.

'I dread to think.'

'I'm scared, Belinda,' he said.

'I know, but no one's going to hurt you tonight. I'm here. We'll decide what to do in the morning. Okay? Come on. I think it's time you went to bed.' She led him into the spare bedroom. 'I'll get you a small brandy. It'll help you sleep,' she told him.

When she returned to the bedroom, he was wincing. 'What's wrong?' she asked, putting the glass on the bed-side cabinet.

'I can't undo my shirt buttons. It's agony.'

She undid them for him. He watched her. Then she removed his shirt. She smiled, and he smiled back. They looked into each other's eyes for a long time, and an unspoken message passed between them.

She removed his shoes and socks, then his trousers, and slid his boxer shorts over his thighs. She pulled back the duvet and gently helped him into the bed.

Then she removed her own clothes and got in with him. 'I don't want you to be in pain. I don't want you to be scared. And I don't want you to say or do anything,' she told him. Then slowly, purposefully, she made love to him.

He stopped shaking and the pain disappeared. He felt calm, soothed, loved. For the first time in years he wasn't scared of failing as an actor, or of facing life without his ex-wife, or of losing Jessica. And he wasn't scared of Sebastian.

When she awoke she reached out for him to find nothing but space. She sat upright.

'Hal?' she called, and jumped out of bed.

'In here.' His voice came from the sitting room.

She dashed in to find him on one of the sofas, drinking coffee. He was still naked.

'You scared me.'

'Sorry. I didn't want to wake you. I needed to think.'

'About Sebastian?'

'Partly,' he said.

'What have you come up with?'

'I have no proof. There's nothing I can do. I just have to get through next week.'

'I don't think he can risk doing anything else, Hal, not now he's gone so far. Keep a low profile, and come back here at night. You should be okay. Then we can talk about what to do in the long-term.'

'Come back here?' Hal queried.

'Yes. I can't have you alone in that flat by yourself. I'd be worried sick.'

'I can't stay here, Belinda. I can't put you at risk.'

'You won't. He thinks I'm pretty, remember? And – please don't take this the wrong way – I don't think you should see Jessica for a while. It will aggravate the situation.'

'I don't think I can avoid it. I'm going to have to talk to her soon.'

'Why's that?' Belinda asked.

'She's going to start divorce proceedings if I don't.'

Belinda looked confused.

'She's still married.'

'Hal!'

'Calm down, Belinda.'

'She's still married! After all that happened between you and Amy—'

'It's not like that. Her husband did a runner when Sebastian was born. She didn't divorce him at the time because she was building up her business, and she didn't want him to rip her off through the courts.'

'What business?' Belinda asked, tensely.

'She owns some shops on the coast somewhere. Her ex disappeared so she just let things lie. She says she hasn't had another relationship until now and—'

'Do you believe that?'

'It's what she says.'

'Poor Sebastian. No wonder he's funny about men and his mother,' Belinda said.

'That's no reason to sabotage tables, switch knives—'

Belinda held up her hands. 'I know. I'm sorry.'

'Anyway, it's beside the point,' Hal said. 'I've got to stop her divorcing her estranged husband on my behalf. And not just because of her psychotic son.'

'I never said he was psychotic.'

'You're not listening.'

'Okay. What other reasons are there?'

'Last night, Belinda.'

'Oh.' She blushed. 'Listen, Hal darling, it was wonderful. I don't regret it. I love you. Well, you know that. But last night was last night. If you love Jessica it must be left at that.'

Hal shook his head. 'I thought I loved Jessica. I thought I loved Amy. But last night . . . Amy was about youthful ignorance and Jessica, well, discovering passion again, or feeling good about myself after a terrible year. I'm not sure.'

'Hal—'

'Do you think it's possible to spend your life looking for something . . . someone, and have them under your nose all the time?'

Belinda's heart-rate doubled. 'Yes.'

'I have to be careful. I have to get this right. I don't want to think I feel something for you because I have problems with Jessica. Or because I'm petrified of Sebastian. I'm almost certain but I have to think this through. I have to go back to my flat, Belinda.'

'No, Hal. Please.'

'Just for a day or two.'

'I'll be worried sick!'

'I'll call you. And I've got a spare set of keys to my flat in my rucksack. You have them. If I don't call by eight o'clock tonight, come over and let yourself in.'

'You carry a spare set of keys?' Belinda asked, puzzled.

'Always. I went through a stage of locking myself out. There's one other thing. You'll have to help me get dressed – my bloody wrist is killing me again.'

The minute Hal got into his flat the mobile rang. He didn't answer it. But he called Belinda as promised, and told her he was missing her.

At rehearsal on Tuesday Hal felt isolated. There was no Jake for support and the cast were avoiding him again. That was fine. It gave him time to think.

Tony spoke to him during the coffee-break. 'A full inquiry has begun into Sunday's incident, Hal, instigated by the powers that be. They want me to reassure you that they'll get to the bottom of it.'

'I doubt that,' Hal said.

'They have some daft idea that you might take legal action.'

'And they're quite right, Tony.'

Sebastian didn't speak to Hal, and as they did not have a scene together in the final episode, they didn't act together either.

As Hal was trying to avoid eye-contact with Jessica he did not know if she was watching him. He didn't want to see or speak to her until he was sure of what he wanted to say.

When she got home Belinda found Hal on her doorstep. 'Hi,' he said. 'I just wanted to see you.'

Half an hour later they were next to each other on the sofa. 'I'm going to tell her it's over,' Hal announced. 'I want out.'

'When will you do it?'

'Not over the phone or at rehearsals. I may get an opportunity at the recording on Sunday.'

'Come back here after today's rehearsal,' she told him.

'I will,' he promised.

Belinda awoke at three thirty a.m. She was troubled. Try as she might she could not get back to sleep. This business with Sebastian didn't make sense. She planted a kiss on Hal's forehead and slipped out of the bed, put on her robe and went into her kitchen. As she filled the kettle she decided to call Jake.

At rehearsal the next day, Sebastian stared blankly into space. He was withdrawn. He clung to his mother. Maybe it was guilt: he was afraid Hal would go to the police over the knife incident.

Hal was unsure. But he had changed. Somehow this made him seem more dangerous. Hal got on with the work.

Belinda retrieved Jake's number from her jacket pocket and called him first thing in the morning. At first he was sleepy and uncommunicative, but she persevered. 'Jake, what were you saying the other night about recognising Jessica? We were saying she looked like someone famous.'

'Oh, yes!' Jake roared. 'But it's her father I really remember. Or, at least, I thought I did. Mind you, I'm going back thirty years or more.'

'Go on.'

'Must I? Couldn't we chew the fat at a more civilised time? Perhaps over a glass of claret?'

'Bear with me, Jake. It may be important.'

'Very well. I was just out of drama school, playing something insignificant in a number-one tour. Gerald, the man I thought was Jessica's father, was playing something equally insignificant. But it was a number-one tour and it probably still ranks as my greatest theatrical success. It was all the sweeter for Gerald because the tour took in the Theatre Royal, Brighton, which was where he lived. His missus had inherited a bob or two, so he wasn't as impoverished as the rest of us, which was probably why I liked him. Always good for a round of drinks, was Gerald—'

'Yes, Jake, forgive me interrupting, but why do you think you recognised Jessica?'

'Well, Gerald had a daughter. Always had her picture stuck above the dressing-room mirror. Never a picture of the wife – she must have had a face like the back of a tram smash, I suppose.'

'Did you ever meet the daughter?'

'Briefly. Gerald and I understudied the leading men. He brought the child to an understudy rehearsal. Had a bit of a career herself – I seem to remember she had the chance to go to America, Disney or some such, but her father stopped her. Couldn't bear to see her go, I think. Is any of this helping?'

'I'm not sure.'

'Only I'm afraid I've rather lost the plot.'

'Oh, I'm sorry, Jake. It's this business with Hal and Sebastian. All these weird happenings. It doesn't make sense.'

'I know what you mean. It's hard to think of the Nation's Poppet as a dangerous loony, isn't it?'

' "The Nation's Poppet"! Where did *that* come from?'

'Some newspaper article. According to Edwin, Jessica thought it up. She's responsible for most of the boy's PR, apparently.'

There was a pause, then Jake said, 'You're worried about Hal, aren't you?'

Belinda sighed. 'Yes. Still, only one more recording, then he doesn't have to see Sebastian again.'

'And if we can persuade him not to see the child's mother either, so much the better.'

'Quite.'

'I'll leave that to you, shall I?' Jake suggested.

Belinda smiled. 'Yes, Jake.'

'Call me if I can be of any further service.'

'I will,' she assured him, and hung up.

Something was niggling at the back of Belinda's mind, trying to prise open a door in her memory . . .

On Sunday, recording day, Jessica came to him in his dressing room. 'Hal, I can't stop. They'll notice I'm missing.'

'Jessica, I have something to tell you.'

'Later. I've found out some things about Sebastian. I think you're right. In fact, I'm certain you are. We need to talk – not here, not today, tomorrow.'

'Jessica—'

'I'll come to your flat. Sebastian's going to Tony's tomorrow. They have a night out together at the end of every series. I'll cook us a meal. I'll be there at seven. Hal, he scares me.'

'Who scares you?' Hal asked.

'Sebastain. Can you imagine that? I'm terrified of my own child. Please say we can talk tomorrow.'

'Okay.'

'I must go. He mustn't know I was here.'

*

After the show Hal did not go to the bar. Instead he went straight to reception where Belinda was waiting as arranged. 'How did she take the news?' she asked, after they hugged.

'I didn't tell her.'

'Oh.'

'I'll explain when we get home,' he promised.

Later they sat on the sofa and Hal recounted the conversation he had had with Jessica. 'She's frightened of her own son. She looks dreadful.'

'So what will you do now?'

'I'll let her cook the meal and tell me what she's found out. I think it best that I do. I want to know if I'm still one of her son's targets.'

'And if she's convinced about Sebastian, are you still going to tell her it's over?' Belinda asked anxiously.

'Of course. It's not just about Sebastian any more, is it? It's about you and me.'

'I'm not sure I like the idea of you seeing her again.'

'I'll behave myself.'

'I know,' Belinda replied unconvincingly.

'Look, I gave you my spare set of keys. If I haven't rung you by nine, you can come round and drag me out. I won't change my mind, Belinda.'

Belinda smiled. After so long, it was finally beginning to look as if she might get to share her life with the man she loved.

26

Belinda sat bolt upright in bed. She had been falling asleep thinking about Hal, Jessica, Sebastian . . . and Jake, when the penny had dropped.

'Poppet!' she said aloud.

She might be wrong, of course.

'Hal!'

He was no longer lying beside her.

She put on her robe and searched for him. She found a note by the kettle in the kitchen.

Hi,

Couldn't sleep. In a bit of a paddy about tonight. Thought I'd better go home and tidy up, etc. Then I can rehearse exactly what I'm going to say. I hate having to ad lib. I'd rather be well prepared.

Don't worry. I'm sure everything will go okay.

Anyway, I had to go home. I didn't have any clean socks or underwear. I hate wearing the same kecks two days running.

Jessica's coming round at seven tonight.

I'll come straight over afterwards, complete with toothbrush and change of undies.

Take care until then.

All my love,

Hal

XXXX

For a moment, Belinda almost laughed.

Then her fear returned.

She thought of telephoning Hal right away, then had second thoughts. What if she was wrong?

She tried to think calmly. She would telephone the office and call in sick. She needed to make some phone calls, do some fast research, track someone down, get things confirmed. She'd do this first, then ring Hal.

As she made her way to the bathroom, she prayed that that was the right thing to do.

Belinda came out of the shower wrapped in a towel, picked up the telephone and called Mary.

'Hello.'

'Mary? It's Belinda.'

'Hello, stranger.'

'Sorry, I've been busy. I've had a house guest.'

'Who?'

'Hal.'

'Way to go, kiddo!'

'I'll fill you in later. Listen, the reason I'm phoning is to let you know I've just phoned in sick.'

'And are you?'

'No. I need to get in touch with someone. I'll "feel better" later this morning. If anyone asks before I get there, you saw me yesterday and I looked dreadful.'

'Got you.'

'Thanks, Mary. Listen, are you free tonight?'

'Lesbianism as well now, is it?'

'Will you behave. Are you around or not?' Belinda persisted.

'Yes. Sadly.'

'Do you mind coming over after work? I could use someone around.'

'Why's that, then?'

'Probably just to stop me being daft.'

'Is that the *Mission Impossible* theme I hear playing in the background?' Mary asked.

'Very funny.'

'Don't worry. I can squeeze you into my busy schedule. And don't think you're going to get away with glossing over your sordid liaison with a TV star.'

'See you later, Mary. Oh, one more thing. You don't remember a film called *Poppet*, do you?'

'Must have been before my time.'

'Never mind. We'll talk later.' Belinda replaced the receiver. 'Belinda, you need to raid the archives,' she told herself.

Belinda sat in the reference library, pages of microfiche strewn about her. It had taken several hours but at last she had found what she was looking for. Three separate articles from *The Times*. The headlines were not huge, the articles not prominent: the film *Poppet* had not been especially successful. Yet as a young girl Belinda had loved it. Her mother had taken her to see it twice. It was an old-fashioned rags-to-riches tale. She decided to go to the office. There was someone she needed to contact urgently.

Seconds after Belinda had arrived Mary bounded into her office. 'I've come to interrogate you,' she said. 'Bring me up to speed on what's been happening with you and lover-boy?'

Belinda gave her a quick précis of events.

'Wow,' Mary said, when she had finished. 'How wonderful. How dramatic. So he's going to tell Jessica it's all over tonight?'

'That's the plan.'

'So all's well that ends well. The Nation's Poppet is

happy – he's got Mummy to himself again – Jessica is out of the frame, Hal's not on the series any more, and you and Hal are going at it like rabbits, and can live happily ever after.'

'I'm not sure it's as simple as that. I have a bad feeling.'

'Oh, Belinda, stop being such a pessimist. I take it the reason you want me around tonight is just in case Hal changes his mind?'

'Not exactly.'

'You're not having second thoughts about him, are you?'

'Of course not,' Belinda assured her.

'Only sometimes when you want something so badly, it can be a bit of a disappointment when you actually get your hands on it. I found that out early when I finally got my hands on a Barbie Doll. I dare say, if Mum had bought me Ken instead, I'd have happily fiddled around with him for hours.'

'No, I'm not disappointed, Mary.'

Mary screwed up her face. 'Then what *is* worrying you?'

'I'll tell you later. I've got to speak to someone first. You *are* still coming round tonight, aren't you?'

'Try to stop me.'

After Mary had left the room Belinda picked up the phone and dialled. 'Hello. Yes, I wonder if you can. Does Geoffrey Gaskill still work there? I see. You don't know where he works now, do you?'

When Hal got back to the flat there was a message on his answering-machine. It was from Sebastian: 'I know you're seeing Mummy tonight. I warned you for your own good. You're a dead man.'

Hal shook his head. 'One more night, you little shit,'

he said, 'and then I'm out of your life and you don't have to worry any more.'

It was five o'clock. Belinda had tried to contact Gaskill once more without success. She had rung him at work and at home, and left messages for him to call her at her flat. She picked up her briefcase, and left the office.

At six o'clock Hal's doorbell rang. 'Who the hell can that be?' he asked himself.

He went downstairs and opened the front door.

'Hello there,' said Jessica. 'Sorry. I had an opportunity to leave early so I thought I might as well come over. It'll give us a bit more time to talk.'

Hal stepped aside and let her in. He noticed she was carrying a small suitcase. 'Don't worry, I'm not moving in. It's full of food for the meal, with some plates and cutlery. I couldn't remember what you had so I thought I'd better come prepared,' she told him.

Hal led the way to his flat. They went in, and he closed the door.

'You don't mind me being early, do you?' she asked.

'Not really, but I'm not ready. I was intending to have a shower.'

'Ooo, can I join you?'

'Er . . .'

Jessica's face fell. 'Only joking,' she said. 'You go and have your shower. I'll pop into the kitchen and start cooking.'

Hal turned towards the bathroom.

'Hal.'

'Yes?'

'I missed you. I know that's not what you want to hear, under the circumstances, and who can blame you? I've found out so much about Sebastian . . . and I feel so bad because I didn't believe you when you said – and I'm scared. And—' Jessica fought tears. 'Anyway, all I'm saying is, please give me a chance to explain.'

'Sure,' Hal replied, then went into the bathroom. He didn't shower. Instead, he just turned on the water, sat on the floor, and thought.

At six-thirty Belinda was pacing around her sitting room.
'For goodness sake, what are you doing?' Mary asked.
'I just want this person to call me.'
'Who?'
'Someone I used to work with.'
'Do they know something about Hal?'
'No.'
'Then what?'
'I'll tell you when I'm sure.'

The table was laid, and the food served at almost exactly seven.
'Thank you,' Hal said flatly, as the pasta was put before him.
'It's the least I could do,' Jessica said. 'Sorry there's no starter but pudding's in the fridge. Wine?'
'Please.'
Jessica poured him a generous glass of red. 'I know red's your favourite. I'm on white, so you have a whole bottle to yourself.'

At seven-thirty the call for which Belinda had been waiting came through. She picked up the phone. 'Hello?'
'Belinda, Geoffrey Gaskill here. Long time no see. I hear you've been trying to get hold of me all day. What can I do for you?'
'I want you to cast your mind back to when I first came to work with you in Brighton . . .'

Jessica put out her cigarette in the glass ashtray Hal kept for guests. 'You were right about Sebastian, Hal. He didn't want us to be together. He knew exactly what he was doing when he fed you the wrong cues that Sunday. He did steal wine from the flat and get Jake drunk, and he told Jake you hated him.'

'I knew it,' Hal said grimly.

'I swear I had no idea. It gets worse. It was Sebastian who loosened the leg on the coffee-table so that you would fall, and he put the letter and that effigy in your rucksack. We do have a set of knives almost identical to the prop-knife. They're not even mine – they belong to Sebastian's agent. They came with the flat.'

'Did he swap one with the prop-knife?'

'Oh, yes. He almost went too far that time. Having said that, his mistake might work to our advantage.'

'Our advantage?' Hal questioned.

Mary got into the car next to Belinda. 'Where are we going, and why the rush?' she asked.

'I'll explain on the way.'

'Have you gone mad? Who was that on the telephone?'

'Geoffrey Gaskill.'

'Who's he?'

Belinda started the car and pulled away from the kerb. 'My old boss.'

'So what was the call about?'

'A former patient of his. Someone I remember him treating when I first joined his clinic.'

'I still don't understand why Sebastian did all those terrible things to me.' Hal felt woozy suddenly, and shook his head to clear it.

Jessica stared at him. She took a drag from yet another cigarette.

He was beginning to feel unwell – lethargic and faint. He swayed on the chair.

'Are you all right?' Jessica asked.

'I feel terrible,' Hal confessed.

Jessica stubbed out her cigarette. 'You need to lie down. Let me help you on to the sofa.' She supported him across the room. He was surprised by how strong she was. She put a cushion under his head.

'Now,' she said, sitting on the floor by the sofa, 'what were we saying? Why did Sebastian pick on you? Yes, I can tell you now. It all began with my father, really. He was an actor, too. So was my mother, before she gave up her career to marry him. My father was also a drunk, an adulterer and a loser. I lost count of the times I saw him drive his fist into my mother's face. And when she hit the floor he used his feet. She tolerated it for years.'

'Jessica—'

'Then one day he finished hurting Mummy and turned on me.'

'Start again, but slow down. You don't have to talk as fast as you're driving,' Mary said.

'Okay. When I went to Hal's flat to look Sebastian over, I thought Jessica looked familiar, like someone famous, or perhaps an old friend, but I didn't dwell on it. Then I saw her in the bar at the BBC. It was something Jake said that triggered my memory.'

'What did he say?'

'He also thought at first that Jessica looked like somebody well known, but then he recognised her. He told me he worked with her father, remembered that she had been a child actress. And that she had been

280

responsible for coining the phrase "The Nation's Poppet". I twigged.'

Mary wrinkled her nose. 'Go on.'

'*Poppet* was the title of a film I loved when I was a child. It was a fore-runner to *Little Orphan Annie*. I wanted to be the little girl in the film. She had red hair and beautiful eyes. The actress who played her was called Jessica.'

'How do you know it was the same Jessica?'

'I've trawled through archive press cuttings. It's her.'

'Was the film famous?'

'Not in its own right. There were far more cuttings about what happened to the little girl's parents. That's what I remembered. That's what I went to look up.'

'I was a success, I could have gone to Hollywood – Disney were interested in me,' Jessica told Hal, 'but Daddy stopped me. He said it was time for me to stop acting, to stay at home and be Daddy's little girl. That's when he started coming to me. He would come into my bedroom and hurt me. "Daddy knows best," he would say, when I cried. My mother said he didn't deserve to be a father, nobody like him did, that he deserved to die.'

'Then one morning, the three of us went for a walk on the cliffs. My father was already drunk. I don't think he'd been to bed. And there we were, all alone, with no one else in sight.'

'The cuttings were about the trial – "Poppet's Father In Tragic Fall", "Poppet's Mother Arrested", "Poppet's Mother Convicted".

'So Jessica's mother went to prison for murdering Jessica's father.'

'Yes. Crime of passion, diminished responsibility, et

cetera. Apparently he'd beaten her. He had a reputation for it locally.' Belinda threw the car into a sharp right-hand turn.

'And when did all this happen?'

'Over thirty years ago.'

'I don't see what bearing it has on what's happening today.'

'I don't think the mother pushed Jessica's father off the cliff. I think Jessica did it.'

'That's a bit of a leap,' Mary said. 'If you'll forgive the expression.'

'I know, but there are more connections. My first decent job was in Brighton. I stayed there for years. My boss, Geoffrey Gaskill, had a particular patient when I first arrived in Brighton, a woman. She was suffering a severe mental trauma after her husband's death. Gradually Geoffrey traced the root of her problem. Her family had lived in Eastbourne, and when she was about eight, her father was pushed off Beachy Head.'

'Oh,' said Mary, 'I'm beginning to see where this is going.'

'We stood there, on the cliff's edge, with my father cursing my mother, calling her a slut and a whore, threatening to beat her again. And I just pushed him over the edge. He fell to his death. He didn't scream, he never made a sound. We stood there for ages.'

'My face,' Hal stuttered. 'It feels funny. Can't feel my mouth.'

Jessica took his right hand and kissed it. 'Don't worry, darling. That will be the drug.'

'Drug?' Hal dribbled. 'How . . .'

'Injected through the cork of the red-wine bottle. And you drank it. What a good boy you are.'

'You've . . . poisoned me.'

'No, darling. I haven't. My mother told me I mustn't worry, that I'd done the right thing. The man wasn't fit to be a father. No actor was. She said people would be cross, but that she would take the blame. She made me promise never to tell anyone. It would be our secret. And they locked her up when I was the one who should have been in jail. She refused to see me. I was fostered. I had a good education and qualified as a pharmacist. I became a good businesswoman, opened a couple of shops. Then I met my husband.'

'How did you know that Geoffrey's patient all those years ago was Jessica?' Mary asked.

'I wasn't sure at first,' Belinda admitted. 'It came to me slowly. I remember Geoffrey telling me about her father and her husband, and the acting connection, and then I remembered him mentioning that film and the trial. But there was something else he recalled when I spoke to him. She never finished her treatment.' Belinda circum-navigated a roundabout. 'When Geoffrey was treating her she was traumatised over the death of her husband. What made things worse was that she was heavily pregnant. The treatment was stopped while she gave birth. She never came back. I presume that's when she high-tailed it to London.'

'And all this was how long ago?'

'About eight years.'

Mary's mind ticked over. 'And Sebastian is—'

'About eight.'

'This is getting serious. What about her husband?'

'It gets worse. He was also an actor.'

'And how did he die?' Mary asked.

'Now here's a coincidence for you. He also died in suspicious circumstances of a drug overdose.'

Mary turned pale.

'John – that was my husband's name – was such fun at first, kind and attentive, so I married him. It was when I moved to Brighton with him that I found out just how like Daddy he was. He drank like Daddy, punched like Daddy, and in my bedroom he hurt me like Daddy too. He didn't stop at drink either – it began with pot, then pills, cocaine and heroin. He was spending all my money.'

'Jessica . . . you said . . . husband . . . ran away . . .' Hal slurred.

'Don't fight the drugs, darling. You can't. Just give in to them.'

'Jess . . .'

'Yes, I know I told you that. I lied. I became pregnant with Sebastian. Still my husband beat me. Then Mummy came back. She'd been out of jail for over a year before she contacted me. She was using a different name – her old stage name, in fact – and was trying to start a new life. She said we shouldn't tell anyone we were related, because people might remember the past. She said she had had many years to brood on it and she was convinced I was a heroine to have killed Daddy.

'Then she met my husband, and she saw . . . she knew. She said I had to act. She said he didn't deserve to be a father. She kept on and on at me. She said he mustn't become a father, because when an actor becomes a father he starts to think that Daddy knows best and we knew what that meant. I couldn't allow it, could I? I couldn't let him visit my child like Daddy had visited me. So, one night, I gave him a little bit more methadone than he needed. He had a stash from the doctor for when he couldn't get his hands on heroin. I just added to the dose. It was easy. And everyone thought it was an accident.'

Belinda handed Mary her mobile phone. She was driving at fifty miles an hour with one hand on the steering-wheel.

'Are you trying to get us killed?' Mary shouted.

'Telephone Hal. I tried to before we left but it was engaged.'

'What's the number?'

Belinda told her and Mary punched it in. 'It's still engaged,' she said.

'It can't be! Something's wrong. Keep trying!'

Mary pressed redial. 'Still engaged.'

'We'd better hurry,' Belinda said, her foot flat on the floor.

'So why is Jessica going after Hal? Fathers? Okay. Husbands? Maybe. But why Hal?'

'Geoffrey found out that she has a downer on actors. But whatever, we're dealing with a very sick mind here.'

'So Hal's just unlucky?'

'I think it's more calculated than that. What about Ian Wilson?' Belinda said.

'The one who committed suicide!' Mary exploded.

'Did he?'

'You don't think Jessica—'

'What if Jessica had an affair with him too? She insisted her thing with Hal was kept secret for Sebastian's sake. What if she did the same with Ian Wilson? And the real reason for the secrecy was so—'

'She could murder him.' Mary finished Belinda's sentence.

'And make it look like suicide.'

'And now Hal,' Mary said.

'I was sick for a long time after my husband's death,' Jessica continued. She was leaning over Hal now, stroking his brow. 'I had to go to the hospital. I couldn't tell them the truth, though, could I? So what use were the nurses and the psychiatrists? Then there was my mother, constantly going on and on. So I came to London. I didn't tell Mother where I was going, I just took off. As Sebastian got older he started to take after his father. He began doing school plays. He said he wanted to be an actor. I couldn't stop it, could I?'

Saliva dribbled out of Hal's mouth. He felt as if he was under water: Jessica's voice echoed, and it was difficult to understand what she was saying to him.

'And then it came to me, the vision. He would be a star and a gentleman. He would be well-mannered and polite, and people would love him. He would show all the low-lifes how it should be done. He wouldn't beat women or drink, like his grandfather and father. He would be the perfect poppet. Just as I was. He would be the star I could have been if my daddy had let me. But Daddy knew best.'

She ran her hands through her hair. 'It took time, but it worked. I made my son a star. Ian Wilson became fond of Sebastian. They were quite close. But then he began acting like a father to him. I couldn't have that. Mother said it mustn't happen. He might hurt Sebastian like Daddy hurt me. Ian even said it. I heard him. He said, "Daddy knows best"!'

'That was . . . his . . . character . . . in the show.' Hal had to force the words out.

'So I began an affair with him.'

Jessica registered the fear in Hal's eyes. 'Oh, does it hurt you, darling, that I had a secret affair with Ian too? Then I cooked him a meal. I drugged him. And then I slit his wrists with a razor blade. I killed him, Hal. He was an easy target. He was depressed. He was a compulsive gambler with huge debts. He owed more money than he could have hoped to repay. Everyone thought it was suicide. But I killed him, my love, just like I'm going to kill you.'

'It's a bit risky, isn't it,' Mary asked, 'killing another actor from the same show?'

'Hal isn't on the show any more, is he? Anyway, it depends on the type of mind thinking it through. Maybe she can see the headlines – "Tragedy Strikes Sit-Com Twice", "The Curse of Playing the Nation's Poppet's Father", I don't know. I think she may have gone beyond rational thought. Or perhaps something has forced her hand, making her move faster than she would have liked. The stunt with the knife seems to suggest that.'

'Hal's probably okay, then. She may want to string him along until she feels safe before she tries anything. We're probably panicking for nothing,' Mary suggested.

'Mary, Hal is going to tell her it's all over tonight. That may leave her with no choice.'

'I just hope we're in time,' Mary whispered.

'We're nearly there.'

Mary picked up the mobile phone from the dashboard, and began to dial. 'You won't get through to Hal. I'm certain of it,' Belinda told her.

'Get ready to give me his address. I'm ringing the emergency services – police, ambulance, fire engines, the lot. If we're dealing with a murdering lunatic we're going to need all the back-up we can get.'

'You're a little unlucky, my darling,' Jessica told Hal. She sat astride his prone body, stroking his chest. 'You weren't supposed to die yet. We were going to have a few more months of fun together. Events conspired against you. That old fool Jake recognised me, remembered my father. It was only a matter of time before he remembered how my father had died. And with Sebastian pulling all those stupid stunts, drawing attention to us like that . . . Then there's your mousy little quack. What did she tell you, Hal? You can't trust psychiatrists. They manipulate your thoughts, try to make you see the world their way. They think they have all the answers, but they're more fucked-up than the rest of us. They're the easiest people on this earth to fool. Once you've dealt with one, you can deal with them all. They all look the same and sound the same. Did she massage your brain to get you into bed, Hal? I know she's bedded you. I knew you'd choose her over me.'

Hal looked into Jessica's eyes. He felt like a baby, defenceless, reliant, vulnerable.

'You almost told me it was over in your dressing room, but you would definitely have told me tonight. So you're to blame too, darling. You're forcing me to kill you now, before I miss my chance.'

Hal stared at the woman he had once thought he loved. There were tears in his eyes.

'Do you want to know something funny?' Jessica asked him. 'You were completely wrong about Sebastian, Hal. He liked you. He was trying to save you, can you believe it? After Ian died, Sebastian was very upset. I had to tell him. Mummy wanted me to tell him. I explained all about my daddy, and his daddy, and Ian, and how actors become terrible men when they are fathers and how they would have hurt Sebastian and why I could not let that happen. He knows why Mummy is doing this. We talk. Like Mummy talked to me. Why did he try to save you? I don't understand.'

Hal tried hard to focus on Jessica's speech. He tried hard to cling to life.

'All that time, all those tricks he played, you thought he was trying to kill you?' Jessica threw back her head and laughed. 'You thought Sebastian had you sacked from the series. Well, I did it. I needed that to happen. It was part of my plan. Then I could carry on manoeuvring you until I was ready.'

A husky gargle emerged from Hal's throat.

'He went too far with the knife – Sebastian, I mean. He might have ruined everything. It was all going wrong. Jake, Belinda, you and even Sebastian were spoiling my plans. Then it came to me in a flash of inspiration. I suddenly realised how to turn it to my advantage. Wait there, darling,' she said, climbed off him and crossed the room to her suitcase. She crouched beside it. The telephone plug, which she had pulled from its socket, lay on the carpet where she had left it. She opened the lid of the case. Inside were cleaning fluids, polish, rubber gloves, large black bags, everything she would need to wipe away the evidence of her presence in the room. She found what she wanted, removed it, and carried it back across the room to where Hal lay. 'Recognise this?' she asked him, holding up the blade.

Hal's eyes widened.

'That's right. It's the same knife. Those idiots at the BBC must be searching for it. Don't you see how perfect it is, Hal? You're depressed. Everyone has noticed how nervous and paranoid you've become. You've lost your starring part in the country's most popular television series. You've already been seen attempting to slash your wrists with this knife. Think how delighted the suits at the BBC will be to find it wasn't their mistake. That you *intended* to hurt yourself. That you stole the knife to finish the job. Here, in your flat. Suicide.'

She sat on the edge of the sofa.

'This is it, my darling. It's time to end it now. I have to leave soon.'

Jessica saw the panic in Hal's eyes. 'Oh, you're

frightened. You have every right to be, my love. No one can save you. It's time for you to die.'

'Check the map again,' Belinda screamed. 'It's one of these roads on the left, I know it is.'

Jessica picked up Hal's right arm and laid it on his right thigh, palm upwards. 'I've heard you say it,' she told him, as she picked up Hal's left hand and placed his fingers around the knife's handle. 'Daddy knows best, Daddy knows best,' she repeated, as she helped him scrape the blade across his right wrist. 'Well, Daddy doesn't know best!'

'My . . . part . . . in show . . .' Hal whispered slowly. 'Same . . . as Ian's . . .'

'Daddy knows best,' she chanted, and helped him drag the blade across his left wrist, severing the stitches from Hal's previous 'accident'. 'Well, you don't. You'll hurt Sebastian. I can't let that happen. Mummy wouldn't want me to. I can hear her telling me.'

'Mother not here . . . any more . . . Help . . . me,' were the last words Hal uttered.

'Of course she's here,' Jessica snapped. 'She found me, she always finds me, she never stops talking to me.'

Jessica let his left arm hang limply down the side of the sofa. 'My, what a lot of blood,' she crowed. 'Forgive me for not sitting with you. I'd love to watch you bleed to death, my darling, but I haven't time. I have to wash up, remove my fingerprints, and pack ready to leave.'

Hal couldn't hear what she was saying now. He hadn't felt the blade on his wrists. He couldn't feel the life pouring out of him. He slipped into unconsciousness.

Belinda parked in the middle of the road.

'Where are the police? They should be here by now,' Mary said.

'We can't wait. We have to go in now,' Belinda said, and unbuckled her seat-belt.

'Don't be ridiculous! There's a madwoman up there. She's dangerous, Belinda.'

'Hal's up there too, remember. I've got to help him. Show the police up when they get here.' Belinda opened the car door.

'Be sensible, Belinda! How are you going to get in?'

'I've got Hal's spare keys.' Belinda leaped out.

'Shit, shit, SHIT!' Mary cursed, as she watched Belinda running towards the flat.

Jessica was washing dishes, humming to herself, when she heard banging. She froze.

Then she heard Belinda cry out, 'Hal!'

Jessica removed the rubber gloves. She heard footsteps on the stairs.

Calmly, she walked across to the sofa and picked up the knife.

Belinda turned the key in the lock and opened the street door. 'Hal!' she yelled. She unlocked the door at the foot of the stairs, climbed them quickly, then fumbled for the key to open the flat. She burst in. 'Hal?'

Jessica came upon her from behind. She slammed Belinda against the wall, winding her, then turned her round, and flung her at the wall again. The back of Belinda's head collided with the brick. Then Jessica's hand was around her throat, squeezing. 'You interfering bitch. You should have stayed at home. How dare you interfere? Messing with people's heads.'

Jessica raised her left hand until Belinda could see the knife she held. 'You think you know it all, don't you? Well, know this. I'm going to cut your throat. You're a dead woman.'

'Stop right there, you psychotic tart.'

Before Jessica could move, Mary had gripped her left hand and banged it against the wall.

Jessica dropped the knife and let go of Belinda's throat.

Belinda slid to the floor, choking for breath.

'Just 'cause you're pretty doesn't mean you can go around killing people, you know,' Mary told Jessica, as she closed her massive arms around her. 'Now behave your fucking self.' She hurled her across the room.

Jessica crashed into the dining-table.

'All those years wrestling sixteen-stone madmen on the wards had to come in useful sometime,' Mary observed, as she rolled up her sleeves and strode towards Jessica.

She didn't notice Jessica pick up the glass ashtray. It hit her head with a sickening thud.

Mary slumped instantly to the floor, blood trickling from her right temple.

'Mary!' Belinda screamed, clambering to her feet. 'You bitch,' she shouted, and charged at Jessica, who swung her fist and drove it into Belinda's face.

Belinda dropped to her knees, holding her nose.

'Come to save your precious actor, have you?' Jessica asked. She grabbed Belinda's hair and turned her head to face the sofa. 'It's too late. He's dead,' Jessica gloated.

Belinda stared at Hal's lifeless form, saw the blood pouring out of him. 'Hal!' she screamed, and tried to stand up, but Jessica drove her knee upwards, connecting with the underside of Belinda's jaw. Then she walked across the room and picked up the knife. 'Looks like there's going to have been a lovers' suicide pact,' she announced. She sat astride Belinda and raised the knife. 'Time to make the ultimate sacrifice,' she cried, and plunged it towards Belinda's throat.

Instinctively Belinda caught hold of Jessica's arm with both hands.

'Don't make it harder for yourself.' Jessica forced the knife closer to Belinda's face. 'Your beloved Hal's dead. What's the point of living without him?' she asked.

The sound of police sirens filtered into the flat. Jessica was distracted, if only for a second, but it was enough for Belinda to gather her strength. She used her legs to force Jessica over, and fought to gain the upper position. Slowly but surely she forced the knife towards Jessica's face.

'*No!*' Jessica shrieked.

Belinda's muscles were tiring. And then Jessica struck.

With a hoarse cry, she flipped Belinda on to her back.

She felt the knife penetrate her skin, and knew the extent of the damage. She felt the heat, pain, moisture and depth of the wound. 'Hal . . . save me,' she whispered, as blood spilled from her mouth, over her lip, on to her chin, and she felt the life ebb from her.

One Year Later

Hal shook his old friend's hand as he sat down at the table in the wine bar. They hadn't seen each other for over six months. 'So how's life back at Aunty Beeb?'

'It's good, Jake. How about you? How's life in Norwich?'

'Wonderful, dear boy.'

'How did you get that gig?'

'An old friend saw my episode of *Bringing Up Ralph*. He got in touch. Chap's now a television producer in the sticks and he remembered I was a bit of a wine buff. They were looking for someone characterful, articulate, and needless to say, good-looking, to present the wine slot in a regional daytime cookery programme. I was the answer to their prayers, dear boy.'

Hal laughed. 'Are you enjoying it?'

'I get to do my three favourite things in life. Talk, drink, and show off. What's not to enjoy? What's this drama serial you're shooting?'

'Ironically, I'm playing a detective on the track of a serial killer.'

'A little close to the bone, perhaps?'

'I thought long and hard about the implications,' Hal confessed, 'and there's no doubt I've been cast partly because of what I've been through. But it's a very different story line, and I felt the need to act again.

In some ways, I'm finding it quite a cathartic experience.'

'I take it you don't bleed to death at the end of episode six, then?'

Hal smiled, ruefully. 'No.'

'That's one of the few things you haven't told me, actually. How you managed to avoid doing so on that night?'

'All down to the paramedics. They somehow managed to patch me up until they could get me to a hospital. It was touch and go for a while. However, several gallons of blood later, for which I am eternally grateful, and I'm still standing.'

'Thanks to the heroic Belinda, who, I suppose, was lucky not to have been prosecuted, when you think about it. Over Jessica Taylor's death. I mean, you hear of dafter things.'

'Her name wasn't Taylor, you know. That was actually Sebastian's stage name, which Jessica conveniently adopted. It separated her from her former identity. Her married name was Murray. Apparently the knife pierced her chest when she forced Belinda onto her back. You could almost say Jessica committed suicide. No, there was never really any chance of Belinda being prosecuted. It was self-defence.'

Jake sighed. 'It's terribly tragic, whichever way you look at it. How is the boy these days?' Jake asked.

'Sebastian? He's getting there. I haven't seen him since. Belinda doesn't think he's ready. She's treating him, by the way.'

'Is that allowed?' Jake asked.

'I think a few strings had to be pulled. Under the circumstances, since he was trying to save my life when he pulled all those stunts, we both wanted to help the lad.'

'Where is he living?'

'He was in care for a while. Just like his mother, funnily enough. But he's with a good foster family now. Belinda visits him. He doesn't like hospitals.'

'Belinda, the new Mrs Morrisey.'

'Yes indeed.'

'Sorry I couldn't make the wedding. I was working and it was short notice.'

'Yeah, bit of a rush job.' Hal blushed. 'We had a great day though. It just felt so right. Of course, Mrs Worrel insisted she'd seen it in the tea-leaves all along.'

'Mrs Worrel?'

'My old landlady remember? She also said she saw something about being a father putting my life in danger too. Anyway she was healthy and in good form. Mary was there too. When Belinda tossed her bouquet, I've never seen anyone plough through so many people with such determination. She was like an American football player going for the try line. Upshot is, she's engaged as well.'

'And did you feel obliged to marry Belinda, dear boy, because she had saved your life?'

'No. I love her. I'd spent a long time looking for the right kind of love and getting it all wrong. The crazy thing is, Belinda, the woman I'd been searching for, was sat right under my nose all the time. I just couldn't see it.'

'All's Well That Ends Well, as the Bard once said,' Jake observed. 'Now, how about the filthy rich star of TV drama buying the pitifully paid cameo performer on regional television another drink?'

Hal laughed and made his way to the bar.

Belinda was gathering her notes together and putting them into a suitcase. Mrs Daniels, Sebastian's foster mother, always allowed them to use the sitting room for their sessions. She made them a large pot of tea, and left them to it.

Belinda had been pleased with Sebastian today. He was starting to take an interest in football, pop music, junk food, the things most nine-year-old boys are into. It was a good sign that normality was returning.

She stood up. 'That went very well, Sebastian. I'm pleased. I'll see you next Tuesday.'

Mrs Daniels walked into the room, followed by another woman. 'Sorry to interrupt. You have another visitor, Sebastian.'

Belinda recognised the stranger immediately. 'Hello, it's . . . now, don't tell me . . . it's Elizabeth Sage, isn't it?'

'Yes, that's right, dear.'

'You were in *Bringing Up Ralph* with Sebastian. What are you doing here?'

'I've just come to visit the boy – you know, what with everything he's been through, the poor little chap. I think a few of the other cast members have already popped in to see him.'

'Really? You didn't tell me, Sebastian.'

'Sorry.' Sebastian blushed.

'It doesn't matter.' Belinda knew that faces from the past might be good or bad. Still, Sebastian seemed to be doing okay. 'Well, I must be getting back to the hospital,' she said, and made to leave, but Elizabeth put out a hand to stop her.

Then she patted Belinda's stomach. 'Happy event on the way?' she asked.

Damn! Belinda had hoped her clothes were still disguising her pregnancy. She hadn't been sure it was a good idea for Sebastian to know yet.

'Yes,' Belinda confirmed, her back to Sebastian, her finger to her lips.

Elizabeth understood. 'Mum's the word. Congratulations,' she whispered.

'Okay, I'm off, then. Have a nice time, you two.'

'You haven't told her anything, have you?' Elizabeth asked Sebastian.

The boy shook his head.

'Good. I knew I was right to find your mother, persuade her to get me a part on that show of yours where I could keep an eye on you. Your mummy got confused, Sebastian. She couldn't tell fact from fiction. But now that girl's pregnant by Hal Morrisey. And we know what happens when they become fathers, don't we, Sebastian? They do terrible things to children because they think . . . What do they think?'

'Daddy knows best,' Sebastian replied.

Elizabeth Sage looked closely at him. He seemed suddenly pale.

'Don't worry, dear, everything will be all right. I won't let any harm come to you.'

Sebastian nodded.

'Come here, Sebastian. Come and give your old granny a hug.'